MW01518227

THE HUNT

NICK WILKSHIRE

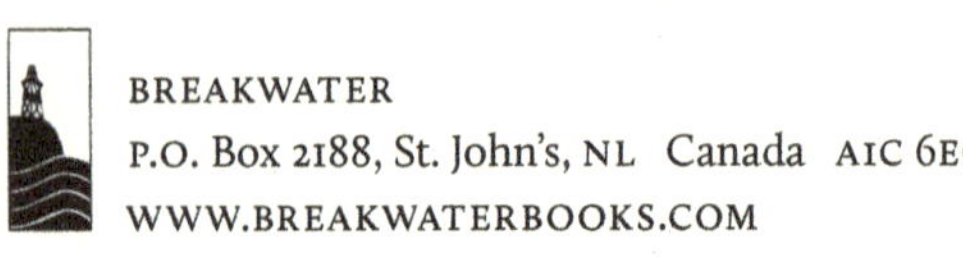

BREAKWATER
P.O. Box 2188, St. John's, NL Canada A1C 6E6
WWW.BREAKWATERBOOKS.COM

LIBRARY AND ARCHIVES CANADA CATALOGUING IN PUBLICATION

The Hunt : a novel / by Nicholas Wilkshire.
Wilkshire, Nick, 1968– author

Canadiana (print) 2025017457x | Canadiana (ebook) 20250174588

ISBN 9781778530630 (softcover) | ISBN 9781778530647 (ePUB)

LCGFT: Novels.

LCC PS8645.I44 H86 2025 | DDC C813/.6—dc23

AUTHOR PHOTO: Lindsey Gibeau
COVER DESIGN: Beth Oberholtzer, Oberholtzer Design Inc.
COVER PHOTOGRAPH: Joris Beugels
PAGE LAYOUT: Nadine Hodder

THE PUBLISHER GRATEFULLY ACKNOWLEDGES THE SUPPORT OF

The Canada Council for the Arts
The Government of Canada through the Department of Heritage and
The Government of Newfoundland and Labrador through the Department of Tourism, Culture, Arts and Recreation

PRINTED AND BOUND IN CANADA

Breakwater Books is commited to choosing papers and materials for our books that help to protect our environment. This book is printed on paper made of material from well-managed forest.

For my father,
who will always give me someone to look up to

CHAPTER 1

Ben Matthews yawned as he took the cup of coffee from the brewer and walked over to the living room of his Georgetown apartment. Settling on the sofa, he glanced out the bay window onto 30th Street below, already busy with morning joggers intent on beating the heat in the shade of the old-growth trees. He smiled as he followed the progress of a battered hatchback towing a U-Haul trailer, the car's rear shocks straining under the load as it crawled toward the nearby campus. College was more than a decade gone for Matthews, but he had always loved September and he still felt the same sense of renewal as each summer drew to a close.

Until a couple of days ago, he had been looking forward to spending the coming fall in London, with its exciting career prospects and a staff apartment in Mayfair that was the perfect base for forays into unexplored parts of the iconic city. His smile faded as he recalled the impromptu summons that had changed everything – he would be spending the fall somewhere cooler than Washington all right, but it wouldn't be London. He had been assured that the last-minute change was in his best interests long term and, while he recognized some truth among the platitudes, he couldn't help thinking the reassignment had more to do with what had happened in Boston a month ago. He reminded himself that he had been officially cleared of any wrongdoing, but he also knew that didn't guarantee he wouldn't carry the stain of failure in the eyes of some in upper management. Still, he was determined to make the most of his situation and the scowl that had settled on his face lifted as he got up and made his way to the bedroom, pausing in the doorway to watch the sleeping form on the bed. The lightly freckled skin at the tops of her shoulders rose and fell with each breath, her face concealed by a strawberry-blond tangle. Then she stirred and two sparkling green eyes opened wide and became visible through her hair as she spoke.

"What are you looking at?"

"I didn't know you were awake."

"Mmmmh," was all she said as she brushed the hair from her face. He sat on the edge of the bed. She pointed to his coffee. "Do I get one of those?"

"Maybe." He set the cup down on the bedside table and slipped under the sheets next to her.

"That's not very chivalrous," she said, wrapping her arms around him.

"You want me to be chivalrous?"

She climbed on top of him, and her golden locks tickled his face. "Hell no," she said, leaning down to kiss him as his hands slid over her hips.

"You still thinking about London?" she said, as they lay side by side in the rumpled sheets, the back of her hand grazing his hair.

"Hmm?"

"You'll come out fine, Ben. I know you will."

He smiled and turned to her, taking in the intricacies of her face in the morning light. "*We'll* come out fine, Caroline. That's a promise."

Her lips formed a smile, but her eyes darted away and focused on the ceiling. Watching her, the feeling of contentment that had enveloped him a moment ago was gone, replaced by a chill despite the warm cocoon of the bed.

"What's wrong?" he heard himself say, his voice sounding distant and alien.

"I can't," she said, after an agonizing pause. "I'm sorry, but I just can't."

"Can't what? What are you talking about?" He was up on one elbow, searching her face for a tell, but the stony resolve he saw told him the other shoe had just dropped.

"I'm sorry, but I can't go with you."

"What happened to us embarking on an adventure together, somewhere new?"

Her mouth drew into a pert frown. "That was when you were going to London, not Ottawa." A defensive edge had crept into her voice and the room echoed with silence as he sat up and considered his dwindling options.

"So, that's it, huh? The first bump in the road and you're done?"

"*Bump in the road?*" She let out a little snort. "What the fuck am I supposed to do in *Ottawa*?"

"Come on, Caroline," he said, refusing to give up. "It's close enough that we can commute every weekend if we want to. We won't have to give up our place here. I'm telling you, this could be really good for us."

"Oh, sure. And we'll eat back-bacon flapjacks every morning, drizzled in fresh maple syrup straight from the tree." She paused and when he refused the bait, she pressed on. "Are you actually listening to yourself? It's *Canada*. Nothing happens in Canada. Have you thought about that?"

"Ortiz says it's become one of the key posts in the current environment, with a lot more upside than most of the Euro . . . " He trailed off as he recognized the first hint of pity in her eyes. They sat motionless for a while, the awkward pause broken only when an ambulance wailed past somewhere to the east. "When were you planning on telling me?"

"I was waiting for the right moment," she said, running a hand through her hair as she sat up. He bit back a sarcastic retort, his mind focused on a more pressing question: how could he not have seen this coming?

"Is this to do with Boston?"

"Don't make this any harder than it has to be." She was getting up now, beginning the search for her clothes. "I'm a big city girl, and I just can't see myself in flannel," she added, with a smile that teased the anger that had been building inside him as he sat there, watching her surgical disengagement from his life. He tamped it down and tried a smile.

"I checked the weather in Ottawa this morning. It's a couple of degrees warmer than here."

"It's August. Let's compare temperatures in February."

"It's probably pissing rain in London," he countered.

"It's not about the weather, Ben. Besides, I can always get an umbrella," she added, fastening her bra behind her back. Her smile faded just a touch as her eyes met his, then she looked away and busied herself with her skirt.

He slid to the edge of the bed. "You're going to London . . . *anyway?*"

"What happened to my other shoe? You really are a brute, you know that?" Her laugh sounded genuine, but even she couldn't keep up the pretense as she came face to face with his incredulous stare. She pulled her shirt over her head and let out an impatient sigh.

"This *is* about Boston, isn't it?" he said.

She seemed to consider her response for a moment as she adjusted her hair. "I already told you, I don't think Boston was your fault."

"But others do," he said. "And you don't want to be tainted."

"What do you want from me, Ben? I said I was sorry."

As he watched her leave the room, it occurred to him that this was just the beginning. If he didn't find a way to set the record straight, Ottawa would be his last posting. He didn't dare acknowledge the other thought lurking at the far reaches of his subconscious – maybe his detractors were right about what had happened in Boston. Maybe he *didn't* have what it takes.

CHAPTER 2

Richard Perry stepped onto the porch and looked out over Marsh Lake, its glass-smooth waters reflecting the starlight from above. He drew the crisp night air deep into his lungs, just as he had done when he first stepped out of the sterile air of the private jet onto the tarmac at the Whitehorse airport around midday. The flight up from Vancouver had been spectacular, with an endless supply of snow-capped peaks to gape at from the comfort of a leather captain's chair. But it wasn't just the beauty of the landscape that had made the approach into Whitehorse so fascinating. Perry had logged some serious air miles over the years and had seen some incredible sights, but never had he been anywhere so . . . untouched. The valley that cradled the city of Whitehorse held just under thirty thousand people. There were only another ten thousand in the entire Yukon – an area larger than the state of California with its nearly forty million inhabitants. He supposed that was why the air was so pristine.

Glancing across to the opposite shoreline of the large lake – located thirty minutes southeast of Whitehorse along the Alaska Highway, at the head of the Yukon River – he saw no sign of life other than a twinkle of light here and there. The vast majority of the cottages were on the eastern shore, including the large, rustic pine inn where he now stood.

"I hope you packed your woollies."

Perry turned to see his old friend, John Townsend, standing there with a couple of glasses. "I just can't get used to the air up here," he said, accepting a snifter of fragrant Cognac.

"Wait'll we get up to the high country tomorrow."

Perry nodded. "I'm so glad I finally made it up here, and I'm grateful to you, John, really," he added, raising his glass. "It's the trip of a lifetime."

"To the hunt." Townsend tapped his glass off Perry's and they stood against the railing, letting the warmth of the drink counter the coolness of the air around them. "Speaking of which, I just got off the phone with the outfitter and everything's set up for tomorrow." Townsend paused as a smile creased his face. "I've got to tell you, when I suggested this in Washington – what was it, twenty-five years ago? – I didn't know if you'd ever get around to it."

Perry smiled. "I think it's closer to thirty now, and I don't know why I didn't do it sooner." They both stood there for a while, taking in the moonlight glinting off the water, until Townsend broke the silence.

"Do you miss those days?"

"Sometimes, sure," Perry said, swirling the liquid in the glass, watching as it clung to the sides. "But it was a different time." He frowned as he turned to face Townsend. "The world's changed and I'm not sure I'd have the stomach for the job anymore. I'll bet you don't miss DC one bit," he added, with a chuckle.

"I miss the sheer excitement of those days," Townsend said, then shook his head. "But you're right about it being a different world."

"It's a young man's game, John, and we're both getting a little long in the tooth."

Townsend laughed as the sliding door opened and a member of the staff announced that coffee was waiting for them by the fire. "Well, enough about the past," he said, draining his glass. "I've got to make a quick call. I'll see you inside."

Perry watched as his host slid through the door and into the A-frame foyer with its massive stone hearth. He shivered in response to an onshore gust and wondered what his accommodations twenty-four hours from now would look like. Then again, he had grown up hunting and he told himself he still had the fortitude to rough it when he had to, despite an intervening half-century of luxury. This trip had been on his bucket list for a long time, and he was going to enjoy every minute. He stared out into the gathering darkness and tried to suppress the nagging thought at the edge of his consciousness that had been growing since leaving Vancouver. No matter how much his reason told him they were just the unfounded rantings of a disgruntled and disillusioned man, the persistent thought still lingered.

What if they're not . . .

"Sir?"

He turned to see a fit man in his early thirties in the doorway, the familiar trace of concern underlying the stoic expression.

"I'm coming, Garcia," Perry said, summoning an easy smile to conceal the disquiet bubbling just below the surface, a skill honed by a lifetime's practice.

CHAPTER 3

Gian Dhillon returned to his hotel feeling drained, not from the short walk up from the waterfront in the warm, late afternoon sun, but from the knowledge that he had squandered a precious opportunity. It was all the more frustrating since everything leading up to the unexpected encounter had fallen into place so perfectly, as if by fate: The timing of his visit to Seattle, the opportunity for an impromptu side trip to Vancouver, and the chance meeting yesterday with a man to whom access would normally have been impossible. Surely, these were all signs that destiny was on his side. It was only a few short minutes, but it was enough time to make his pitch. At least it should have been. While Dhillon had always flourished in the laboratory, where the precise and delicate chemical interactions he orchestrated spoke more persuasively than any words ever could, interpersonal communication was another matter.

He replayed the whole exchange in his mind as he walked through the lobby of his hotel, scouring his memory for anything he might have missed in the encounter that could indicate that his message had been received and, more importantly, accepted. But he knew it was hopeless. His carefully prepared speech – hastily delivered as the other man stood watching him with a cool detachment that had only made Dhillon more nervous – had missed the mark. Despite the reassuring smile and silver-tongued parting banter from the wily old pro after the pitch was done, Dhillon had known he was being dismissed. Passing the front desk, he was too absorbed in his disappointment to hear the clerk at the reception desk calling his name, but she caught his eye and he recognized her friendly face from check-in.

"I have a message for you, Mr. Dhillon."

"A message?" Very few people knew he was in Vancouver, let alone where he was staying. He watched as the young woman rummaged around behind the counter and came up with an envelope with his name scribbled on the front.

"Thanks," he said, taking it and tearing it open. "When did this come in?"

She shrugged. "It was here when I started my shift an hour ago."

He thanked her again and headed toward the elevators, unfolding the single piece of paper inside the envelope as he walked. He stopped as he read the three typed lines.

> I believe you
> I have information to prove you are right
> East Cordova and Main at 10 p.m.

Dhillon stood in front of the elevators as the bell rang and the doors opened, disgorging a family burdened with luggage. He remained frozen as they navigated their trolley around him, and when he turned to watch their progress across the empty lobby, he scanned the sofas in the little seating area by the fake fireplace to confirm that they were empty. Returning his attention to the typewritten words, he tried to process the competing thoughts running through his mind. On the one hand, he was excited by the possibility that there was someone else out there with the means to help him prove what he knew to be true. The burden of his discovery was heavy enough, but being powerless to do anything about it was even worse, and it had taken its toll. But his cautious side worried over the anonymous nature of the message. Why not just meet him face to face, or pick up the phone? And how could the sender have known of Dhillon's meeting less than twenty-four hours before, much less the subject of the brief discussion? His heart raced as a new possibility dawned on him – perhaps his awkward pitch *had* hit home, just not right away. The public nature of their initial exchange might have explained an initial reticence, with a subsequent private meeting with a middleman being a cautious but reasonable next step.

Returning to the front desk, Dhillon took one of the tourist maps and located the address, which was not much more than a thirty-minute walk from the hotel.

"Are there any good places to eat in this area?" he asked, pointing to the intersection where the mysterious meeting was to occur.

"There're a lot of good places in Gastown," she said, tapping the map to indicate an area to the west, then gave a little frown. "You don't want to go too far east, though.

"What's wrong with this part of town?" he asked.

She followed his finger east of Gastown. "It's just not a great area, especially at night. We don't generally recommend it to guests." She brightened. "But our concierge can help you find what you're looking for."

"I'll check with him before I head out," he said, then returned to the elevators, his excitement over the ten o'clock meeting undiminished by the warning. He would be careful, but he had spent time in much more dangerous places.

Dhillon checked his watch as he approached the intersection of Main and East Cordova, wishing he hadn't opted for that second beer as his full bladder sent a shiver through his system. Crossing the street, he glanced in the window of a little convenience store - the only open business within sight - and decided to check it out. A man in his early twenties with greasy hair and shabby clothes stood by the entrance and shot a yellow grin Dhillon's way as he entered the store. After a quick tour of the shelves and the cooler at the rear to confirm the place was empty, Dhillon returned to the front and gave the bored clerk a nod as he exited, then walked headlong into the same man he had seen on the way in.

"Sorry, dude!" the man said, as Dhillon recoiled from the noxious cocktail of body odour, stale beer, and tobacco.

"No problem," Dhillon said, backpedalling as he watched the other man cross the street and then turn into a nearby alley. He was just recovering from the encounter when he heard a voice call out from behind him.

"Mr. Dhillon."

He swung around and looked in the direction of the voice, seeing nothing in the dim light, until a large form emerged from behind an old pickup.

"Yes?" His voice sounded higher in the night air.

"I leave message at your hotel." The speaker lingered in the shadows, just out of range of the light from the store window. "I'm glad you have come. I have information to support your claims."

Dhillon took a step forward, ignoring the red flag his subconscious was waving as his brain tried to place the strange accent that accompanied the other man's words. "Who are you?" he asked, as the figure took a step backward so that he was standing by the front bumper of the pickup, the otherwise deserted and darkened lot behind him.

"Someone who believes in you. A friend."

"Well, come on out here and let's talk." Dhillon stood at the edge of the sidewalk, determined not to go any farther without knowing who he was talking to.

"I am . . . afraid. I think they follow me," the stranger said, as a screech of tires from out on East Cordova startled Dhillon, causing him to flinch and instinctively turn for an instant.

"Who?" he asked, turning back just in time to see a large blur in front of him. He had no time to defend himself against the disorienting blow to the side of his head, and he barely felt the blade plunge into his midsection, focused as he was on trying to pry away the thick forearm around his neck, cutting off his air supply. He was powerless to dislodge the arm or the gloved hand covering his mouth as his assailant dragged him back into the darkened lot. He tried to call out, but the hand clamped tighter over his mouth and, as the vise around his neck constricted, his vision blurred and his remaining strength ebbed away. His final thought before his eyes flickered and then shut was *why?*

CHAPTER 4

Ben Matthews watched through the window as a woman in athletic gear trailed behind a white Shih-poo out on Sussex Drive. She returned his gaze and added a smile before disappearing beyond the frame and leaving him with a view of the imposing stone fortress across the street that housed the US Embassy in Ottawa – his new home. The sound of his lunch partner's voice brought him back to reality.

"So, you're getting settled?"

Matthews looked across the table at Jim Hatcher, a good-natured State Department lifer in his mid-forties, and puzzled over the motivation for the unusual lunch invitation. It had caught him so off guard that he had been unable to come up with an immediate excuse for refusing that didn't seem rude. The two men occupied offices down the hall from one another, after all, though they operated in completely different spheres, and both knew that Matthews's official job description had little to do with his actual work. Surely Hatcher wasn't expecting Matthews to divulge any particulars of his immediate plans, so what did he expect to gain from the meeting?

Matthews had a hard time believing it was just a thoughtful gesture to a new arrival, but whatever Hatcher's motive, he decided to play nice. Besides, Matthews had his own agenda.

"Yeah, I'm getting my bearings," he said, taking a sip of his ice water.

"You got your housing all set up?"

Matthew nodded. "I'm just over there." He gestured beyond the window and east down Sussex Drive.

"The condos on Murray Street? I hear they're nice. I haven't had to deal with any complaints at all yet." Apart from other administrative duties, Hatcher was responsible for accommodation for all American nationals posted to the city. "And you sure are close to work."

"How about you? Are you nearby?"

"New Edinburgh. A pleasant walk in this weather. Not so much in January, but that's a long way off," he added quickly. "I guess you're getting up to speed on—"

He returned Hatcher's easy smile as the server appeared and took their orders. They chatted as they waited for the food to arrive, the subjects ranging from border security to the difference between American and Canadian beer, with Hatcher's gentle probing of Matthews's work being just as gently rebuffed with deft changes of topic.

"So, where was your last posting?" Matthews asked, after the server had deposited their plates.

"Rome. I was there for three years."

"Must have been interesting," Matthews said, spearing a cherry tomato with his fork and wondering what Hatcher had done wrong to get cross-posted from Rome to Ottawa.

Hatcher frowned. "It's overrated. The property file's a mess and once you've seen the sites, Rome just seems overcrowded and polluted. Kind of the opposite of here," he added with a smile that faded a bit in the face of Matthews's sombre expression. "It's not that bad, believe me."

"I'm sure it'll be fine." Matthews tried for a conviction he didn't feel.

"I can tell you're skeptical, but you'll learn to love it, I promise you. I know Ottawa's got a reputation for being a little staid," Hatcher continued. "*The town that fun forgot*, and all that."

"I hadn't heard that one." Now it was Matthews's turn to frown. Maybe things were even worse than he had thought.

"There's actually plenty to do here, and Montreal's only a two-hour drive," Hatcher said, like a beachfront resort manager extolling the benefits of a week's rain to a disgruntled vacationer. "A little more to Toronto. But Ottawa's a great place, especially for kids. You don't have kids, though, right?"

"Nope." Matthews shook his head. His domestic situation was quite a few steps back from having kids, but he wasn't about to get into having just lost his so-called girlfriend of almost a year. Or the fact that she had gone off to London – where he was supposed to have been posted – without him.

"I'll take you to a football game," Hatcher continued, seeming to sense his colleague's spiralling mood. "The whole three downs thing is weird at first, but it makes for an exciting game – lots of passing." He took an enormous bite of his burger and Matthews tried not to focus on the mayonnaise at the edges of Hatcher's mouth. "Say, you look like you're in pretty good shape," Hatcher mumbled, reaching for his soda to ease a sizable portion of the burger down his throat. "You play any hockey?"

"I played at Providence before transferring to Georgetown," Matthews said, spotting the server and resisting the urge to make the sign for the cheque. Hatcher looked like he enjoyed his dessert.

"I assume you mean intramural."

Matthews shook his head. "Division I, actually. I had a partial ride."

"You're kidding me, right?" Hatcher's eyes had widened noticeably as he put down his burger. "You played NCAA hockey? Holy shit, wait 'til the Marines get a hold of you. They've been trying for years to ice a team that can hold its own against the Canucks."

Matthews held up his hand. "It's been a few years—"

"But you don't mind if I let them know, right?" Hatcher had stopped chewing.

"Sure, I guess." Matthews shrugged. He waited for Hatcher to take another bite of his burger, then broached the only topic he wanted to discuss. "Any word on my accreditation?"

"It's coming," Hatcher said, taking another sip of his drink. "XDC – that's the protocol folks – are pretty efficient."

Matthews nodded. His last-minute posting had meant a delay in the processing of his diplomatic accreditation – a rubber stamp for the most part, but its absence did present some administrative obstacles, including to travel. They continued to chat over coffee and Hatcher's dessert and then they were back out on Sussex Drive, taking the short stroll back to the front entrance of the embassy. The midday sun made the coolness Matthews had felt when leaving his condo at eight that morning seem alien.

"When does it start to get cold, anyway?"

"November, usually, but it's different every year." Hatcher reached for his pass as they approached the gate. "Speaking of which, I should have you over for a barbecue while it's still nice, give you a chance to meet some people."

"Sounds great," Matthews lied, picturing a yard full of embassy employees he had nothing in common with and their kids, Hatcher sweating over the grill. He found himself having to fight off what had become a recurring image: Caroline in one of her sleek, black numbers, a glass of Pinot in her hand as her companion fought off the advances of an assortment of charming Brits at a West End gallery. Matthews had only become aware of the full extent of her betrayal after he had arrived in Ottawa and learned that the man who had replaced him in London was someone she had been romantically involved with a couple of years back. The speed with which it had all happened made it clear that she had known it was in the works for some time – how could he have been so blind?

"What?" Matthews found himself staring at Hatcher, who was looking concerned. "Sorry, I was just thinking . . . a barbecue would be a great icebreaker," he said, with no intention of attending such an event. He recalled the recent criticism from his immediate superior about his tendency against co-operation, but teamwork was a two-way street and if his recent experiences had taught him anything, it was that he was better off trusting no one.

Matthews walked into the ByWard Market bar with a handful of his teammates and followed them to a table at the rear of the room.

"I'll get the first round," he said, making a detour to the bar. As he waited for the bartender and reached for his wallet, he noticed a tall man farther down the bar and recognized the lantern-jawed defenceman on the team he had just played. They had done battle in front of the net a few times and the guy had also tried to embed Matthews's head into the corner boards with his elbow at one point. As their eyes met, Matthews tensed but the other man's face broke into a broad smile. "Good game," he called down the bar and pointed at a full pitcher of beer. "This one's on me."

"Thanks," Matthews said, thinking it was true what they said about Canadians and their hockey – polite as hell until they strapped on a pair of skates, then look out. He made his way down the bar and they shook hands.

"It was a close one."

"That was a nice move," the other man said, referring to the deke Matthews had deployed to fool the opposing goaltender in the dying seconds and bring the American side to within a goal.

"Our goalie's still lookin' for his jockstrap," he added, sliding the pitcher over.

"Cheers." Matthews gestured to the table. "You gonna join us?"

"Be right there."

Matthews returned to the table where his teammates were dissecting the game. Far from lamenting the defeat, they seemed ecstatic not to have lost by a landslide.

"Hatcher wasn't kidding when he said he found a ringer for us," one of the older guys, a trade officer, piped up. "You've got some serious game."

Matthews laughed and took a seat as they shared out the beer into glasses and raised them in a toast. It had been less than a week since his lunch with Hatcher, but his new teammates had wasted no time signing him up and had even cobbled together a set of equipment when they learned Matthews hadn't bothered to ship his gear. As they joked about their future as pros, a handful of players from the Canadian side, including the defenceman from the bar, came over and joined them. The pitchers seemed to appear out of nowhere as the friendly banter continued and the bar became more and more crowded, the players mixing with the other patrons.

At one point, Matthews turned from a heated discussion with one of the Canadian players about who was going to win gold at the next Olympics to find a woman in her late twenties standing over him.

"Do you mind?" she said, pointing to the small space next to him on the bench seat.

"Be my guest." He ignored the wink from his teammate, who helped him out by not sliding over more than an inch.

"It's not usually this crowded on a Wednesday," she said, squeezing onto the bench next to him. "I'm Renée by the way."

"Ben. Nice to meet you."

"Love your accent."

"Really?" He hadn't said much, and he didn't know he even had a distinguishable accent.

"Where you from?"

"Pittsburgh area," he lied.

"You here on business?" she asked, as a passing server with a tray full of drinks forced her to press up against his arm. He couldn't help noticing that she was wearing a plaid shirt, and he allowed an image of Caroline's most disdainful expression to flash briefly across his mind's eye.

"I just moved here, actually."

"In that case, welcome." She raised a half-empty glass and tapped it against his own, giving him a smile as they both drank.

"Thanks," he said, gesturing to a passing server. As she swung by and took his order, Renée pressed herself even closer to let someone by behind them and Matthews could smell the perfume rising up from her neck in the close air.

"So, what brings you here?" she asked. He fought back the retreat instinct that had become his natural response to this type of situation lately, reminding himself that he was no longer with Caroline and that every cloud has a silver lining.

"Just a couple of post-game beers," he said, returning her smile.

"Did you win?"

He shook his head. "Close, though. Four-three."

"That's okay," she said. "The night's still young."

Matthews sat in Kent Dorsey's office two days later, taking in the view of the Ottawa River and the rolling hills of Gatineau beyond as Dorsey fiddled with his computer. Matthews knew the head of administration was a career bureaucrat, and the pretend urgency he was dealing with now, and the ten minutes he had made Matthews wait outside the office, were sure signs that Dorsey didn't like him. Whether it was personal or due to the nature of his work, Matthews had seen it before and didn't much care. Besides, he thought, as he looked out at the gold and red canopy of leaves across the river, his own office was a windowless tomb where he planned to spend as little time as possible, so the view from here suited him just fine.

"Sorry about this," Dorsey said, looking away from his monitor with an apologetic smile. "I'll be right with you."

"No problem."

"There." Dorsey hit the Enter key with a flourish and turned in his chair to face Matthews. "So, how are you settling in?"

"Good, thanks."

"Housing's okay?"

Matthews nodded. "Yup."

"First time in Ottawa?"

"Yeah."

Feel free to cut the shit any time . . .

"Well, I think you'll find there's plenty to keep us busy, and the locals are very friendly."

Matthews fought the image of his encounter with Renée the other night. It had been promising enough to start and had seemed just what he needed to forget Caroline. But by the time they got back to his place from the bar, his ex was all he could think of, not Renée – however lovely she was. The whole thing had turned awkward and left him feeling even worse. Dorsey snapped him out of his funk as he got to the point. "So, what can I do for you?"

"I was hoping you could expedite my accreditation," Matthews said, donning his most congenial smile.

"These things take time, but I'm sure it won't be long." Dorsey's expression did little to conceal the frost in his voice.

"I'm sure you're right, but I need to head out to Vancouver, ASAP."

Dorsey frowned. "I hope you're not thinking of dabbling in consular."

It took Matthews a moment to make the connection to the broadcast email that had appeared in his inbox as he was ordering his morning cappuccino. "The scientist," he said with a nod. "Is the Vancouver PD even calling it murder?"

"Who knows, but I'm sure our people at the consulate have it well in hand."

"I'm sure they do," Matthews said. "But I'd be happy to tack it onto my other business if you want a second set of eyes on it."

Dorsey's frown deepened as he leaned back in his chair and folded his arms. "I don't, and I'm surprised you're hopping on a plane less than two weeks after arriving here, what with all the cutbacks in travel. At least for my staff," he added. "It's a big country out there," he said, gesturing outside. ". . . and we have these things called phones, the interne—"

"Some things are better face to face," Matthews said. "But if you're saying there's nothing you can do, then so be it. I'm sure no one will think you gave anything less than a hundred per cent support."

The two men stared at each other in silence for a few seconds, then Dorsey's lips formed into a smile so razor-thin that his bloodless lips almost disappeared. "Come to think of it, I think your accreditation came through this afternoon."

"Good thing I dropped by, then," Matthews said, getting up.

"Just remember." Dorsey leaned forward, elbows resting on his desk. "You may not report to me, but you're still a member of this mission."

Matthews paused at the door and gave him a thousand-watt smile. "No, I don't report to you."

CHAPTER 5

Richard Perry looked out the window of the Cessna 180 Skywagon, marvelling at the view of the rugged Yukon landscape from two thousand feet. The plane had been modified for bush flying, its stock landing gear switched out for softer, oversized tires that could handle the rough terrain below. Normally a six-seater, two of its seats had been sacrificed and the plane's interior had been stripped down to the bare necessities to accommodate more cargo and fuel.

"Kluane Plateau's just up there, northeast of the park."

Perry followed the pilot's outstretched hand and looked northeast as the plane banked slightly, then straightened up on a new heading. Dale Oyler was an experienced bush pilot, hunter, and guide who looked precisely the part in his tan outback jacket and black leather cap, complete with fur-lined ear flaps. He slid his side window open and tossed his cigarette butt out – in violation of a handful of laws and regulations – as Perry took in the incredible vista before them of snow-capped mountains nestled among the greenery of Kluane National Park. In fact, there was nothing but mountains and trees as far as the eye could see and, at their low altitude, they seemed almost level with the peaks. They had been following the Alaska Highway as they headed northwest from Whitehorse and, other than the smattering of buildings at Haines Junction, it had been wilderness all the way.

"That's quite a view," Perry said, turning to John Townsend, who was sitting in one of the rear seats, next to Garcia.

"And we'll have it all to ourselves." Oyler grinned.

"I made sure of that," Townsend said. "Just in case anyone finds out Richard, here, is in town."

"What are you talking about?" Perry turned and gave him a quizzical look.

"When I was in town yesterday afternoon," Townsend said, "I might have mentioned to a couple of people that I was headed up to Mayo."

"You mention it to Gopher?" Oyler said.

Townsend nodded "Of course."

"That's better than any social media post," Oyler said, with a nod of appreciation before turning to Perry. "Gopher supplies all the local outfitters with dry goods and let's just say he likes to flap his gums."

"Where's Mayo anyway?" Perry asked.

"Great hunting ground," the pilot said. "But it's a good four hundred clicks northeast of here. You're a sneaky one, John. Then again, you always were," he added, with a cackle that had everyone on board the little plane laughing along.

"Looks like the weather's gonna hold for today, at least," Oyler said after a while, looking off to the west. They had dissected several forecasts the previous evening and again that morning, all warning of the possibility that a storm was making its way toward them from the coast. Parts of Alaska had been hit with an early blizzard but weather patterns this far north were anything but predictable. They had plenty of warm clothing and supplies for several days of hunting and, despite some initial resistance from Garcia, who would have preferred they wait a few days, they had decided to stick with the original plan. The temperature had dropped to near the freezing point by the time they had taken off, but the clouds were still a ways off, making the flight in very pleasant.

"John tells me this isn't your first sheep hunt," Oyler said, as he adjusted a dial on the instrument panel.

Perry shook his head. "I grew up in Texas, and I used to go out with my dad and uncle when I was a kid. Bagged my first one when I was sixteen – never forget it." A lifetime away from Texas had rounded off his accent and with his tall, slender frame, angular good looks, and silver hair, Perry seemed more suited to a boardroom than behind the scope of a hunting rifle, but he had made a career out of surprising people.

"Well, conditions are perfect, so I'd say you're about to bag another." Oyler nodded. "I don't know what you've got in Texas, but the last few years, we've seen a lot of big rams up here."

"I hope you saved a couple for us, Dale," Townsend said from the back seat.

Oyler nodded. "Most years, this might be a little late for the rams, but there hasn't been enough snow up in the mountains to force them down yet, so I've got a good feeling. You guys sure you don't want me to come along?" He glanced first at Perry, then at Garcia, seated directly behind him. He sensed the younger man would prefer that Oyler did join them, but they had been through the logistics in detail and agreed that Townsend was familiar enough with the hunting grounds to lead them. "I know you're in good hands with John, here," he added, the only hint of any sort of deferral to men of power like Perry and Townsend. To Oyler, all men were equal when they came out here.

"We're good, Dale," Townsend said. "But it's nice to know you're only a phone call away," he added, pointing to Garcia, who had paired his phone to a satellite communicator that would allow for texting and calling beyond cell tower range. "Besides, I have a feeling it won't take us long to bag a trophy."

They continued to chat easily as the plane banked again and headed away from the highway below that they had followed up from Haines Junction.

"That's Tee-Pee Peak." Oyler was pointing to a snow-capped mountaintop up ahead and to the left. "The one off in the distance is Hazel Peak," he added. "The base camp's in between, on the plateau there." The passengers were checking out the view as the plane began to descend, buffeted by a sudden gust of wind. Oyler glanced at Perry out of the corner of his eye, but if he was expecting a trace of anxiety on the other man's face, he was disappointed. "Bit of weather comin' in from Alaska maybe," he said, gesturing to the clouds off to the west.

"There's snow on the peaks," Garcia said from the back seat. "Is that normal for this time of year?"

"Snow flies early up here," Oyler said, wrestling the control wheel against another gust and straightening the plane out. "Usually starts in August, but it can be earlier. It's on account of the panhandle."

"You mean that we're not far from the coast?" Perry asked.

Oyler nodded. "If we get ten centimetres in Whitehorse, it might be forty up here. Same goes for anywhere in the western half of the territory, for that matter, but it doesn't look like a lot of accumulation up on the high ground, so we should be good." He pointed out the front windshield, to the left. "That's where I'm gonna put her down," he said, pushing the control wheel forward and nosing the plane into a steeper descent as Perry and the other passengers craned their necks to make out a narrow opening between the peaks.

"You're gonna land *there*?" Garcia had leaned forward between the front seats and was pointing through the windshield, a grave expression on his face.

"I could land a friggin' 747 on that," Oyler said, with a snort. "You should see some of the turkey trails I've put this baby down on," he added, tightening his grip on the wheel as another cross-draft shook the little plane. Moments later, they were skimming the treetops at the near end of the mountain plain and then the Cessna touched down with a jolt, bouncing from side to side before it settled. It continued to rumble down the makeshift runway and came to a stop a hundred feet from a collection of cabins and other wooden structures near the treeline.

"What'd I tell you?" Oyler said with a grin as he shut off the engine and the prop gradually stopped spinning. "Real pilots land where they want to."

"I see you haven't lost your touch," Townsend said, as he unstrapped his belts and opened the door. The base camp, which would normally accommodate up to four different hunting groups, was deserted by special arrangement between Townsend and Oyler – the exclusive use a part of the hefty fee he and Perry had agreed to pay for the hunt. The fact that they had been able to book anything on less than two years' notice was another. As for the requirement that all non-Canadians be accompanied by a Yukon outfitter, Oyler was prepared to look the other way, trusting that these particular clients had sufficient pull to get him out of hot water if anyone found out and made a fuss.

They unloaded their gear and did a last check before slinging their packs over their shoulders. Oyler had offered them horses, but Townsend had been insistent that they wouldn't need them. They wanted to hunt the high ground, and they were prepared to do the walking to get there.

"You sure you remember where the spike camp is?" Oyler asked, referring to the ridge a day's hike away, where he always brought his hunters to make camp, close to their quarry.

Townsend snorted. "Quit fussing like an old woman, Dale. You forget I've done this hunt five times in the past ten years. I know where Eagle Ridge is."

"All right, all right." Oyler put up a hand, deciding there was no point mentioning the fact that he had always gone along as a guide on those hunts.

"We'll be fine," Townsend continued, noticing Garcia's grim expression. "You just make sure you come back for us in a few days, Dale."

Oyler nodded and tugged at the collar of his outback jacket. "You'd best get movin'," he said, looking up at the clouds that were coming in from the west. They looked darker than they had from the air. As the party of three headed toward the foothills with Townsend and Perry in the lead, Garcia fell into step behind them, subtly reaching into his jacket and pulling his Beretta from a shoulder holster to check the fifteen-round clip.

CHAPTER 6

Ben Matthews watched as the young man he had just spent the last twenty minutes with walked out the door of the Burnaby coffee shop and into the warm, midday sunshine. As the man disappeared around the corner, Matthews couldn't help feeling that his own career prospects were along for the ride. To say that the meeting had been a disappointment was an understatement, both in terms of the lack of useful information conveyed and the quality of the source. Human intelligence was everything in Matthews's line of work, and he had been led to believe that he had found a valuable source, connected to the decision makers in the local expat Hindu community, including a small group of violent extremists. In fact, while he might turn out to be very useful in the future, the young man's current access was limited to low-level players in the organization. He had been unaware of any local plots targeting Sikh activists in the area, let alone a rumoured plan to assassinate prominent members of the pro-Khalistan movement south of the border, in California. The disruption of such a plot was one of the best outcomes in counter-intelligence, and successful operations were often used to justify increased budgets, not to mention thwarting murder. After what had happened in Boston, Matthews needed a win – a big one – and he had thought he was onto something. Now he had nothing, and he was right back to square one, with the clock ticking.

Picking up his phone to summon an Uber to take him back to Vancouver, Matthews noticed a couple of new emails on the State Department system, including an erratum with respect to earlier messages regarding the US citizen killed in Vancouver who had been originally identified as John Dillon but whose actual name was Gian Dhillon. Matthews puzzled over the message for a moment, wondering who had managed to get the name so wrong in the first place, but as he stared at the correct name, something occurred to him that had him jump from his seat and hurry for the door.

Matthews sat in a meeting room at the Vancouver Police Department's headquarters on Cambie Street, reviewing the copy of the police report that the young investigator had given him before heading off for more coffee. The greeting from the Vancouver PD had been friendly enough, though they did seem a little puzzled by his presence. Perhaps it was because they had already been in touch with the US Consulate in Vancouver about the unfortunate but apparently routine mugging of a US citizen.

"Here you go," the investigator said, reappearing with a couple of coffees and a bag of condiments bearing the ubiquitous logo that was familiar even to a recent arrival to Canada like Matthews.

"Thanks. There really is a Tim's every five feet, isn't there?"

"Right across the street." The cop took a seat as Matthews pointed to the report.

"It says there might have been a witness, but I don't see a statement in the file."

"A homeless guy – Travis something or other – hanging around by a dumpster at the rear of the parking lot where the attack went down." The young cop popped open the lid of the cup and took a sip of the coffee. "I talked to him myself. He told one of the uniforms at the scene that he saw it all; but when I started asking questions, it was pretty clear he didn't see shit. He was fifty feet away and the lot was unlit. He was just looking for a bit of attention."

"So, no description of the perp, then? Not even a general height, build, skin colour?"

There was a slight pause as the investigator sipped at his coffee. "He mentioned something about a military look."

"Military, how?"

"I don't know – it's probably all bullshit, anyway."

Matthews was debating whether to keep pressing when the door opened and a woman in a pantsuit stepped into the room. She had an imposing look, not just because of her height but also the fact that Matthews could feel the scrutiny of her gaze from the doorway. After a few seconds, her focus shifted to the investigator seated opposite him.

"I'd like a minute with Mr. Matthews," she said, prompting the young investigator out of his chair and through the door in a matter of seconds.

"I'm Lieutenant Karen Armour," she said, after shutting the door.

"Ben Matthews." He stood and held out his State Department ID, but she waved it off.

"I know who you are, just not why you're here. To what do we owe the pleasure?"

He smiled and sat back down. "A US national was killed – standard procedure."

"We went through standard procedure with your colleague at the consulate. She didn't mention anyone flying in from Ottawa – not for what looks like a mugging gone wrong." She stayed on her feet by the door.

"I happened to be out here on other business," he said, with a smile. "I thought maybe I could lend a hand."

Armour seemed to consider the statement for a moment, then shrugged. "It's your dime, but from what I've been told, it's a pretty straightforward case. Not that we won't be working it very hard – we take homicide pretty seriously in this country."

"I'm sure you do. And I'm not here to make something out of nothing," Matthews said, opting not to challenge her initial assessment, given that no wallet or phone had been recovered at the scene – consistent with a crime of opportunity. "I just want to make sure we tick all the boxes."

Armour stared at him, as though running him through some internal bullshit meter that eventually told her to give him the benefit of the doubt. She glanced at the file folder in front of him. "I assume Duncan gave you what you need."

"He was nice enough to throw in a Tim Horton's too," he said, tapping the top of the coffee cup.

"Well, let me know if you need anything else." Armour started to turn toward the door.

"What about the location of the attack?"

She paused in the open doorway. "East Cordova and Main. What about it?"

"That's not a great area, right?"

Armour frowned. "It's at the edge of the East Side, but it's close enough to Gastown that it's not unusual for a tourist to have ventured there."

"What makes you think he was a tourist?"

Her eyes narrowed. "He's a retired scientist, or something, isn't he?"

"Yes. Retired to South Carolina, where he lived with his wife of forty years, who has no idea why he was in Vancouver."

Silence reigned as they looked at each other for a moment, neither displaying anything other than pinched smiles. Armour crossed her arms and cocked her head to the side, as though reassessing him.

"Well," she finally said. "Like I said, we're happy to let you make your inquiries, but Duncan's got a full slate of—"

"I understand, believe me," Matthews said, his hands up in a gesture of concession. "I'll keep out of your way."

"In that case, happy hunting."

Matthews got out of the cab and walked up West Pender Street to the intersection with Hornby and the entrance to the hotel where Gian Dhillon had stayed. It was no five-star but it wasn't a dump, either. About right for a retired scientist, he thought as he walked into the lobby and headed straight to reception. A twenty-something blond woman looked up from her monitor and gave him a broad smile as he approached the counter.

"Good morning," she said.

"I was wondering if I could have a word with the manager?" Her smile faded as she seemed to go through an internal assessment of how serious a complaint the man before her was about to make, from the size of the bed to the speed of the Wi-Fi. "I just have a couple of questions about the guest who was killed the other night," he added, flashing his State Department ID and hoping it looked law enforcement enough to overcome her reticence. She picked up the phone and five minutes later, he was sitting in the office of the manager – a fussy man in his forties who seemed put out by the fact that, of all the hotels in Vancouver, Gian Dhillon had picked his to stay at before inconsiderately getting himself killed.

"And you're with the US Consulate here?"

Matthews shook his head. "The US Embassy, in Ottawa."

"I see. Well, I've already told the Vancouver Police everything I know about Mr. Dhillon, which really isn't much."

"Yes, I know." Matthews had been through the notes in the file, which told him little other than the fact that Dhillon had booked a single room for three nights and appeared to be unaccompanied. "I was hoping to talk to the concierge who was on duty the night Mr. Dhillon was killed. I'd also like to take a look at the video from your lobby cameras."

The manager flicked a piece of lint from his lapel and consulted a printed schedule pinned to a bulletin board next to his monitor. "The concierge on duty that afternoon starts his shift in less than an hour. In the meantime, I can take you along to the security office, where you can have a look at the video." He paused as a frown creased his forehead. "Are you looking for something in particular? I mean, the police told us this was a random incident."

Matthews waved a hand. "I have no reason to think otherwise. I just want to be thorough."

"Well, if you'd care to follow me." The manager stood and gestured to the door, then led the way down the hall, into a room filled with screens featuring views of every public section of the hotel. "This is our head of security," he said, introducing Matthews to a heavyset man in his late fifties who stood and gripped his hand in a meaty paw. "He'd like to have a look at the lobby cam, to see if we have anything on Mr. Dhillon, the guest who was killed the other . . . Well, you know who he is. I'll leave you to it."

Matthews took a seat while the other man searched through some digital files.

"I've already been through all of the files for that day, and these are the only three that Mr. Dhillon was on."

"You did this for the Vancouver PD?"

The security manager shook his head. "They didn't ask. I was just curious."

"Well, I'm glad for that." Matthews smiled as the other man pulled up the first file. It was from the hall on the fifth floor, showing Dhillon leaving his room and walking toward the elevators. The time stamp read just after six p.m. and Dhillon was dressed in khakis and a light jacket, looking like any other guest headed out for dinner. The next file featured Dhillon alone in an elevator, checking his phone before slipping it into his jacket pocket as the door opened and he stepped out. The last was seven seconds of Dhillon crossing the lobby to the concierge desk, followed by another ninety seconds of him talking to someone in a hotel uniform - presumably the concierge Matthews was soon to meet - before exiting through the main doors.

"That's it?"

"'Fraid so."

"Can you replay that last one?"

A few clicks of the mouse later, the security manager had the last file ready to play again. "Do you want it in slow-mo?"

"Sure." They sat in silence, watching the same scene play out at half speed. First, Dhillon emerging from the elevator, then crossing the lobby. Matthews noticed a couple standing at the reception counter who appeared to show no interest in Dhillon as he passed them on his way to the concierge's desk.

"You want to see it again?"

Matthews shook his head. "No, but I'd like to talk to the concierge."

"He should be here soon. If you'd like to wait out in the lobby, I'll let him know."

"Thanks."

Returning to the lobby, Matthews waited for the guest at the front desk to finish checking out before approaching the same young woman he had spoken to earlier.

"I'm sorry if I upset you earlier, Darlene," he said, noticing her name tag. "I was just wondering if you had any interaction with Mr. Dhillon?"

"No, well, I handed him a message, that's all," she said

"A message? Did you see what it said?"

She shook her head. "It was in an envelope with his name on it."

"Did you see who dropped it off?

"No," she said, with another shake of her head. "It was here when I started my shift at three."

He asked a few more questions, but it was clear she had nothing more to offer, and with no sign of the concierge, he returned to the security manager's office and knocked on the door.

"Sorry to bother you again," he said. "Turns out someone dropped off a message for Dhillon the day he was killed. According to the front desk, it would have been sometime before three.

"I can have a look. Might take a while, though. I'm doing interviews for most of the day."

"Here's my number," Matthews said, handing him a card. "Appreciate it if you can send me anything you find."

Back out front, he took a seat on one of the lobby sofas. As he sat there waiting for the concierge, his mind began to wander, and it wasn't long before he began to question what he was doing digging into a mugging in Vancouver when he should be in London. He could picture the bustle of Piccadilly, its sidewalks crammed with well-heeled Londoners, a trendy Mayfair apartment just a short Tube ride from the US Embassy on the South Bank. His brain conjured a lazy Sunday morning sleep-in, the sunlight creeping in through the oversized windows and rousing him from a contented slumber as Caroline lay curled up next to him. Pulling out his phone, he checked his messages and found nothing to distract him from a creeping despair.

"Mr. Matthews?" He looked up to see a young man in a hotel uniform standing over him. "The security manager said you wanted to talk to me."

Matthews stood and shook his hand. "Ben Matthews. I wanted to ask you a couple of questions about Mr. Dhillon. Here okay?"

He gestured to the sofa. "I understand you were the last person he talked to at the hotel."

The concierge shrugged. "I guess so."

"I just watched the footage from the lobby cameras and saw that you had a ninety-second conversation with him."

"He asked about places to get a beer and a bite to eat."

"Did you recommend somewhere?"

The concierge nodded. "He was looking for pub fare in the Gastown area."

Matthews pulled out one of the hotel's maps of downtown Vancouver and pointed to an X he had marked at the intersection of Main and East Cordova. "This is where he was killed, which is a little east of Gastown, right?"

The concierge looked at the map and nodded. "It's the start of East Side, which isn't a great area, but that's not where I told him to go." He pointed a few blocks west. "I gave him the names of a couple of pubs over here. What time was he . . . attacked, anyway?"

"Around ten p.m., according to the police report."

The concierge frowned. "Main and East Cordova should have been okay around then, anyway."

"Look, I'm not here to suggest you did anything wrong," Matthews said. "I'm just wondering if there was anything else he said that might be of interest."

"I don't think so."

Matthews thought he recognized relief in the other man's eyes. "He was going to dinner alone?"

A quick nod. "I think so."

"He didn't ask where he might find some companionship, anything like that?"

The concierge gave an even quicker shake of the head. "No. Like I said, he just wanted a beer and a burger. I could tell from his accent that he was American, but we didn't really get into much of a conversation."

Matthews nodded. There was no evidence that Dhillon had strayed farther east than recommended to satisfy one vice or another, but if there was one thing he had learned, it was that people could always surprise you.

Matthews checked the sign at the intersection just down the street from the Quickie Mart that Sergeant Duncan had mentioned. If Travis – last name Wolfe, according to the police file – was going to be anywhere, it would be here. He glanced around and spotted a couple of men in their thirties in tattered clothes huddled in a doorway. Setting off in their direction, he noticed a solitary figure down an alley, sitting on a cardboard box next to a dumpster. He had dark hair topped by a tattered Vancouver Canucks hat and a patchy beard covered the bottom of his face. As Matthews approached, he recognized the sunken eyes and sallow skin of an addict.

"Are you Travis, by any chance?"

"Who's askin'?"

Bingo . . .

"I just wanted to ask you a few questions about the incident you witnessed the other night."

"And who the fuck are you? You ain't no cop."

Matthews grinned. "What makes you say that?"

"Vancouver PD can't afford nice suits like that."

"You're pretty observant. I'm glad I came to see you."

Wolfe grimaced, suddenly a hustler being hustled. "Why should I talk to you? I told the cops everything I know."

That's more like it, Matthews thought, pulling a twenty out of his pocket. "How about this, for starters," he said, as Wolfe eyed the bill.

"You told the cops you saw the attack go down."

"Maybe."

"What did he look like? The attacker."

Wolfe looked at the bill in silence, until Matthews handed it to him and he tucked it quickly into his shirt pocket. "Kinda like you."

"Like me, how? Wearing a suit?"

Wolfe shook his head. "Naw, I mean he was a big fuck. And he had short hair. His was blond though."

"So, big guy, six-two, six-three, with short blond hair. What was he wearing?"

Wolfe shrugged. "I dunno. Light wasn't good, but I'd say it was a dark jacket, or sweatshirt. He looked military to me."

"You mentioned that to one of the cops," Matthews said, with a nod. "What did you mean? Like he was wearing camo pants, or big boots?"

"Naw, I just mean . . . It takes one to know one."

"You were in the military?"

Wolfe nodded. "Bosnia in the nineties. I saw shit there no one should have to see. This guy reminded me of one of those fuckers . . . natural born killers."

Matthews waited as Wolfe went quiet. "You said you saw the attack?" he prompted, but Wolfe was staring at his feet. "Travis?" he said, his tone a little firmer.

"Yeah, I saw it. Heard it, more like it."

"What did you hear?"

"I heard him choking that poor bastard out, that's what."

Matthews nodded, thinking of the coroner's preliminary report. Dhillon had a single stab wound to the abdomen from a very sharp knife – likely delivered by a left-handed killer – and bruising in the area of the left temple, but the coroner seemed certain that the cause of death was asphyxiation. It seemed an odd combination of wounds for a mugging gone awry.

"And where were you?" Matthews asked.

"I was on the other side of that dumpster." Wolfe pointed to a large green bin at the rear of the parking lot behind the Quickie Mart. It wasn't as far as the fifty feet that Sergeant Duncan had mentioned, but it was at least thirty. As he glanced around the deserted lot, he saw only one light pole at the opposite rear corner. He noticed that Wolfe didn't elaborate on what he was doing at the time, whether it was sleeping, shooting up, or something else.

"So, you didn't actually see the victim before he was attacked?"

A shake of the head. "I was just mindin' my own business. The guy took off down that alley . . . after." Wolfe gestured to an alley running parallel to the side of the lot. "I caught a glimpse of him when he walked by the fence, over there," he added, pointing to a fenced-in area behind a commercial building that had a pair of security lights attached to the wall at the near end. Matthews didn't see any cameras, but he made a mental note to check.

"Anything else about this guy that stood out?"

"Let me think," Wolfe patted the pocket where he had tucked the first twenty, waiting until Matthews pulled out another one and handed it over.

"He said something."

Matthews leaned in. "Who, the killer? What'd he say?"

"I don't know." Wolfe was shaking his head again. "It sounded Eastern European, maybe?"

Matthews noticed Wolfe's expression had changed and realized that he was looking not at a streetwise hustler but a deeply damaged human. He reminded Matthews of someone back home – the older brother of a high school friend who had enlisted in the army and returned from Iraq broken. He reached into his pocket for his last twenty and handed it to Wolfe.

"For your trouble."

CHAPTER 7

"Here you go, Mr. Bosko," the clerk at the rental agency said, handing a set of keys across the counter and pointing through the window. "It's the silver one, right out front. Don't forget to have a quick look for damage," he added, with a smile. "Just so you don't get charged for stuff you didn't do."

The other man took the keys and returned the smile before heading for the door, thinking they could charge whatever damage they liked to the fictional Mr. Bosko. There was five thousand dollars on the credit card, after which they would be at a dead end, literally. The rental was a risk, but an unavoidable one, given the car he had driven up from Vancouver had refused to start that morning. He suspected the alternator, but he didn't have time to fix it himself and he couldn't bring it to a mechanic. If he had known the original trip from LA to Seattle was going to be extended to Vancouver and then Whitehorse, he would have had the car tuned up before he left, but there was nothing to be done about it now. He supposed he should be thankful that it hadn't chosen to crap out in the middle of nowhere out on the Alaska Highway. It was parked at the rear of a commercial parking lot where it would draw no attention and he had rented the pickup for a week. He planned to be long gone by the time it was due back.

Getting behind the wheel of the Ford F150, he ignored the welcome greeting from the built-in GPS, preferring the paper map he had brought with him and focusing on the location he had circled on Chadburn Lake Road. His tasking in Vancouver had been unusual to say the least, but he had just enough information to make it work, though he didn't have much time. He double-checked the destination and the route from his current location, then pulled out of the lot and headed down into the valley cradling the city of Whitehorse. He drove south through the city, though it seemed to him more like a town, crossed the Yukon River, and entered a residential area that eventually led to Chadburn Lake Road. Five minutes later, he was back in the wilderness, working his way along the edge of Schwatka Lake, then the Yukon River as it snaked east until it flowed into Chadburn Lake. Halfway along the lake, he spotted the sign for Sourdough Outfitters and turned off the dirt road. The gravel driveway took him through dense trees before opening up into a large clearing that featured a main lodge and several outbuildings, including horse corrals and sheds. Farther along, at the foot of a gentle incline leading up from the water, he saw a pair of bush planes parked next to a large Quonset hut that looked big enough to shelter them both.

He parked the truck in front of the main building and scanned the parking area, empty apart from a dented old Chevy at the far end. As he opened his door, he smelled woodsmoke and looked up to see a white cloud billowing out of the chimney above the lodge. He was getting out of the truck when a young woman appeared on the front porch, carrying what looked like a wooden crate. A large black-and-white husky followed her out through the door and stopped to take in the stranger.

"Good morning," he called out, with a disarming smile. He could feel the knife tucked into the left sleeve of his jacket, but he was hoping he wouldn't have to use it just yet.

"Mornin'," the woman replied, apparently unconcerned by his presence. "You lookin' for Dale?"

"I have some questions about your guided hunts."

"Just gimme a second. I've gotta get some wood. And don't worry about him," she said, gesturing toward the dog, who was now sitting by the door staring at him. "He wouldn't hurt a flea."

He waited as she disappeared around the side of the lodge and re-emerged a couple of minutes later with the box full of chopped wood.

"Let me help you," he said and as he got closer, he realized she was barely more than a girl, maybe only twenty years old.

"It's lighter than it looks, but you could get the door for me."

"Of course." He stepped past the dog and held the door, then followed her inside.

"I just put coffee on. You want some?" the girl called out, as she deposited the wood box in front of a large stone hearth where a fire was already crackling.

"No, thank you."

"You're interested in a hunt?"

"Yes, I read your materials online and it seems like perfect for me."

"Love your accent. Where you from?"

"Poland," he said, glancing around the lodge. There was an open living area in front of the fireplace, a couple of rooms off to the side with both doors open and a loft that ran the length of one end of the structure. It seemed that the girl was alone. "I plan a trip for my brothers. They love to hunt."

"They're all coming over from Poland?"

"No, they are living in America now, like me."

"Cool. When were you planning on doing your hunt? We tend to book up a long time in advance."

"Yes, I see this on your website. I hope for next fall."

The girl moved off toward the back of the room and he heard the clink of a china mug. "You sure you don't want a coffee?" she called out.

"No, thank you," he said again as he edged closer to a cluttered desk to the right of the entrance, staring at a small calendar pinned to the wall behind it, just out of sight of the entrance. He walked around to read it as he heard the girl pouring coffee. Most of the boxes marking the days of the current month were filled with entries in ink of various colours. He checked the box for a day ago and saw *JT +2 – VIP* in red ink, whereas the rest of the entries were mostly in black or blue. The only other entry in red ink was in the box four days from the current date, but he couldn't make out what it said. He reached over and tore the top sheet of the calendar off, stuffing it into his pocket as he stepped back toward the main entrance just as the girl returned.

"So, what kind of game are you after?"

"Sheep. Yukon is best place to get them, yes?"

The girl smiled as she sipped at a mug of steaming coffee. "We've been getting some big rams in the past few weeks."

"All of your hunts are guided?"

"Yup," she said, as the dog curled up at her feet. "Dale was supposed to be on a hunt right now, but it's a . . . special case. He'll be in tomorrow if you want to talk to him."

"Not today?"

She shook her head. "He flew up to Dawson and he's stayin' the night. He's an early riser though, so he'll be back first thing in the morning."

"I come back to see him," the man said, nodding. He pulled a copy of the outfitter's brochure from his pocket and pointed to the map printed on the back. "He always hunts the same area?"

"Yup. Kluane Plateau's good huntin', whether you're lookin' for sheep, moose, or grizzly."

He asked some more questions while the young woman sipped her coffee, then he stood to leave. "Thank you for your information. I come back tomorrow and see Mr. Dale."

"Do you want to leave a name?"

"Bosko. Piotr Bosko," he said, giving the room one last sweep with his eyes before they settled on the girl and her trusting smile. If only she knew.

CHAPTER 8

Richard Perry stopped breathing the moment the bullet left the gun, and he felt its power in his spine as the ear-splitting crack of the shot ripped through the icy air and echoed against the mountainside above. He released his breath in a cloud then looked through the long-range scope at the top of the .303 rifle and saw the big ram stumble, twist, and then eventually topple onto its side.

"What a shot!" John Townsend held his binoculars at eye level for a moment, before dropping them down and patting Perry on the shoulder. "That's got to be three hundred and fifty yards, and he's *down*!"

Perry lowered the rifle, adrenaline still surging through his system. They had spotted the ram over an hour ago, but it had disappeared behind some rocks before anyone could line up a shot.

"I thought we'd lost our chance," he said, taking the binoculars from Townsend and locating the ram on the distant mountainside, now motionless on its side.

"There's some pretty rugged terrain to get over there." Garcia was scanning the ram's location with his own binoculars, panning down to the narrow pass that connected it with their current vantage point.

It might only be three hundred and fifty yards as the crow flies, but the difference in elevation and the terrain could easily mean a two-hour hike.

"I ever tell you you worry too much?" Perry said with a grin. "We can set up a fly camp by the treeline if we can't make it back to Eagle Ridge." He handed the binoculars back to Townsend, who followed where he was pointing and nodded, then looked up at the thickening clouds. The sky had been clear when they set out from the spike camp at Eagle Ridge but now, almost two in the afternoon, the clouds looked ready to burst. He hoped it wouldn't take too long to reach the ram, or they might find themselves out in the open in a blizzard. Setting up the lightweight tent they had brought along would be no fun in a snowstorm.

"We should probably get moving." Townsend gestured up to the sky. "We want to get our camp set up before this blows in."

Perry was on his feet first, a smile on his face as he prepared to see his kill up close. He drew in a deep breath of the mountain air and looked around. To the north and east lay mountain slopes, their upper limits dusted in white; to the southwest, green valleys leading into Kluane National Park, its mountains just visible in the distance. Nowhere was there any trace of another human being – something both unfamiliar and awe-inspiring. "It really is unbelievable up here," he said, with a sweep of his hand.

Townsend slapped him on the back. "What's unbelievable is that shot you just made, from four hundred yards."

"It'll be five hundred by the time we get back to base camp." Perry was laughing as he shouldered his rifle and they donned their packs. The only one who wasn't smiling as they set off over the rocks was Garcia, who paused to scan the valley below and the climb that would follow on the other side. He looked up at the darkening sky and noticed the first flakes of snow, frowned, and then fell in behind the other two men.

Perry snugged the bottom corner of the tent and hammered in the last of the pegs with the back of a hatchet, then double-checked the knots on the ropes holding the overhead tarp in place, his fingers raw and stinging from the cold. The wind had picked up as the temperature dropped over the course of the afternoon and he was really noticing the difference as he finished his work. It was dark now, but as he rubbed his hands together to get the circulation going, he was heartened by the sound of a crackling fire burning under a small outcrop of rock that seemed to be keeping most of the snow from the flames.

"All squared away?" Townsend asked, as Perry joined him and warmed his hands by the fire.

"Anything short of a hurricane and we should be good. Where's Garcia?"

"He's stashing the meat," Townsend said. "We don't want a grizzly rolling up on us in the middle of the night."

Perry nodded. It had taken them over two hours to hike up to where the ram lay dead and another to field dress it and cape it out. They had divided what was left between the three of them and the hike back down to the treeline had been heavy going, with their progress further hampered by snow squalls that had increased in intensity as the day wore on.

"We're lucky we made it back down without anyone busting an ankle," Townsend said, as Garcia appeared at the edge of the firelight, his black watch cap covered in snow.

"We good?"

Garcia nodded, removing the hat and shaking off the snow, then dusting off the sleeves of the lightweight shell he wore over a warm fleece.

"It's really coming down now." Townsend looked up at the thick flakes swirling beyond the overhang of rock.

"What's the latest forecast?" Perry turned to Garcia, who shook his head and dug into his jacket pocket.

"My phone wasn't working last I checked, sir."

"Well," Townsend said, "we're not going anywhere tonight anyway, and we've got all we need."

"Speaking of which, is anyone else hungry?" Perry reached for his pack and pulled out three packets of freeze-dried food. "We've got chicken teriyaki and rice, bacon and cheddar and mashed potatoes, or . . . noodles with beef and mushroom sauce."

Townsend was shaking his head. "To hell with that. We've got ribs on the menu tonight, gentlemen."

The others watched as he laid a canvas bag that had been attached to his pack on the ground and pulled out a thick side of the ram's ribs. He threaded a wooden skewer through the ribs and laid them across the flames, resting the ends of the skewer on two rocks he had placed on either side of the fire.

"I was wondering what they were for," Perry said, pointing to the rocks as Townsend reached for the second side of ribs.

"These are gonna taste a whole lot better than that freeze-dried crap," Townsend said, slapping Perry on the shoulder. "Besides, it's tradition."

"Dessert anyone?" Townsend said, pulling out a thick slab of chocolate after they had polished off the ribs. Perry declined and Garcia accepted a chunk as Townsend filled a pot with water for coffee.

"Any luck?" Perry asked, turning to Garcia as he fiddled with the satellite communicator and his phone.

"I'm afraid not." Garcia's expression was as stoic as usual, but it was clear he was concerned.

"You downloaded the updates before you left?" Townsend asked, turning from the fire.

Garcia nodded. "I'm sure I did."

"It's probably the weather." Townsend pointed up at the sky. "It can disrupt the satellite signals sometimes, but I'm sure this'll blow over tonight. Then it'll work just fine."

Perry nodded. "He's right, Garcia. I know what you're thinking, but it's fine."

Townsend said nothing for a moment, not wanting to interrupt what seemed to be a continuing but unspoken dialogue between the other two men. "We'll hunker down tonight and then hike back to base camp tomorrow. I can't wait to see Dale's face when he sees those horns, or when he finds out you took that ram out from three hundred and fifty yards."

Garcia gave a rare smile from the other side of the fire. "That *was* a helluva shot, sir."

"Ah, I got lucky." Perry gave a dismissive wave. "But there's no need to tell anyone else that when we get back," he added, with a chuckle.

Townsend smiled. "And did I say three-fifty? It was four hundred yards, at least."

CHAPTER 9

Dale Oyler was gassing up a chainsaw out by the garage when he saw the silver F150 pull up in front of the lodge. He watched as a tall, blond man emerged from the driver's side of the pickup.

"Mornin'," Oyler said, rubbing his hands with an oily rag.

"You are Mr. Oyler?"

Oyler nodded, trying to place the accent. It had a Germanic tinge, but he had guided so many Germans over the years – they just couldn't get enough of the Yukon's wide open spaces – that he knew it didn't sound quite right. "What can I do ya for?"

"I am interested in reserving a hunt."

"You the fella was by yesterday, got a group from Poland?"

"Yes. Piotr Bosko," he said, extending a hand.

Oyler shook it but began to frown. "I don't know if Marcie told you, but we're pretty booked up."

"I am interested in next fall."

"Well, come on in and I'll have a look-see at the schedule and give you the low down on what we offer here at Sourdough." Oyler led the way inside and offered the other man a seat on one of the sofas by the fireplace, but Bosko lingered near the cluttered desk instead. "You are very busy," he said, with a lopsided grin that Oyler found odd.

"Like I said, we're pretty much booked solid until the end of October."

"Why you're not out on a hunt right now?" It wasn't the grammatical peculiarity of the question but its underlying tone that made Oyler reconsider his answer in the silence that settled over the interior of the lodge, deserted except for the two of them. Marcie had the day off and he wasn't expecting anyone else that morning. "You drop someone off, yes?" Bosko continued, pulling the page he had taken from the wall calendar the day before and pointing to the red ink on the calendar square for a few days earlier.

Oyler looked at the crumpled page, then at the wall calendar. "Listen, Mr. . . . What'd you say your name was?"

"Bosko."

"I don't discuss the particulars of my hunts, Mr. Bosko. You'll understand that people come from a long way away and spend a lot of money to be alone up there in the mountains." He softened the message with a smile, but he hoped he had been clear enough.

"I understand this completely. But it surprise me you are not guiding this . . . how do you call him? Guest?" Oyler felt a shiver at the back of his neck as he took in the big Pole, realizing he was blocking the path to the shotgun he kept inside the front hall closet. The other man followed Oyler's furtive glance, then smirked before returning his focus to the calendar page in his hand and tapping the box representing a few days from now. "This is when you pick them up, yes?"

"Look, I don't know who you are, or what you want, but I think it's time you left."

"But you have not told me what I need to know."

"I'm not telling you a goddamn thing," Oyler said, his face flushing as anger and adrenaline pushed up his heart rate and blood pressure.

"I think you will," the other man said, sliding a semi-automatic out of his jacket pocket and pointing it in Oyler's direction.

"Now listen—"

The speed and force of the blow to the side of his head seemed impossible to Oyler, especially since his attacker had closed a three-foot gap without giving him the chance to get his arms up to defend himself, let alone consider a counterattack. But there was no denying the stinging pain above his right ear, left by the butt of the gun.

"Come," the other man said, gesturing to the front door with the gun. "We take trip together. Get your plane ready."

"My plane? What the fu—" Oyler's further protests were halted by the sight of the gun raising in Bosko's hand until the barrel was level with the bridge of his nose.

"Will they be at base camp, or still in mountains?" Bosko said, looking out the window at the expanse of wilderness below.

"How the fuck should I know?" Oyler yelled. Even with headsets on, the roar of the Cessna's propeller was deafening. He had made a couple of attempts to put his passenger on the wrong path since leaving the lodge on Chadburn Lake, but the guy seemed to be one step ahead of him. He knew the hunting party was up on the Kluane Plateau, and Oyler's attempt to fly near the airport after taking off had been met by a threat of being shot in the gut and tossed out of the plane at two thousand feet – a threat he considered entirely credible coming from the glowering hulk riding shotgun. There was something about the detached way in which he spoke and, combined with his considerable size and those dead eyes, the man oozed menace from his every pore. Even so, Oyler had tried subtly deviating from the course that followed the Alaska Highway northwest from the Whitehorse area but was met almost immediately with the same threat each time.

"I mean, it snowed a fair bit last night," he added quickly, thinking that Bosko might be considering a consequence for Oyler's uncooperative silence. "They probably hunkered down somewhere up in the mountains," he added as the Kluane Plateau became visible in the distance. All he could think was that if he didn't do something soon, he was going to lead this maniac right to the group. "What exactly are you planning on doing once you find them?" he asked, immediately wishing he hadn't when he saw the twisted grin on the other man's face.

"Just get me there and back, and everyone is happy," he said. "I pay you a good fee as well, if you co-operate."

"Sure," Oyler said, focusing on the feel of the six-inch Buck knife tucked inside his right boot.

You keep smiling like you know everything, asshole . . .

CHAPTER 10

Matthews was on his way out for a coffee when he spotted a woman standing on the sidewalk in front of the Cambie Street station, a small plastic bag in her hand. He had seen her photo but it was the unmistakable signs of grief in her lightly lined face that told him he was looking at Cathy Dhillon. He might have kept walking, but she turned just as he reached the bottom step. When their eyes met, he felt an obligation to say something.

"Mrs. Dhillon?"

She seemed lost and hesitated a moment, then gave a mechanical nod.

"I'm Ben Matthews, from the US Embassy. I'm very sorry for your loss."

"Thank you," she said, her brows furrowing. "You mean the consulate?"

He smiled. "I'm in town from Ottawa, but I'm aware of your husband's . . . case. I'm very—"

"Yes, you said that," she said, as an uncomfortable silence descended and Matthews wished he had kept his mouth shut. "I'm sorry if I seem abrupt," she finally said. "It's just that with everything going on, I feel a bit drained."

"I was just going to get a coffee if you'd like to join me?"

She seemed to look through him before a thin smile appeared on her face. "I could use some caffeine."

"I really am sorry for your loss," he said, after they had taken their coffees to a table in the corner. He watched her set the bag containing her husband's personal effects gently on the empty chair.

"I just want to know what happened. There's so much that doesn't make sense."

He saw the incomprehension in her eyes, and it made the official explanation – that her husband had been in the wrong place at the wrong time – seem all the more unsatisfactory.

"I'm sure this must be a very trying time for—"

"Let's cut the diplomatic doublespeak, okay?" she interrupted, as a silence descended over the table, punctuated by ambient jazz, the hiss of steam, and the occasional clink of mugs. He looked at her and saw the intelligence and resolve in her eyes and knew this wasn't going to be easy. "I've had a lifetime's worth of apologies and good wishes in the past few days," she continued, "but nobody's told me a goddamn thing about what actually *happened* to Gian."

Matthews glanced at his hands for a moment, then looked back at her. "Do you know why your husband was in Vancouver, Mrs. Dhillon?"

"It's Cathy, and no. I didn't even know Gian *was* in Vancouver. He left about a week ago, for Seattle. He volunteers with a group called Scientists for Humanity. Their annual general meeting was in Seattle. Vancouver must have been a last-minute side trip."

Matthews frowned. "Did he actually go to Seattle?"

"Yes, of course. He called me from Seattle four days ago, I saw the name of the hotel on the call display."

"He didn't say anything about going to Vancouver?"

"No. He did say he was going to stay on a couple of extra days after the conference wrapped up, but I just assumed he was staying in the Seattle area." She paused for a moment and spun her cup on the table before looking back at him. "That was the last time I talked to him."

He gave her a moment as she looked away and composed herself before he asked his next question. "Did he sound normal?"

A little shrug. "As normal as he's been lately."

"What do you mean? Had he been acting strange lately?"

Another shrug. "He was . . . agitated. I wrote it off to boredom. Gian's been retired from WPI for less than a year, and he's had a hard time with it. His work was always his life. He was dedicated, you know?"

"WPI?"

"Wellstead Pharmaceuticals International," she said. "Gian spent his entire career there."

Matthews nodded. "I see. Any other unusual behaviour in the past few weeks?"

"It's probably nothing, but . . ." She paused, fixing him with those intense eyes before continuing. "He was on his cellphone a lot, which is unusual for Gian. He hates those things almost as much as I do, and he was almost . . . secretive about it. And I know what you're thinking," she added. "But it wasn't another woman."

"I wasn't thinking that."

"You're a bad liar, Mr. Matthews, but it's all right – that's the natural assumption. We've been married forty years, we have no kids, and Gian was in good shape and comfortably off. It's almost what he's supposed to do, right? Trade me in for someone half my age, or just get someone on the side. Not Gian." She was shaking her head.

"Do you or your husband have friends in Vancouver? Maybe a former colleague of his?"

"Not that I know of," she said. "The funny thing is, I called the phone company and got the list of incoming and outgoing calls from our home line and both of our cells, and there's no record of *any* calls on his cell in the past week. Yet I know he was on the phone several times before he left for Seattle."

"That's odd," Matthews said, thinking the most likely explanation was that Gian Dhillon had a second cellphone – probably a prepaid – that he was making the calls on. Perhaps the girlfriend had suggested a dirty weekend in Vancouver.

"I *know* he was not seeing another woman," she said, interrupting the scenario Matthews's mind was rapidly assembling and triggering a wave of guilt. "Even if he were, it still wouldn't explain why anyone would want to kill him."

"What kind of phone did he have?" Matthews asked, thinking of the image of Dhillon in the elevator with a phone in his hands, and its absence from the inventory of the crime scene and Dhillon's hotel room.

"I think it was an iPhone but don't ask me what model – I can barely tell the difference between a smartphone and a rotary dial." They sat in silence for a moment, each preoccupied with their own theories on what Dhillon had been up to in the past few weeks. Then she stopped fidgeting with her cup and looked up at him. "I get the feeling the police aren't going to be doing much investigating."

"They're treating it as a random attack. It was a bad part of town and your husband's wallet and phone appear to have been taken, so I guess their position is understandable."

"And you agree?"

He shrugged. "There's not much to suggest any other motive," he said, though the unusual nature of Dhillon's wounds still bothered him. Then again, they didn't rule out a random mugging that had escalated for one reason or another.

"That's not what I asked."

"I'm not really in a position to tell the Vancouver PD how to go about their investigation."

She crossed her arms over her chest. "Well, you may be willing to go along with the Vancouver Police's whitewash of this, but I'm certainly not."

"I understand a forensic autopsy is in the works. Hopefully that will provide some answers."

That seemed to appease her for the moment, then she glanced at her watch. "I should be going soon. I have to go back to my hotel before my meeting at the consulate."

He nodded as he avoided her eyes. "I'm sure you're in good hands."

Cathy Dhillon's eyes narrowed over her cup as she drank the last of her coffee. "But you're not working with them on this?"

"Like I said, I just happened to be in town, but the folks at the consulate will take good care of you." He drained the last of his coffee. "Before you go, do you mind me asking whether Gian was Sikh?"

"What does that have to do with anything?"

"Probably not much. I just know there's a large Sikh community in the greater Vancouver area and I wondered—"

"His parents are fairly active in the Sikh community in Raleigh - that's where they ended up when they emigrated from Punjab. As for Gian, he's . . . he was proud of his heritage, but he wasn't really involved in any expat communities that I'm aware of and he hadn't been to a gurdwara in years. Maybe even decades." She glanced at her watch again. "I really should be going."

"Can I offer you a ride to your hotel?"

"Do you have a limo parked outside, with an American flag on the hood?"

Matthews smiled. "Just an Uber, I'm afraid."

Matthews took a sip of beer and glanced around the bar in the lobby of his hotel. It was a relatively sparse pre-dinner crowd, too late for happy hour but too early for the serious drinkers. An attractive woman in her late thirties sitting at the opposite end of the bar smiled as his scan of the room brought them into eye contact. She was a bit older than Caroline and apart from the hair colour and general build there was little resemblance, but that didn't prevent him from thinking of her as he returned the smile and went back to his beer. Caroline was probably in some swanky after-hours club in Soho, or already home in bed, tucked up with . . . The ringing of his phone broke his train of thought before the bitterness turned to bile.

"Matthews."

"What the fuck are you doing?"

Matthews took a moment to gauge the level of anger in his boss's voice. He had a pretty good sense of Vanessa Ortiz's snapping point and while the timbre of her voice told him she wasn't quite there, he knew it wasn't far off. "What do you mean?"

"Don't give me that. I just got off the phone with the consulate in Vancouver – the head of consular, to be precise – who's all pissed off because you've been sticking your nose into one of their cases? What the fuck?"

"I'm not sticking my nose into anything."

"He says you met with the widow?"

"I didn't *meet* with her. I bumped into her and offered her my condolences, that's all. I don't know why the consulate's getting all bent out of shape," he added, laying the bemusement on thick. "I just bought her a coffee."

"Don't bullshit me, Ben. I know you think you're smarter than everyone else, but you need to learn to stay in your lane."

"I'm in my lane, believe me."

"What's so interesting about this consular case, anyway?" Ortiz said, after a pause to catch her breath. Matthews smiled, knowing her curiosity was even more all-consuming than his own.

"On the surface, it's a mugging gone bad. Routine stuff."

There was another pause as Ortiz seemed to assess the credibility of his statement. "And beneath the surface?"

"The wounds were a bit unusual for a mugging, and the victim was Sikh."

"You think that's why he was targeted? That it's related to the cell you're looking into?"

"You have to admit it's pretty coincidental," Matthews said, sensing some leeway. "We get wind of a rumoured plot against American Sikhs cooked up by an extremist cell in BC and low and behold – an American Sikh gets murdered in Vancouver."

"Was the victim politically active?"

"Not sure," he said, thinking Dhillon's widow had been clear that he wasn't, not that her assessment was conclusive – Dhillon might have kept his activism to himself.

"What does your source say?"

Matthews paused. He wasn't prepared for this conversation yet, but it was only a matter of time before he had to come clean. "The source is a dead end."

"What do you mean a dead end? I thought he was the whole reason you went out there?"

"He doesn't have the kind of access we need," Matthews said, adding quickly: "Not yet anyway. I'm working another possible angle, too, but it's gonna take a little time."

"Doesn't sound like a productive trip."

He sighed. "You know how these things go. What do you want me to say?"

"I don't want you to say anything, but what I want you to *do* is to stay the fuck out of consular's way, understood?"

"Understood. So," he added after a pause, "you don't want me to rule out a connection betwee—"

"I said I don't want any more calls from the consulate."

"Right," he said, before realizing that the line had gone dead, leaving him to try and figure out if she was telling him to keep digging or get on a plane. He had barely put the phone down on the bar when it rang again. His first thought was that it was Ortiz calling back, either to clarify her instructions or to give him another lambasting, but instead he saw the name of the Vancouver PD's Major Crimes Unit member he had spoken to after returning from his interview with Travis Wolfe.

"Matthews."

"It's Sergeant Dave Lam, Vancouver PD. I just wanted to follow up on a couple of things."

"I'm all ears," he said, leaning onto the bar.

"I wish I had better news. We struck out on security footage from the alley. The camera above the fenced-in area was out of commission and the only other view of the alley was too far south."

"That's too bad." Matthews spun his beer glass around, sensing there was more bad news to come.

"And we double-checked with ident – the crime scene guys – and there was no phone found at the scene and it's not in the inventory from his hotel room either."

"Perp must have taken it. Shit." Matthews recalled the image from the elevator camera that clearly showed Dhillon checking a phone on his ride down to the lobby. His last ride, as it would turn out. The fact that his killer had taken it was hardly unusual – it could have been the sole motive for the attack for all Matthews knew.

"You know what kind of phone it was?"

"An iPhone. Not sure what model but pretty recent."

"We can put the word out to our CIs in the area," Lam said, referring to confidential informants. "It'd be a hell of a long shot, but you never know. Are you back in tomorrow?"

"Yeah, I'll be in first thing."

"Well, let me know if there's anything else I can do for you."

"Appreciate it, thanks." Matthews hung up the phone, wondering what the cop was really thinking. Probably that Matthews's flight out to sniff around a mugging just meant the US State Department had too much time and money on its hands. He glanced around and caught the brunette looking his way again, then returned his attention to his phone as a new message from the security manager at Dhillon's hotel came in. He clicked open the attachment and watched a few seconds of grainy footage of a man handing something across the desk before turning and leaving. The woman behind the desk was engaged in a conversation with a guest and it didn't look like she had spoken to whoever had delivered the message. Matthews returned to the email and learned that the security manager had spoken to the desk clerk himself and confirmed that all she remembered was a man in his thirties or forties saying the envelope was for a guest: Dhillon. Matthews replayed the attachment, pausing the video several times but the best he got was a grainy profile of a man wearing a flat cap. Whether he had known where the camera was or timed his delivery for when the woman at the desk was most distracted, Matthews didn't know, but the result was the same – a poor image and little to no physical description from the hotel staff. He forwarded it to Lam with a covering email just in case, but he had a feeling it was a dead end.

"Fuck."

"Bad news?"

He looked up, surprised to see the woman from the end of the bar was now two seats from his own. Up close, she really did look like Caroline and whatever initial attraction he had felt was gone. If he had learned anything from his experience with Renée back in Ottawa, it was that he wasn't ready to move on.

"Sorry . . . it's nothing. Just work," he said, putting some bills on the bar and pushing back his stool. "Have a nice evening."

In no rush to return to his sterile hotel room, Matthews headed outside and made his way northwest from West Hastings Street in the waning daylight, his mind sifting through different subsets of information but ending up with the same question – why was he so convinced that there was more to Gian Dhillon's death than the official explanation? Matthews had found no evidence that Dhillon was a Khalistani or even politically active at all, much less to an extent that would warrant a state-sponsored attack, so why was he clinging to the remote possibility?

By the time he reached the seawall near Coal Harbour, he couldn't avoid the answer anymore. He felt exhausted as he slumped onto one of the few vacant benches lining the walkway and looked out over the water at North Vancouver. He could just make out the outline of the mountains beyond in the dim light, but his thoughts turned to Boston and the line from the report that had burned itself into his subconscious ever since he had first read it: *It is unclear whether all actions commensurate with the urgency of the situation were taken . . .*

What had followed read like a full exoneration, but there was no denying the caveat and that it had been included for a reason. Yes, the plot to murder two MIT scientists had failed, mostly because of Matthews's work following a combination of instinct and raw intelligence to locate an intermediary with knowledge of the planned assassinations. But one of the scientists, a woman in her late twenties, had been attacked and seriously injured before an FBI agent had taken her assailant down, and Matthews knew she would bear the physical and mental scars of the attack for the rest of her life. The fact that minutes – possibly even seconds – could have prevented that damage was something he'd never be able to forget. Far worse than the blemish on his record was his own assessment that he had not only failed but had done so in a way that he had tried so hard to avoid ever since he had first told his father that he wanted to be a cop back in high school. The dismissive look had been more powerful than any words could ever have been in conveying his father's response – that he didn't think his son had what it takes.

Matthews turned at the sound of laughter as a young couple strolled by hand in hand, the woman leaning into her partner in a playful shove before kissing him on the cheek. Matthews watched their progress for a while, then turned his attention back to the water, watching it darken as the last of the daylight faded and there was nothing to do but return to his hotel room.

CHAPTER 11

Dale Oyler kept his eyes straight ahead as he flew the Cessna along the line of the Alaska Highway, far below.

"Where are you going?" The hulk in the passenger seat said with a scowl.

"You want me to take you to base camp, so I'm heading to base camp," Oyler said, trying to appear unshaken as he continued to stare out the windshield of the little bush plane.

"Plateau is over there, between those mountains. West."

"What are you talking about?"

Bosko glared at him, something between a grimace and a grin forming as he pushed the barrel of the automatic into Oyler's flank. "Stop fucking around – I have seen your brochure, and your website, you remember?"

"You're so sure, why don't you fly the goddamn plane," Oyler muttered as he adjusted course, the hard steel of the gun still pressed into his rib cage. It occurred to him that a quick jerk of his arm might give him a chance to disarm his unwanted passenger. But it could also earn him a bullet in his gut, and even if he could knock the gun away from him, Bosko was built like a truck and to take him at close quarters and maintain control of the plane was impossible. He had even considered a controlled crash-landing, but doing so with this big ape sitting next to him presented the same problem. He had to be patient, he told himself, still feeling the knife inside his boot and thinking the best time to use it was when he got some separation from his captor. That opportunity would come after they landed. It would have to, or he would have to make it happen.

"I see it," Bosko said, removing the gun from Oyler's side and looking out through the windshield as he pointed to a collection of brown dots representing the base camp lodge and outbuildings, located at the near end of a mountain valley surrounded by a series of peaks of varying height.

"Yeah, but there's nobody home," Oyler remarked, enjoying a brief rush of relief.

Bosko frowned. "They will be in mountains still."

"Who are you, anyway?" Oyler turned to face him. "And don't tell me you're Polish, either."

"Just fly fucking plane . . . why we're not going down?"

"Relax, the ground's smoother at the north end, and it's a gentle incline. I'm going to bring us around and come in from the north . . . unless you want to take the chance of hitting a boulder at the south end, or running out of landing strip."

The other man grunted and gave a subtle nod, placing the gun back against Oyler's ribs. "Don't do something stupid."

"You think I want to crash any more than you do?" Oyler gave a shake of his head as he flew past the plateau. He kept going as long as he could before he felt questioning eyes boring into the side of his head and was forced to begin a banked turn. Instead of heading west toward the spectacular scenery of Kluane National Park, as he would normally do when flying in a hunting party, Oyler banked east toward the Alaska Highway. He swung the Cessna in a wide arc out over the highway and scanned for cars, spotting a couple of vehicles far below. As he straightened out, he dipped the wings to one side, but before he could complete the second half of the manoeuvre, Bosko's hand shot out and grabbed the control wheel.

"Do that again and I blow *fucking* head off!"

"I'm straightenin' out, for Christ's sake."

"You're dipping wings, to send distress signal," Bosko yelled, then swatted Oyler's cheek with a fist that felt like granite. "Get back on course and land fucking plane!"

"All right, all right! Take it easy." Oyler rubbed his cheek and adjusted course, heading toward the plateau again. Neither man spoke for the next few minutes as Oyler lined up for a landing at the northern end and edged the plane into a final descent. As the rugged but familiar terrain below came toward them, he flirted again with intentionally clipping the treetops, but he held his course until the tundra tires connected with the ground and the little plane bounced along the makeshift runway, gradually losing speed as he applied the brakes and they climbed the slight natural incline. He continued to taxi along until they were within a hundred feet of the base camp buildings. Oyler felt relief seeing them unoccupied.

"What now?" He looked at the other man as he shut off the engine.

"We get out," Bosko said, waving the gun. "Very slow."

Oyler nodded, unfastening his seat belt and opening his door while the other man did the same. He felt the air in his nostrils as soon as he stepped outside, the temperature a good ten degrees Celsius colder than when they had left Chadburn Lake. He made a show of stretching from side to side, then bending at the waist.

"My friggin' back," he said with a groan.

"Show me inside," Bosko said, gesturing toward the lodge as he stepped up behind Oyler, who was still bent over at the waist.

"Just let me finish stretching," Oyler said, then straightened up suddenly, slashing at Bosko's gun hand with the razor-sharp Buck knife. He felt it tear through flesh, and watched the gun fall from the other man's hand.

"How's it feel without your gun, big man?" he said, taking a step forward and thrusting the knife to keep Bosko from recovering the weapon that lay between them. Oyler didn't dare try and reach for it himself, sensing that was the opening the other man was anticipating. Bosko seemed not to notice his bleeding hand and was staring instead at Oyler's knife. But it wasn't concern, much less fear of the knife or the sudden turn of events, that appeared on Bosko's face as he crouched and moved slowly to the side. An ugly grin curled the man's lips as his dark eyes narrowed.

"Now, I will kill you."

"Good luck," Oyler said, bravado concealing the panic he felt as he watched the other man's face morph from smirk to snarl – those dark, merciless eyes fixing on him as he circled. Oyler thrust the knife forward a couple of times to back him away from the gun still lying on the ground, but Bosko seemed uninterested in it, content for them both to move away. Oyler slipped on a snow-covered rock but caught himself before losing his balance, his relief fading as he realized that Bosko now held a belt in his hands.

What the fuck . . .

He hadn't even noticed him unclasp the buckle, let alone slip the belt from around his waist. Now, he watched with a feeling of dread as Bosko wrapped the thick leather around his hand and began to swing the belt from side to side, its heavy buckle making a swooshing sound as it cut through the air. Oyler had spent his life around guns and knives, and he had been in his share of bar fights over the years, but the only thing he had actually fought with a knife was a cougar, and that had been when he was in a BC mining camp in his twenties. He still had the scars on his arms, but he had ended up with the cougar's pelt, and he wasn't going down without a fight now. He began moving to the side, forcing the bigger man to rotate around to follow, hoping to take advantage of a stumble on the rocky ground.

"I was going to kill you anyway," Bosko said, assuming a wide stance as he stepped over the rocks at his feet and maintained the same distance from Oyler. "You just save me some time," he added. Seeing the smirk on his face, Oyler's rage swelled up and he lunged forward, hoping to bury the blade of his knife in something vital. Bosko seemed to expect the move, parrying it with the thick leather belt, then clutching Oyler's extended arm at the wrist and wrenching it until he dropped the knife. Bosko continued to twist Oyler's arm up behind his back until the tendons in his shoulder almost popped, and the next thing he knew, Oyler was face down on the ground. Ignoring the pain in his shoulder, he whipped himself over just in time to avoid the thrust of his own knife, now in Bosko's hand. Rolling out of the way, he swept Bosko's feet from under him in the process, so that they were both on the ground. They separated and got back on their feet, Oyler concealing a rock he had plucked from under the snow in the palm of his hand.

As the bigger man attacked, Oyler dodged the knife and caught Bosko on the side of the head with the rock. Instead of the temple area he was aiming for, he made contact behind his ear and Bosko didn't even flinch. He came at Oyler again, aware of the rock this time and feinting to draw it out. He anticipated Oyler's first punch, but not the second, aimed at his knife hand, and Oyler felt the solid contact and sensed that the knife was out. His adrenaline surged as he watched it fall to the ground, less concerned by Bosko's left hand making its way toward his midsection – until he felt it burn into his stomach. When he looked down, Bosko's hand was drawing back, a five-inch blade protruding from between his second and third fingers, its steel slick with blood.

"Surprise," Bosko said, straightening up.

"Where—" Oyler sputtered, clutching at his stomach before staggering back and toppling over onto his back. Bosko stood over his victim for a moment, a glint in his dark eyes.

"It's my favourite knife, Mr. Oyler," Bosko said, looming over him as he opened his fist and Oyler saw the thick blade was attached to a steel ball that fit in the palm of his hand. "I make it myself. Do you like it?"

"Fuck . . . you."

Oyler was powerless to resist as the razor-sharp blade swept across his throat and the rest of his life drained away.

Bosko straightened up, wiped the knife on Oyler's coat, then ran his finger lovingly along the edge of the blade before slipping it back into the makeshift sheath on the inside of his jacket sleeve. He stood and looked around him, breathing in the crisp air and taking in the view – nothing but mountains, trees, and snow as far as the eye could see. To most, an inhospitable wasteland. To him, it felt like home.

CHAPTER 12

"It's just over that rise," Townsend called out over his shoulder, stopping for a drink of water as Perry and Garcia caught up. Even with the younger, fitter Garcia taking the heaviest parts of the ram, the two other men were still carrying a much heavier load than when they had first set out.

"You said that an hour ago," Perry quipped, accepting the flask of water as he leaned the weight of his pack against a big rock and caught his breath.

"That was just to keep your spirits up. This time, I mean it. We're a twenty-minute hike from the base camp, if that." Townsend's light tone concealed a profound relief at having almost made it back. They had left their camp early that morning, but the path they had originally chosen to take them over the first of several rises on the way back had been made treacherous by the previous day's snowfall, which had continued late into the night. In many places, the overnight plummet in temperature had made for icy footing, and they had lost several hours retracing their steps and finding an easier route. To make matters worse, they had wasted most of the clear morning weather, forced to walk though intermittent snow squalls the rest of the day. It had tapered off to light flurries in the past thirty minutes, but they were still wet and cold despite the best outdoor gear money could buy.

"I'll be glad when this hike's over," Perry said, looking up at the sky.

Townsend nodded and offered the flask to Garcia, who declined as he watched Perry straighten and shift the weight of his pack.

"Let me take that, sir."

Perry shook his head at the younger man and smiled. "You've got far more than your share already. Besides, we're almost there, and base camp's gonna seem like a five-star resort."

Townsend stowed the flask and looked up at the last rocky outcrop between them and their destination. "Last push, guys," he said, as they set off again. Fifteen minutes later, they were at the top of the outcrop, looking down at the mountain plateau that doubled as a landing strip.

"Is that Dale's plane?" Perry was peering through the dusting of fine snow coming down through the fading light.

"Looks like it," Townsend said. "Though I don't know why he's here early." They had been unable to get through on the satellite communicator to tell Oyler they wanted to head back ahead of schedule. "Too bad we spent half the morning backtracking or there might have been enough light to get us back to Whitehorse tonight. Then again, resting up and heading out first thing tomorrow won't be so bad and, knowing Dale, he's got some pretty good whiskey tucked away in that lodge." Townsend started off toward the base camp. "Come on."

They made the descent carefully but quickly, spurred on by the prospect of a warm fire and dry clothes. They were almost at the floor of the mountain valley, several hundred feet from the main lodge, when Townsend stopped and pointed.

"There he is."

The three men stopped and took in the familiar tan outback jacket and ear-flapped cap, and as the distant figure turned in their direction, Townsend waved. After returning the gesture, the silhouette stepped back inside the lodge. A few minutes later, after the trio had come within a hundred feet of the lodge, the figure re-emerged.

"Hope you've got the fire on, Dale," Townsend yelled, but there was no response from the front porch. He turned to the other two men. "You'd think he'd come out and give us a hand with these damn packs," Townsend muttered, getting a guttural laugh from Perry. He glanced toward Garcia, who had stopped walking and was staring intently in the direction of the lodge. Garcia's eyes flashed suddenly, and he began a yell that caught in his throat as he jumped in front of Perry. A dull thud stopped the two older men in their tracks, with the echo of a gunshot tearing through the silence of the valley and ricocheting off the surrounding mountains a split second later. Townsend stared as Garcia slumped and fell to the ground, motionless. He remained transfixed as Perry grabbed him and pushed him behind a nearby boulder just as something pinged against the metal frame of Townsend's backpack and another echo rang out over the plateau.

"What the hell . . . that can't be Dale!"

"Whoever he is, he knows how to handle a rifle," Perry said, glancing toward Garcia's body, five feet away, out in the open.

"No." Townsend grabbed him by the arm and held him back, then slung his rifle off his shoulder and loaded a shell. "Get down," he yelled, as he felt something whiz by his ear. They both crouched as tightly as they could behind the boulder, then Townsend took a deep breath, leaned out, and lined up his shot, diving back behind the rock as he saw the long barrel of a rifle pointed right at him. A second later, a puff of snow behind them announced that the shot had gone high. Townsend rolled out to the left of the boulder this time, taking quick aim and getting a shot off.

"You got him!" Perry yelled.

Townsend kept the scope at his eye long enough to see the man on the porch clutching his arm before disappearing behind the wall of the lodge. Any hope that Townsend's shot had done serious damage was dashed a moment later, when the man reappeared with the rifle still in hand. "I just winged him," he said, glancing over at the treeline to their left. It was only fifty feet away, and it was now or never. "There's nothing you can do for him," he said, pulling Perry by the arm past Garcia's body toward the trees as he fumbled in his vest for another shell.

"Garci—"

"Come on," Townsend yelled, dragging Perry along as they both sprinted across the uneven terrain toward the trees. The echo of another gunshot rang out just as they reached the safety of the treeline, and a nearby branch splintered as they kept running into denser forest.

Bosko considered another shot but shouldered his rifle instead – he would have plenty of time to track them down later. Leaving the lodge, he walked toward the motionless figure on the ground and realized as he approached that the man was still alive. He closed the gap quickly and saw the man struggle to move his hand toward his waist. As Bosko drew closer, the dying man's movements slowed and he let out a final gasp before going still. What Bosko had assumed was a concealed weapon looked more like a miniature walkie-talkie, and when he pried it out of the dead man's hand, he examined the odd-looking device and noticed a little red light flashing on its side. He threw it to the ground and crushed it with a few stomps of his heavy boot before heading in the direction of the woods where Townsend and Perry had just disappeared. Then a throb in his right upper arm reminded him of his wound. It was just soft tissue and the pain itself was nothing, but blood loss would eventually slow him down if he didn't apply a quick field dressing. He spat on the ground and scowled toward the treeline. He would have to wait a bit, but he would find them soon enough, and when he did, he would make them both pay.

CHAPTER 13

Matthews was in a business lounge at the Vancouver airport, standing in front of a shiny silver-and-black machine trying to decide between a latte and a mocha, given that, despite its impressive size and flashing lights, it seemed currently unable to make a cappuccino. He finally decided on a latte, thinking as he pressed the blue button to start the process that he probably should be drinking water instead.

Finding a chair in a quiet corner, he set his cup down on the table and took a seat, determined to enjoy a moment without thinking about work. But he had barely taken his first sip before an involuntary frown had settled on his face as he considered the report he would have to file when he got back to Ottawa, and how he could possibly avoid the conclusion that his trip had been a complete waste of time. His highly touted source into West Coast anti-Sikh extremists – some possibly state-sponsored – had turned out to be a dud, and despite a strong hunch that the Gian Dhillon death was not what it seemed, he had found no evidence of political, much less terrorist, motivation. In fact, when he considered the evidence objectively, his attempt to make such a connection reeked of desperation. Ortiz had backed him after Boston, but even she was only going to give him so much leeway and, without her support, he knew his prospects were not good.

An image of Dhillon's grieving widow appeared unbidden in his mind's eye, prompting a fresh pang of guilt as he considered his motive for involving himself in her husband's case. In trying to salvage his own career, had he given her false hope that he would help her find answers? In the end, he had been able to do precisely nothing for her, other than to try and grease the bureaucratic wheels a little so that her dead husband's remains would be repatriated in a matter of days, instead of weeks, after the coroner's office had conducted a post-mortem. Whether the forensic autopsy would bring her any more answers as to what had really happened to her husband was another question. The secretive phone calls she had mentioned could explain Dhillon's being in Vancouver without his wife's knowledge – the concept of an older man with someone on the side wasn't exactly a stretch, despite her protestations to the contrary. And as for why he was killed, there was nothing to suggest anything other than being in the wrong part of town at the wrong time, with a late-model iPhone and a wallet more than enough motivation for a desperate addict. As for the nature of Dhillon's injuries, whether his attacker had been high or things had escalated for other reasons, the wounds weren't so atypical as to change the overall conclusion of a random mugging gone terribly wrong.

Sipping his latte, he pondered Travis Wolfe's vague reference to the attacker having a military air, as well as the young Vancouver PD investigator's assessment that Wolfe was just trying to get a little attention. He couldn't help wondering if Wolfe's comments on the description and accent of the killer were just theatre, designed to string Matthews along just enough to collect sixty bucks. When his phone began to buzz with an incoming call, Matthews saw Vanessa Ortiz's name on the screen and let out a sigh.

"I don't care what the consulate told you," he said. "I haven't been anywhere near the Dhillon cas—"

"Are you still in Vancouver?"

"Yes," he said, taken aback by her tone.

"Where?"

"At the airport, waiting for a flight to Ottawa. What's going on?"

"There's a . . . situation. You're being tasked on an urgent basis. Hang on."

"Vanessa?" he said, hearing only rustling on the other end of the line.

"Wait . . . All right, that's good. We've got access to a Lear to transport you."

"Transport me where?"

"Whitehorse."

"Where?"

"Get yourself a fucking map. It's a two-hour flight north of you. You'll be met by local law enforcement at the airport."

"What's the tasking?"

"We got a distress message on a priority asset up there. Not a lot of intel so far, and we've been unable to make contact."

"Who's the asset?" Matthews waited as the silence stretched for several seconds. "Who the hell is it?"

"Richard Perry. You need to get to the executive terminal."

Another question – many questions, in fact – had formed in Matthews's mind but hadn't made it to his lips by the time the line went dead.

"Holy shit," he said as he slid his phone into his pocket and began to move. It wasn't every day that a former US vice president went missing.

CHAPTER 14

It was almost ten p.m. by the time Matthews stepped off the plane in Whitehorse into drastically colder air than he had left behind in Vancouver. It occurred to him that the suit jacket he was wearing and the thin cashmere-blend sweater in his carry-on probably weren't the best choices, but it was too late now. When he entered the terminal, he immediately spotted a uniformed RCMP officer waiting near the gate and walked over to identify himself.

"No luggage to pick up?" the young Mountie asked, looking at the sleek carry-on at Matthews's feet.

"I like to travel light."

"Then you can come with me."

Matthews soon learned that the constable knew little to nothing about the purpose of his visit, so the talk on the short drive into town was mostly friendly banter while he tried to get his bearings in his strange new environment. From what he could tell in the dark once they left the Alaska Highway and drove down into the river valley, the city was laid out on a compact grid, with a Western-style main street, minus the wooden sidewalks. His knowledge of

Whitehorse was limited to what he had gleaned from the internet on the flight up from Vancouver, before the Wi-Fi crapped out. He knew its population was about thirty thousand, that it sat just north of the 60th parallel, and that it had a subarctic continental climate, which he already knew was a hell of a lot colder than Vancouver's. He had seen some references to mining and economic output, but none of the data or pictures captured the sensation he had felt upon walking out the front door of the terminal – like it was the last frontier. He had the same feeling even down in the heart of the little city, as they drove along Fourth Avenue. When they passed Main Street, Matthews made out the RCMP detachment on the right and a few minutes later, they were inside the main building, where they were met by a burly man in khakis and a fleece.

"Sergeant Bill Armstrong," he said, enveloping Matthews's hand in a firm grip before directing them to a nearby conference room. "I've been asked to offer whatever support I can," he said, shutting the door.

"Thanks," Matthews said. "I could use an update."

Armstrong took a seat. "It looks like Mr. Perry came up for a hunting trip three days ago – private charter out of Vancouver. We understand that he stayed at the Pine Lodge out on Marsh Lake three nights ago, and that was the last contact anyone had with him, until late this afternoon."

"And what was the nature of the contact this afternoon?"

"A partial text from Perry's Secret Service officer, Mateo Garcia. It went to the service provider, who looped in search and rescue at CFB Trenton," Armstrong added, referring to the Canadian Forces base.

Matthews frowned. "What did it say?"

"SOS Perr—" Armstrong said, spelling it out. "Don't know if the rest of the text got lost in the ether, or . . ." Armstrong trailed off as they both considered the other possibility.

"Do we know *where* the message came from?" Matthews asked, after a pause.

Armstrong shook his head. "Normally, there's a GPS signature, but that function either wasn't activated or it wasn't working."

"Well, we must know where Perry was supposed to be going," Matthews said, undeterred. "The Secret Service would never let him—"

"Apparently this hunting trip was . . . unofficial. Off the books."

Matthews was frowning again, as his unease grew. "What does that mean?"

"We know he had a one-man personal security detail and that he was accompanied by another hunter, but that's about it."

"Who's the other hunter?"

"John Townsend – former Canadian ambassador to the US," Armstrong said. "He and Perry knew each other when they were both in office."

"Did Townsend not have his own security detail?"

Armstrong shook his head. "Former ambassadors aren't assigned close protection in Canada."

Matthews took a minute to process the information. A former US vice president and a former Canadian ambassador were now missing. This was getting worse by the minute. He glanced at the map on the wall.

"And you're saying we have no idea where they were hunting?" He got up and walked over to the map, tapping it as he tried to remember the total area. "In a territory with an area the size of the state of Montana?"

"It's more like California, actually," Armstrong said, with a shrug. "Just a little bigger, and a whole lot less populated."

Matthews sighed. "So, we're basically looking for a needle in a haystack."

"Maybe not. We think they were hunting Dall."

"Dall?"

"Sheep," Armstrong said. "You'd know them as bighorn sheep, though Dalls are technically thinhorn."

"Right," Matthews said, beginning to feel seriously out of his element. He had been in grade school when Richard Perry had been in office, but he vaguely remembered something about him being a bit of an outdoorsman from Texas. Matthews saw the expectant look on the Mountie's face and decided he didn't have time to pretend he had the first clue about hunting, whether it was for sheep or anything else. "And the fact that they were hunting sheep is important because?"

"They would have been with an outfitter . . . a hunting guide," Armstrong continued. "To show them where to go, supply them properly – that kind of thing."

"But I assume no outfitter has checked in to say he's guiding this particular group, and that they're lost, so I'm still not sure how—"

"Outfitters operate in distinct areas," Armstrong said. "They all have their own turf. We know from the operator of the lodge out on Marsh Lake that they were talking about hunting sheep, so that might narrow it down a bit," he added. "We find out what outfitter they're using, we have a good idea where they are."

"Okay." Matthews was nodding at the first positive-sounding news he had heard so far. "So how do we find out which outfitter they're using?"

"We've been going down the list but they're hard to reach at this time of year – it's still peak hunting season for everything from moose to grizzly," Armstrong said. "And the ones we have gotten in touch with have no idea. Whoever it is must have been keeping it pretty quiet, 'cause these guys talk to each other a lot. But there's a guy out by the Carcross turnoff – he's retired RCMP. If anyone knows who might be involved, it's him."

"So let's call him."

Armstrong shook his head. "I was waiting for you. He doesn't have a phone."

Matthews's eyebrows shot up. "He doesn't have a . . . never mind. How far's the Carcass turnoff?"

"Carcross."

"Whatever."

Armstrong shrugged. "Fifteen minutes."

Matthews gestured toward the front door. "Then let's go."

"So, who is this guy we're going to meet?" Matthews asked, from the front seat of the RCMP Suburban. Within minutes of leaving the detachment, Armstrong's lead foot had them up Two Mile Hill and headed south on the Alaska Highway.

"Name's Cory Sawchuk. He was a member for thirty-five years, a lot of them spent up North – in Yellowknife and here in Whitehorse. He's also hunted pretty much anything you can kill all over the territory. His reputation as a hunter's almost as good as it is for his police work."

"Sounds like our kind of guy," Matthews said, imagining a grizzled, bearskin-clad man-tracker with a shotgun over his shoulder and a Bowie knife between his teeth. Glancing at his phone in the dim interior of the truck, he saw no new messages since he had landed. "Do you get normal cell signal up here?"

"It's pretty good in the Whitehorse area," Armstrong said. "Not so good outside."

As if to highlight the remoteness of their location, the truck's headlights lit up a ramshackle shed by the side of the road with smoke pouring from the chimney. A 1970s pickup sat out front, the top half of a set of adult antlers visible in the box.

"Looks like Smokey got himself a moose." Armstong's comment was half grunt, half chuckle. "Jeez, it's a big one too, by the look of those antlers."

"I guess hunting's pretty big up here?"

Armstrong nodded. "You bet. Between the locals and the hundreds of Cheechakos that come up around this time of year, the territory's pretty crowded."

"Cheechakos?"

"It means southerners," Armstrong said, with a little smile. Clearly, he was lumping Matthews into what sounded like an unflattering category. "And not just from the rest of Canada and the US. We get lots of Europeans, too. Germans especially."

"Now it's working," Matthews said, looking down at his phone, where an incoming email appeared on the screen. "Says here John Townsend was the Canadian ambassador to the US from 1993 to 1999. That overlaps with Perry's tenure as VP from '89 to '96. Perry was one of the youngest VPs in recent US history at forty-four."

Armstrong nodded. "I think I remember that. Townsend was young for the Washington posting too – something to do with getting NAFTA over the finish line."

"Makes sense that they connected if they were both young for their positions. Though they're both in their seventies now," Matthews added.

As they passed a junction with a sign for Carcross, Armstrong slowed and turned onto a gravel road, followed by another turn onto an unlit dirt road that gradually grew narrower. It was little more than a cart path by the time they were half a kilometre in.

"Cory's place is just up here," Armstrong said, swinging the truck around a turn and lighting a clearing with his headlights, at its centre a tidy log home with wood piled up on the side.

"Looks like his truck's here," Matthews said, though the Mountie's expression didn't suggest the same optimism as they stepped out of the SUV and walked up the front steps. Armstrong rapped on the door, then gave a harder knock after a few seconds of silence.

"Someone's got a fire on," he said, pointing up at the cloud rising over the house and sniffing the woodsmoke in the crisp night air. He was about to knock again when the door swung open. The person standing there looked quite a bit different from what Matthews had imagined. Nothing like it, actually, apart from being close to six feet tall. Her athletic frame was clad in worn jeans and a red thermal long-sleeve with Yukon Girls Kick Ass stencilled across the front, and her blond hair was tied back in a ponytail. She seemed oblivious to the smudge of black across one cheek as she looked at the two men standing on her front porch. Whereas Matthews's eyes seemed to have grown in diameter and the bottom half of his jaw descended slightly, Armstrong didn't seem the least bit surprised.

"Oh, hi Lee"

"You lookin' for Dad?"

Armstrong gave a friendly nod. "He in?"

She shook her head, with an inquisitive glance toward Matthews. "He's down South."

Armstrong frowned. "Vancouver?"

"Quito, Ecuador."

"*Ecuador*?" Now Armstrong did show his surprise, whereas all Matthews felt was disappointment and an urgency to get back to the detachment and on to Plan B, regardless of how attractive the woman at the door happened to be.

"Sorry to have bothered you," he said, tapping Armstrong on the shoulder. "Come on."

"What's going on?" Sawchuk said to Armstrong, with a sideways glance at the outsider.

"We've got a situation and we were hoping to get your dad's help."

"This have anything to do with John Townsend going missing?"

Matthews stopped in his tracks. "How did you know about that?"

"It's all over the radio. I was on my way—"

"So much for security," Matthews muttered, shooting a glance at Armstrong, who shook his head.

"Lee here's RCMP – Major Crimes Unit."

"We don't wear the red serge all the time, you know," she said, seeing Matthews's surprise. "Or is it that I'm a woman?"

Matthews felt a flush on his cheeks as Armstrong spoke.

"Mr. Matthews here is with the US State Department."

Sawchuk tilted her head and took in his suit and gingham button-down that had seemed the perfect attire in Vancouver. "So, it's true," she said. "Townsend really *did* bring a former vice president up here."

"We need to get going." Matthews gestured to the Suburban.

"What did you need Dad for?" Sawchuk asked, turning to Armstrong.

"Well, we were hoping he might know where they might have gone for sheep."

Matthews sighed. "We really don't have time for this. I need to get back—"

"Just a sec." Armstrong held up a hand. "You wouldn't know, would you, Lee?"

Sawchuk shrugged. "Pretty obvious they're up on Kluane Plateau."

"Why's it obvious?" Matthews asked, his dismissive tone doing little to conceal his interest.

"'Cause that's Dale's turf."

"Who's Dale?" Matthews said, beginning to feel like the kid at a birthday party without a chair when the music stopped.

"Dale Oyler," Armstrong said, his eyes still on Sawchuk. "Local outfitter."

"And what makes you think this Oyler guy is the outfitter they went with?" Matthews persisted, prompting another shrug from Sawchuk, her silence suggesting she was enjoying leaving him hanging. "Because John Townsend's used him before," she finally said.

"My father was in Townsend's security detail way back when. He came up here on a sheep hunt ten or so years ago and Dad hooked him up with Dale. Townsend's been coming up regularly ever since and he mostly uses Dale."

"How far's Klu—this plateau?" Matthews asked, unsure whether to be addressing the question to Sawchuk or Armstrong.

"Coupla hundred clicks," she replied. "But we should probably check Dale's place first, no? He's on Chadburn Lake."

Matthews looked to Armstrong, who nodded. "It's near enough, and it's worth a visit before we go rushing off to the Plateau. Hang on a sec," he said, as his phone began ringing. He answered the call and walked down off the front porch, becoming engrossed in a conversation as Matthews and Sawchuk stood there in awkward silence.

"You've got something there," Matthews said, pointing to her cheek. She rubbed a hand across the black smudge, then examined her finger.

"It's soot. Damn chimney flue was half blocked. All gone?" she asked, after a couple of passes with the sleeve of her shirt had succeeded in spreading the smudge to her entire cheek.

"Yeah, you're good."

"So, you're up here from Ottawa, or Washington?"

"I was in Vancouver, actually."

"I was gonna ask what kind of planes the State Department had that would get you here so quick."

Armstrong returned, tucking his phone back in his pocket. "I've gotta get back to the detachment for a conference call with HQ. Apparently, your team is delayed," he added, looking to Matthews. "I'm gonna have to ask you to take him out to Dale's, Lee."

Sawchuk nodded. "Sure, I can take him. Just gimme a sec," she added, disappearing inside.

Matthews turned to Armstrong. "What do you mean, delayed?"

"Problem with the plane or something. There's a bunch of State Troopers coming in from Juneau tonight, but it looks like the rest of your crew won't be here until tomorrow morning."

Matthews checked his phone again, but there was nothing new. He looked up as Sawchuk re-emerged wearing a brown coat lined with off-white shearling. She held out a well-worn parka to him.

"Here, you might need this."

"I'm fine," Matthews said, eyeing the sawdust on the sleeve of the coat.

Armstrong glanced at Matthews's thin suit jacket then shared a knowing look with Sawchuk. "Don't say I didn't warn you," she said, tossing the coat back inside and closing the front door.

CHAPTER 15

With his arm patched up, Bosko went outside and kicked fresh snow over the trail of blood he had left after dragging Garcia's body out of sight. Back inside the lodge, where Dale Oyler's body lay on the floor by the fireplace, he returned to the room at the back where he had found the .303 rifle and took an extra box of shells. He still had the 9mm, but he preferred the accuracy and range of the rifle. Moving on to the kitchen, he stuffed some energy bars he found in a cupboard into his pocket and took a wool hat and some gloves from the shelf over a closet by the front door on his way out. He felt the drop in temperature as soon he stepped outside and knew it would continue to plummet overnight, but that didn't bother him in the least. In fact, he felt at ease in this climate, and he intended to use that to his advantage. As for being outnumbered two to one, he liked his odds. He knew the men he was chasing were the type that had been steeped in a lifetime of privilege that had made them soft. As he set out toward the treeline, he glanced around and drew in a deep breath of the mountain air. It reminded him of Grozny, where the odds were much different and his prey of much tougher stock. Tracking and killing those men had been a challenge. This wouldn't be.

He found their trail easily enough soon after entering the trees, though he knew exactly where they were headed in their desperation and fear. Slinging his rifle over his shoulder, he set off deeper into the trees, where the ground soon began to slope downward, toward the Alaska Highway ten or fifteen kilometres to the east. He would beat them there and lie in wait, or intercept them en route. Either way, they wouldn't make it out of these woods alive.

CHAPTER 16

Matthews sat in silence as Sawchuk drove them farther along a dirt road that was as desolate as it was dark. But just inside the fifteen minutes predicted by Armstrong, the truck's headlights lit up a sign for Sourdough Outfitters and Sawchuk directed the pickup off the main road, onto a narrower dirt track that led them to a darkened lodge.

"It doesn't look like he's here," Sawchuk said, putting the truck in park and switching off the engine.

"Is that his plane over there?" Matthews gestured to a red bush plane parked near a large Quonset hut with a floodlight over the open doorway.

"Yeah, but he's got a couple of planes," Sawchuk said, opening her door and getting out. They walked up to the lodge and knocked on the door. After trying the handle and finding the door unlocked, she pushed it open and they both stepped inside and scanned the dimly lit interior.

"Dale?" she called out. "Anyone home?"

Matthews felt around until he found a switch and flicked it on, bathing the entrance in light.

"He's definitely not here," she said, as Matthews went to the stone hearth and inspected the fireplace.

"There's some embers still smouldering in here."

Sawchuk joined him and leaned down, prodding the ashes with a poker. "It ain't much. Either way, he hasn't been here for hours."

Matthews scanned the main room of the lodge and the unlit loft above, then turned his attention to the cluttered desk to the right of the front foyer beneath a wall-sized map of the Yukon. He walked up to the adjacent wall calendar and scanned the various initials and shorthand scribbles handwritten into most of the boxes. It took him a moment to realize that he was looking at the month of October. He turned to say something to Sawchuk, but she was stepping outside with her phone at her ear, so he began flipping through the papers on the desk.

"I was just calling Transport Canada," she said, when she returned a few minutes later, "to see if Dale filed a flight plan. It's not required unless you're flying near the airport – it's what we call local flying." She followed his gaze to the calendar. "What's up?"

"The page for September is missing."

"That's weird," she said, as he took the calendar down from the wall and examined it more closely, focusing on a couple of smudges of red.

"Looks like the ink bled through in some places. Everything else is in blue or black ink," he added, gesturing to the entries for October. "Any reason he might have used red?"

Sawchuk shrugged. "A special party maybe?"

"And look," Matthews said, tilting the calendar into the overhead light. "You can almost see the impression. Is that—"

"It looks like '*JT +2 VIP*'," Sawchuk said, with a nod.

"And by the placement," Matthews said. "I'd say it means that Oyler took John Townsend, Perry, and his Secret Service man out two days ago."

Sawchuk pointed to another smudge of red ink a few boxes to the right. "Looks like the pickup was for the day after tomorrow."

"Unless someone convinced him to head back earlier," Matthews said, watching as her frown grew more pronounced. "What?"

"It's just weird that he wouldn't have gone with them. Dale's usually a stickler when it comes to the rules."

"What rules?"

"Any non-Yukon resident has to be escorted, or guided, on a hunt anywhere in the territory."

"Unless Perry paid for a special arrangement?" Matthews said. "You said yourself, Townsend's been coming up here on hunts for a long time."

She shrugged. "Could be, but Dale's always done his own flying. He'll bring in help to guide now and then, and there's Marcie, but she doesn't fly."

"Who's Marcie?"

"Girl who helps him run things. I think she's his niece, or something. Hang on," she said, holding up a finger as her phone started ringing. She answered it on the second ring and nodded a few times, asked a few short follow-up questions, then hung up.

"No flight plan today. He did file one two days ago though, for a flight to Kluane Plateau."

"Maybe he stayed?"

She shook her head. "The plan he filed was for a return flight the same day."

They both stood in silence for a moment, looking at the calendar and the adjacent map. "You were saying his niece helps out here?" Matthews said, gesturing to the cluttered desk.

"She's usually more organized than this," Sawchuk said, tutting over the mess. "I'm tryin' to remember her last name. It's on the tip of my tongue."

"I'll have a look around outside while you're thinking," Matthews said, heading for the door. "You got a flashlight?"

"Kilpatrick," she said, snapping her fingers. "Won't take a minute to find her number." She pulled out her cellphone as he walked toward the front door. "Flashlight's in the glovebox," she called out after him.

Matthews walked outside and opened the door of her truck and rummaged around in the glovebox for a second, finding the flashlight next to a loaded Beretta. So much for Canadian cops not carrying weapons, he thought to himself, tucking the flashlight into his back pocket. When he shut the door, he saw Sawchuk standing on the front porch.

"If you wanna borrow the piece, go ahead. It's my backup," she said. "Marcie's on her way out here. She'll be about twenty minutes."

"I'm good," he said, closing the door to the truck. "You should probably lock it though, don't you think?"

She pulled the same annoyed face he had seen earlier, then gestured to the truck with a fob and he heard the click of the locks engage. "Does she know where Dale is?" he asked, walking toward a battered pickup parked at the side of the house.

"Hasn't heard from him all day. It's her day off, though, so she didn't really expect to." Sawchuk stepped down off the porch and followed him around to the side of the lodge.

"Is that Dale's truck?" Matthews asked.

"There's only one piece of shit looks like Dale's," she replied, with a nod.

"What's down there?" He swept the beam of the flashlight past the front of the lodge and onto the nearest of a series of outbuildings.

"Corrals for the horses, Quonset hut for the planes."

"Is his other one a float plane?" Matthews asked, setting off down the sloped lawn with Sawchuk behind him.

"No. Float planes use Schwatka Lake. It's fifteen minutes away, to the northwest. Dale might have one there, I'm not sure. But he flies bush planes for most of his hunts."

"What's the difference?" Matthews heard himself ask, though he wasn't sure why. Whether it was her manner or something else, he felt off-kilter in her presence. Sawchuk paused just the right amount of time before delivering the tart response.

"Bush planes don't have floats."

There was an emphatic silence as he stopped to play the beam left and right. "I guess that was a stupid question," he said, thinking he saw what might have passed as a sheepish expression on her face, at the edge of the flashlight's beam.

"Bush planes are usually modified for landing in rough terrain," she said. "Tundra tires, reinforced suspension . . . that kind of thing. Dale's got a base camp near a long stretch of fairly even ground up on the Kluane Plateau that makes a pretty good runway, and he's got lots of flat land here for takeoff and landing. Bush planes don't need much."

"Plus, the not having floats on the bottom probably helps," Matthews deadpanned. They were twenty feet from the Quonset hut when he saw a glint in the flashlight beam.

"Dale have any other vehicles?"

"Not that I know of."

They reached the entrance to the large hut and the rear corner of a silver pickup came into view.

"That's way too shiny for anything Dale'd drive," Sawchuk said, as they walked around the truck and Matthews slid the cuff of his sleeve over his hand before trying the door, then looked through the window.

"Locked."

"I'll call Dave. Get him up here to open it up for us."

"Who's Dave?"

"He runs the rental agency by the airport."

"How do you know it's a rental?"

She smiled and then stepped aside to reveal the sticker on the rear of the tailgate she had been blocking with her hip. "You State Department guys aren't too observant, are you?"

"You may think this is all a big joke," he shot back. "But I don't."

"Don't get pissy with me," Sawchuk said, her smile nowhere to be seen. "It's not my fault you guys let your former VP loose up here, so if you don't want my help, just say so."

They stood in awkward silence before Matthews broke it with a sigh. "Look, it's been a long day and—"

"Do you know Richard Perry? I mean, personally?"

Matthews shook his head. "No."

"Well, I do know John Townsend, and I've known Dale since I was in pigtails. If your Mr. Perry dragged him into any kind of trouble, that's as serious as it gets to me, so don't ever question my commitment to finding them, got it?"

Matthews stayed put as she stormed off back up the hill toward the lodge.

"Got it," he muttered as he set off after her.

CHAPTER 17

Townsend turned his face from an icy gust of wind and ducked back into the trees. Sheltered from the cold, he stopped and looked around as Perry sat heavily on a fallen trunk.

"There's no way he's gonna find us now," he said, his breathing laboured.

"Here." Townsend handed him a bottle of water from his pack. They had been walking for a couple of hours, headed east into the woods at first, before Townsend had turned them north and then back out beyond the treeline. The rocky, windswept terrain did a good job of concealing their tracks, but the temperature had plunged as soon as the sun had set.

"You don't think we lost him?" Perry asked, after he had caught his breath. "If he's even following us, that is. You definitely hit him."

Townsend frowned. "I winged him, that's all."

"So we head to the highway. We're far enough north now and he would have lost our trail as soon as we came back out of the woods." Perry nodded, as though to emphasize his own point. "What are you thinking?" he added, in response to his friend's uncharacteristic silence.

"I'm thinking I'd rather reach the highway at first light than in the dark. There's gonna be no one on it at this time of night, for one thing."

"So we're just gonna keep walking around these woods all night?"

Townsend shook his head and took a sip of the water. "We head a little farther north, then we hunker down until daylight."

"Why not head east now?"

"The highway's the only way out of here and we have to assume he knows that. I don't want to take the chance of stumbling into this guy in the dark." Townsend patted his vest pocket. "I've only got a couple of shells. The rest were in my pack," he added, wishing he had grabbed it when they bolted. At the time, he had been more concerned about getting to cover in one piece than thinking through what they would do if they reached it.

"Mine were in my vest," Perry muttered, then looked away.

"I've got a couple of energy bars in here, if you're hungry." Townsend gestured to his coat pocket, but there was something about Perry's demeanour that seemed off. "Anything vital in your pack?"

"No, just some supplements."

"What kind of supplements?"

"I have low iron," Perry said, almost apologetically. "It affects my energy levels, but I'll be fine. I took a pill just before we got back to the lodge."

"Can you keep walking for another hour or so?"

Perry nodded. "I can keep going as long as you need me to. Just so long as we can get the hell out of here – or blow that bastard away, whichever comes first."

They sat in silence for a while, listening for the tell-tale sounds of a pursuer but, other than the rustle of a branch in the wind or the distant squawk of a bird, there was nothing.

"I'll get you out of here, Richard, don't worry."

"I don't doubt it," Perry said, his forced smile fading. "I was just thinking about Garcia. He's been watching my back for three years now." His face darkened with a frown. "That bullet was meant for me."

"Come on," Townsend said, getting up and patting him on the arm. "We'll keep going north for a while longer, just to be on the safe side, then we'll find somewhere to hole up for the night."

CHAPTER 18

Sawchuk and Matthews returned to the main building at Sourdough Outfitters just in time to see a car pull up and a young woman in jeans and a fleece jacket emerge from the driver's side.

"Hey, Marcie," Sawchuk called out. "Sorry to drag you out here this late, but we're looking for Dale."

"What's going on?" the young woman asked, looking first to Sawchuk, then Matthews – her eyes lingering over him for a moment, as though inspecting an unusual species of wild game.

"Can't really get into the details," Sawchuk said. "But we need to know if Dale went out on a hunt, or just dropped off. Look, Marcie," she added, seeming to sense the other woman's wariness, "we're not looking to get Dale in trouble. We just want to find him and make sure he's safe. If he didn't escort someone he was supposed to, we're not gonna make a big deal out of it."

"He brought some mucky-mucks up to the Plateau the other day," Marcie said. "It was just a drop. He's going back in a coupla days to pick them up."

"But you haven't talked to him today?" Matthews asked.

"Like I said, today's my day off. As far as I know, Dale was supposed to be doing some odd jobs around here. He said the truck was due for an oil change."

"One of the planes is gone," Sawchuk said, as Marcie began to walk toward the Quonset hut, taking in the red plane parked in front.

"He hasn't been flying the Cub lately."

"Something wrong with it?" Sawchuk asked.

Marcie shook her head. "It runs like a top. He just likes to alternate them. Plus, the Cub's no good if there's more than one passenger."

"There's a truck down there, too, that I'd like you to take a look at," Sawchuk said, as they all headed down toward the water. When the rear of the silver Ford F150 came into view, Marcie's eyes lit up.

"There was a guy here yesterday, drivin' a truck just like that."

The sound of Sawchuk's phone pierced the still night air. She put it to her ear.

"Hi, Dave," she said, glancing at Matthews as she stepped into the hut to take the call. He turned to Marcie.

"This guy who was here yesterday. What did he look like?"

She shrugged. "Big guy, blond hair, cut real short. He had a funny accent."

Matthews nodded. "What kind of accent?"

"He said he was Polish, but he lived in the States. He wanted to talk to Dale about setting up a sheep hunt for him and his family – he mentioned his brothers."

"And he asked specifically for Dale?"

Marcie nodded. "I told him he wasn't around, gave him some brochures and stuff." She stopped as Sawchuk re-emerged from the hut.

"The truck was rented yesterday to a man named Piotr Bosko," she said.

"That's the guy." Marcie was nodding.

"We're checking the ID now," Sawchuk continued. "Ident's on the way for prints, and Dave'll be here in two shakes with spare keys."

"Marcie was just saying this Bosko guy came by to see Dale yesterday," Matthews said. "Asking about setting up a sheep hunt."

"I as much as told him he was nuts." Marcie huffed. "Hunts book up a coupla years in advance. But he said he was interested in next fall."

Matthews looked up toward the lodge. "You said you gave him some brochures. Was he inside the lodge?"

She nodded. "I offered him a cup of coffee."

"Did he have one?" Matthews asked.

She shook her head and he glanced at Sawchuk, who appeared to be thinking the same thing – that Bosko could easily have seen the calendar on the wall, torn off the page for September, and figured out where and when the hunting party had been dropped.

"Speaking of coffee," Sawchuk said, glancing at Matthews shivering in his suit.

"I'll put a pot on." Marcie gestured up to the lodge.

"Much appreciated." Sawchuk turned to Matthews. "I have a feeling it's going to be a long night."

It was almost three a.m. by the time the identification team packed up their things and left, having been through the pickup and Quonset hut with a fine-toothed comb and come up with some good prints. They had followed Marcie's directions inside the lodge, taking prints from the desk, the wall calendar, and whatever else the man calling himself Bosko might have touched on his visit the day before, though they all knew that most of the prints taken were likely to be Oyler's or Marcie's. Sawchuk was already on a call with her boss when Matthews's phone began to blow up. First, a series of emails from Vanessa Ortiz in Washington, which he was just finishing up with when his phone began to ring.

"Matthews here."

"This is Special Agent Brent Croft, from the Seattle Field Office. I just got into Whitehorse."

"I thought you guys were delayed," Matthews said, noting the authoritative tone and recalling Ortiz's instruction to co-operate – for the most part – with the FBI, who were heading up the task force that was being assembled to find Richard Perry.

"The main team from LA is still a few hours out, but I don't intend to waste that time. What's the current status?"

"I'm out at a local outfitter's place – a hunting guide we think might have accompanied Perry."

"What makes you think that?"

"Local law enforcement says Townsend used this guide before." Matthews glanced over at Sawchuk, still on her own call. "It was a couple of years ago, but—"

"I'm looking at statements from three different locals saying that Townsend told them he was headed to a place called Mayo two days ago."

"Where's Mayo?" Matthews whispered to Sawchuk, putting the phone against his chest.

"That's a few hundred clicks due north," she replied, a puzzled look on her face.

"That's nowhere near Oyler's territory," Matthews said.

"Who?"

"Dale Oyler, the outfitter I jus—"

"You have any other evidence that he's with Perry?"

Matthews hesitated, thinking of the impressions in the calendar – was he really sure they were evidence of anything, as opposed to just wishful thinking that he was onto a solid lead? As for the pickup truck parked down in the Quonset hut and the man it had been rented to – Bosko might just be another one of Oyler's clients.

"Not really, but I have a feel—"

"We need to focus what resources we have in the right place," Croft said sharply. "There's a lot of wilderness out there and we don't have a lot of time for hunches."

"It's not just a hunch. I told you," Matthews said, trying to keep the irritation out of his voice, "this Oyler guy has a history working with Townsend,"

There was a pause, during which Matthews and Sawchuk made eye contact as she continued with her own call ten feet away, then Croft finally spoke. "Maybe so, but I'm not hearing anything close to strong enough to override multiple statements, so if you want to keep digging there, I'd suggest you not waste too much time on a wild goose chase."

Matthews was about to respond when he realized the line was dead. He waited for Sawchuk to wrap up her call and set her phone on the table.

"Let me guess," he said, "they told you they think Oyler took them up to Mayo, right?"

She nodded and let out a sigh. "They're not in friggin' Mayo. I tried explaining, but he won't listen. Your friend – Croft? He seems pretty adamant. He's got an ERT and half of JTF2 headed to Mayo."

"He's not my friend," Matthews said. He didn't know Croft, but Ortiz did. Oddly, she had described him as a solid agent and Ortiz didn't have much time for one-track thinking, which made Matthews start to question his own judgment. *Was* he on a wild goose chase? He shook the thought as he tried to refocus. "I assume ERT is emergency response. What's JTF2?"

"Joint Task Force 2 – they're like your Navy SEALs," Sawchuk said. "Did you tell Croft about the truck?"

"I didn't get a chance. Besides, it doesn't really prove anything . . . yet," he added, more doubt creeping in.

"Only reason they think the hunt's in Mayo is 'cause Townsend wanted to make sure they had the Plateau to themselves. I guarantee you they're up there with Dale."

Sawchuk picked up a brass poker and prodded the fire to life, before tossing in a couple of fresh junks of pine. Sitting on the sofa in front of the hearth, she scanned the printout from the rental company, with the photocopied California driver's licence in the name of Piotr Bosko, his picture over a Huntington Beach address. Even in the grainy, photocopied headshot, Bosko looked powerful, and there was something about his eyes that told her they were dealing with someone evil. The licence and credit card he had rented the truck with were being checked, but she thought it was unlikely they would have any real connection to the man who had been there yesterday. Whoever this guy was, she knew in her bones that his name wasn't Piotr Bosko and he was no Californian tourist.

Putting the papers down on the coffee table, she sank back in the soft cushions of the sofa. She glanced over at Matthews, whose phone had begun ringing again a few minutes earlier, prompting him to move gradually to the other end of the lodge, as his conversation seemed to grow more and more intense. She had never met anyone from the State Department before, but this guy seemed like he fit with what she would expect. He was cocky, despite not seeming to know much – not unlike most southerners in her experience – and he was probably missing his climate-controlled office, ergonomic chair, and fancy coffee. She pretended to be engrossed in her phone as he turned toward her, ended his call, and sat at the other end of the sofa.

"Everything okay?" she asked.

"Not exactly. The rest of the team won't be here until mid-morning after all. Some clusterfuck at the airport. How about you – what's the word?"

She shrugged. "They're checking flight manifests, but I've got my doubts we're gonna get anywhere with that, though the rental's a bit of a puzzle."

"Agreed. If this guy was planning on getting up to no good, why would he take the risk of renting a vehicle, even with the best fake ID?" He leaned back into the sofa cushion and crossed his arms. "How long of a drive is it to here from Vancouver?"

"Most people come up from Edmonton," Sawchuk said, looking into the fire as it crackled and spit sparks. "Either way, it's a solid two-day drive to Whitehorse."

They sat in silence for a while just staring at the fire.

"So you know Dale Oyler pretty well then?" he finally said.

She nodded. "Between him and my dad, they taught me everything I know about hunting, the outdoors, and a whole lot more."

"And Townsend?"

"I don't know him near as well," Sawchuk said. "But I've met him a few times, and from what my dad's said about him over the years, I know he's a good man."

"Well, I'm sorry if I snapped at you earlier."

Sawchuk waved a hand. "No worries. I'm sure you're under a lot of pressure to find Perry."

Matthews let out a grim laugh. "You don't know the half of it."

"I thought you were only involved because you happened to be on site?" Sawchuk said, turning to him with a puzzled expression on her face.

"It's complicated," he said, making a deliberate glance at his watch.

"Sun'll be up in a few hours," she said.

"I need to set up a flight to Oyler's hunting ground first thing tomorrow. Maybe a chopper?"

"If you're looking for a ride up to the Plateau, it's sitting down by the lake," she said, gesturing out through the picture window toward the Quonset hut and the lake beyond.

He stared at her. "What about a pilot?"

"I'll take you, if you want."

"Like, now?"

She shook her head. "The Cub's not equipped for night flying, but we can leave at first light. I checked with Marcie before she left – it's all gassed up."

Matthews shrugged. "Sounds like a plan."

"Aren't you supposed to be focusing on Mayo?" she asked, cocking her head to one side.

"Do you think they're in Mayo?"

"No way."

"What makes you so sure? Did Townsend use Dale exclusively for hunts?"

Sawchuk shook her head. "No, and I'm sure John's probably hunted in Mayo before, but if he was bringing someone up for a special trip, he'd use Dale and they'd go to the Plateau. That I can tell you for sure."

"And these statements from people saying they heard Townsend mention Mayo?"

"I told you," Sawchuk said. "Just blowing smoke to make sure their hunt was nice and private. Dad always said Townsend was a wily one."

"All right, then," Matthews said. "The Plateau it is."

"You can take this," Sawchuk said, gesturing to the sofa as she stood. "I'll find us some blankets."

She returned a few minutes later with some wool blankets and a pillow.

"Thanks," he said, as she deposited the bedding at the end of the sofa.

"You sure you're up for this?"

"What do you mean?"

She shrugged. "There's no espresso up on the Plateau, if you know what I mean."

"That's very funny," he said. "I appreciate your concern, but I'll be just fine."

"You might want to borrow some of Dale's clothes," she said, looking at his shirt with a mix of curiosity and disdain. "He's a bit shorter than you, but you could probably find something that fits," she added, focusing on Matthews's lightweight wool pants and calf-leather brogues, in contrast to her own lined jeans, hiking boots, and sturdy outback jacket. "I'm just sayin', it gets pretty cold up there, and I think they had some weather last night."

"You mean, like, snow?"

She looked at him and gave a little snort. "Yeah, I mean, like, snow."

CHAPTER 19

Perry almost ran into Townsend, who had stopped abruptly and was staring up at the sky. It had gotten bright so suddenly that it looked like dawn had come early.

"Aurora borealis," Townsend said, as they both stood on the edge of the treeline, watching as the sky changed from green to blue, punctuated by dancing rays of yellow, green, and red, as though some celestial giant was waving a colourful flashlight from a perch high above the atmosphere.

"I'll be damned."

"This is far enough north," Townsend said, tapping Perry on the arm. "Come on. We'll have lots of time for the northern lights later."

They headed into the trees and down a gradual slope as they proceeded east. After about fifteen minutes, they came to an outcropping of rock that made a natural shelter. Townsend held up a hand for caution as they approached but as they got nearer, he could see in the dim light of the forest that it was empty. He kept walking.

"Where are you going?" Perry was leaning against a tree and pointing to the shelter. "This is perfect."

"It's too perfect. Let's go a little farther." Townsend led them up a little incline to a cluster of trees a couple of hundred feet away. "We'll hunker down here," he said, gesturing to the pit created by an uprooted trunk. "I'll collect some of this deadfall for a roof and for some insulation," he added, as they looked around, their breath rising in white clouds in the frigid air. The temperature had dropped a good ten degrees since the shoot-out up on the plateau.

"Here, take a load off." Townsend pointed to a nearby stump, then set about collecting branches. Fifteen minutes later, he had used some string he had found in one of his pockets to tie the branches together and he had filled the gaps with leaves and whatever other foliage he could find on the forest floor. Perry watched with interest as Townsend expanded the edges of the pit before laying the makeshift cover over the opening. When it was in place, the space was concealed, the cover blending seamlessly in the half-light.

"You're a regular Howard Johnson," Perry cracked, eliciting a smile from Townsend.

"I prefer Hiltons myself, but this'll have to do."

They shared a laugh and then crawled into the space, replacing the cover overhead. It wasn't exactly cozy, but it felt a few degrees warmer than outside.

"I guess a fire's out of the question," Perry said, rubbing his hands together.

Townsend didn't respond. Instead, he set about arranging the rifle so the end of the barrel was concealed in the gap between the cover and the forest floor, the stock resting on a root at the edge of the pit. He threaded a few of the extra boughs around the barrel, leaving just enough space to give him a clear line of sight without exposing them. Lining himself up by the stock, he looked over the rifle's sights at the slope leading up to their little hideaway, and he could just make out the natural shelter they had come across two hundred feet away.

"You really think he's out there?" Perry's voice was barely more than a whisper, but it sounded both muffled and loud in the confined space. It was more a statement than a question, and there was a hint of resignation in the tone.

"I do."

"Even if he is," Perry said, after a pause. "He's gunshot and dealing with the effects of blood loss. Plus, he's probably down at the highway, wondering where the hell we went. You were smart to stay out on the rocky ground where we wouldn't leave a trail."

"Maybe," Townsend said, adjusting the rifle stock slightly, then leaning back against the rear of the pit.

"And if he does, by some miracle, track us here," Perry continued, gesturing to the rifle. "We can blow a hole in him with that."

"As long as I don't miss." Townsend said. "I've only got two shells."

"I don't know what I was thinking, taking off my vest," Perry said with a frown and a shake of his head. He had removed his camouflage vest, and the half dozen shells in it, and put it in his pack for the last part of the walk down to the lodge. They had both left their packs behind in the confusion up on the plateau.

"No sense crying over spilled milk. And it's probably not gonna come to that, anyway. With any luck, we'll make it through the night without freezing our asses off, then walk out to the highway in the morning and flag someone down. There should be plenty of traffic."

When Perry didn't respond, Townsend turned to look at him. "It's gonna be okay, really."

Perry shook his head. "I was just thinking about Garcia. He literally put his life on the line for me. I don't think he was married, but he must have had family. Now that I think of it, I never even asked about his family and now I can't."

"He seemed like a nice guy," Townsend said, after a pause. "But he must have known the risks of the job when he signed up. You can't blame yourself."

"I'm not so sure."

"What do you mean?"

Perry hesitated and then let out a sigh. "I don't know, I just have a bad feeling, and I've dragged you into whatever this is too."

"It's not your fault some wacko came after you and it's him, not you, who's responsible for Garcia's death. As for me, I'm not worried. And if this asshole tries to roll up on us in the night, he's gonna be in for a nasty surprise." Townsend adjusted himself in the shelter and pointed at the rifle barrel. "Maybe we should switch places, though. I still can't get over that shot you made yesterday. Right through the heart at three hundred and fifty yards."

Perry gave a grim chuckle. "Four hundred, didn't you say?"

The shared a quiet laugh and then the silence descended over them, their breathing the only sound. A minute later, a distant howl echoed through the night, followed by another.

"Wolves?" Perry asked.

"Maybe. Could be coyotes. Either way, they're a long way off. Try and get some shut-eye." He gave Perry a pat on the arm. "I'll keep watch."

"Wake me up in an hour and I'll take over," Perry said, closing his eyes.

Townsend scanned the area beyond their perch, down the slope, and toward the shelter in the distance, more visible now that the cloud cover had moved off and the moonlight shone through. Maybe Perry was right. Maybe he had hit something vital with his shot, but something about the way the man had spun told Townsend that he had hit an arm, not the torso. Too bad. Still, they wouldn't have left much of a trail, so the odds that this guy would find them – if he really was still out there – were slim. He listened as Perry's breathing grew more pronounced and regular as he slipped into sleep, wondering what sort of shape he would be in a few hours from now without his iron supplements. If he had to carry him out on his back, Townsend thought, so be it. Alone now, he listened to the dead silence all around him, his ears straining for the slightest dissonance – the swish of a branch or crack of a twig that might alert him to approaching danger. Another howl pierced the silence. This one was noticeably closer and, for the first time since they had stopped walking, he felt fear tickle his spine.

CHAPTER 20

Bosko paused at the sound of the howl. *So, they have those devils here, too.* Well, if they wanted to come out and play, he was up for that. Looking down at the rocky ground, he swore before moving on. He had scoured the trees to the east of the plateau, thinking his targets' most likely route was a beeline for the highway, but he had quickly lost the original trail and had found no further tracks. Then he had turned northwest and made his way back out of the trees, thinking he would have done the same in their place: try to use the rugged terrain to conceal their tracks. Most of the light snow had blown off the rocks, meaning that if they were careful, they could leave almost no trace. He had found some broken branches and footprints in the woods, but nothing fresh. Now, after skirting the treeline for half an hour and failing to pick up their trail, it was time to head east again. They couldn't be far.

He took a drink of water from his canteen, the motion recalling the wound to his arm. But the field dressing had held and he felt strong. If they had hoped to stop him, or slow him down, they were mistaken – they had no idea who they were dealing with. He grinned as another howl pierced the silence. Taking a deep breath of the biting night air, he was about to head into the trees when he noticed something glimmering in the moonlight ten feet to his left on a patch of rocky tundra. He approached it, realizing that it was a frost-dusted twig, not the man-made object that he had first thought. Grimacing, he was about to turn back when he spotted something else on the rocks, just a few feet farther. As he crouched to inspect it, there was no question he was looking at a partial footprint in the dusting of snow that clung to the edge of the rock. It was from a boot, definitely man-sized and, given that the snow had come in overnight, it had to be recent. He scanned the ground surrounding the footprint and found nothing, but continuing north, he came upon another partial print of what looked like the same boot tread a few hundred feet farther. There was no doubt about it, they were following the treeline north.

Abandoning his plan to head east, he continued to skirt the treeline, thinking that if they were planning on laying low for the night before making a break for the highway in the daylight, that suited him just fine. If he didn't come across them in the dark, he would catch them at first light. Either way, he could sense that he was closing in. Whether they died tonight or tomorrow morning was immaterial to him, but neither of the two men he was following would make it to the highway alive.

CHAPTER 21

"Time to get going."

Matthews opened his eyes to the sight of Sawchuk looming over him. He didn't remember going to sleep, but he checked his watch out of instinct and realized he had been out for just over two hours.

"I've got breakfast to go," she said, pointing to a plastic bag and a large stainless-steel thermos in her hand as he sat upright and rubbed his eyes. Opening them again, he looked down at the boots he had found in the hall closet before conking out. They were about as far as could be from his Cole Haans and a little snug at the toes, but they would have to do. He sighed and bent over to put them on.

"I found this in the loft," Sawchuk said, as he was lacing up the boots, tossing him a tattered but warm-looking parka that smelled of campfire and sweat. She seemed to enjoy watching him stare at it for a moment, as though it were made of radioactive material that might be fatal if it came in contact with human skin. His survival instincts kicked in as he caught sight of the fresh covering of snow on the branches outside the window and gingerly pulled it on.

"You might want to look around for some other pants, too. Those look pretty thin."

"I'll pass," he said, walking past her to the door. From the smell of the coat, he wanted nothing to do with Oyler's pants. "I ever need a wardrobe consultant, I'll know who not to call," he said as he caught his reflection in a mirror by the door. With his tousled hair and day-old beard, combined with the well-worn coat and work-boots, he was already halfway through the full-scale conversion to Grizzly Adams. He watched as Sawchuk picked up a 7mm rifle leaning against the wall by the door, along with a couple of boxes of cartridges.

"Thought I'd bring this along."

"Good idea," he said, zipping his jacket up and surreptitiously moving his Beretta from the waistband of his pants to the jacket's inner pocket as Sawchuk slung the rifle over her shoulder. It was still dark as they walked outside, but there was a faint glow behind the mountains to the east.

"It'll be light enough by the time we get up in the air," she said.

"Sooner we get there, the better."

They walked down to the Quonset hut in silence and loaded what little gear they had into the plane. Seeing it up close for the first time, Matthews was surprised at how old it looked.

"What kind of plane is this, anyway?"

"Piper Super Cub," Sawchuk replied, hopping into the cockpit, as though to pre-empt any further questioning. He walked around to the passenger side and opened the door, noticing with some alarm the grating squeak it made. He pulled himself up into the seat and looked around, feeling like a kid in an aviation museum, playing in a scale model of something from a previous era.

"How old is this thing?"

"They stopped making them in '80 or '81, I think. This one's probably from the last few years of production."

"It's almost *fifty* years old?" He let the statement hang as she fiddled with the controls. She eventually looked over in his direction and, seeing his expression, she rolled her eyes.

"What were you expecting, an A380 with a bar?" She returned her focus to the instrument panel.

"Seriously, are we sure this thing can make it to the Plateau, or even off the ground?"

As if to answer, she pressed a button that started a series of noises that ended with several large splutters and a bang as the propeller started to turn, slowly at first, as though miffed at being woken from a long and pleasant slumber. Within seconds though, the engine noise had settled into a satisfying hum and the blades of the propeller had disappeared into a greyish blur. She looked over at him and smiled, either despite or because of the continuing skepticism she saw in his face.

"Relax," she yelled, over the engine noise. "The Cub's the best bush plane ever made, bar none. This one's had the engine totally rebuilt, and Dale treats his planes like gold. It runs like new, believe me."

Matthews gave a reluctant nod and shut his door, then strapped himself in.

"Here," she said, handing him a headset as she donned the other one. "Testing: 1, 2, 3," she said, a tinnier version of her voice coming through Matthews's headset. "Can you hear me?"

"Loud and clear," he said, giving her a thumbs-up as she began to nudge the plane forward. When he saw that she was lining it up with a short strip of flat land along the waterfront, his alarm returned.

"These things are designed for short takeoffs and landings," she said, as the engine revved higher and they began to pick up speed. "Don't worry!"

He gave as convincing a nod as he could manage and said a silent prayer as the engine revved higher and the plane trundled on toward a fast-approaching line of trees. Then suddenly, it was up and they were over the treetops and headed into the dawn sky. As he looked down, he noticed the trees were all white, as though dusted in icing sugar.

"Hoarfrost looks nice, huh?" Sawchuk said, as the plane straightened on a westerly heading and the sun behind them lit the vast swath of forest ahead. She made a few adjustments to their course and when they levelled off a few minutes later, she picked the bag up off the floor between the two seats and set it on her lap.

"Here," she said, handing him a foil-wrapped lump. "Hope you're not allergic."

He shook his head and peeled back the foil to reveal a peanut butter and jam sandwich on thick-cut bread. "Thanks." He took a bite and reached for the thermos. "Coffee?"

She nodded and he filled a travel mug with steaming coffee and handed it to her, then poured another for himself and took a sip, the aroma filling the inside of the small cockpit. They ate in silence as they flew south of Schwatka Lake and then she turned the plane gradually a little to the north.

"What's the flight time?" he asked between bites of his sandwich.

"Little over an hour."

He nodded and sipped his coffee, looking out as the sun at their back filled the sky with a red-orange glow. "So how long have you had your pilot's licence?"

"Who said I had a licence?"

He looked at her, waiting for the smile to indicate she was joking, but she remained stone-faced.

"Are you fucking kidding me?"

"Relax," she said, with the smile he had been waiting for. "I've been flying these things for years with my dad."

"You had me going there for a . . . so, you're saying you *do* have a pilot's licence, right?"

"Licence, no licence – what difference does it make? I can fly the damn plane. You want to get up to the Plateau or not?"

He continued to stare as she calmly sipped her coffee, one hand on the yoke, and he decided not to pursue it any further – he had the feeling he didn't want to know.

"So, what's your story, anyway?" she said.

"What do you mean?" He took another bite of the sandwich.

"How does a diplomat end up on a rescue mission for a former vice president?"

He shrugged and looked out the window. "I told you, I was in Vancouver, so I was the nearest when the call came in. It's an all-hands-on-deck kind of deal."

"Except you don't seem like much of a sailor."

"What's that supposed to mean?"

"Nothing," she said, as they both chewed in silence for a while. Then she took another sip of coffee and turned to him with an inquisitive frown. "I didn't know State Department guys carried."

"What are you talking about?"

"I'm talking about the 9mm in your pants," she added, matter of fact. He squeezed his arm instinctively, to make sure the gun was still in his pocket, where he had moved it. "I like to know who I'm travelling with," she continued. "So why don't you cut the shit and tell me who you really work for. FBI?"

"I think we should focus on what we're—"

"CIA?" She turned to face him, staring him down for a second. He held her gaze until she eventually let out a little laugh and looked away.

"Does it really matter?" he asked. "The main thing is we both have a vested interest in locating these guys – and fast."

"It matters to me. Are you CIA or not?"

"I'm CIA," he said, after a moment's hesitation. "Though I was telling you the truth when I said the only reason I'm involved in this at all is because I happened to be in Vancouver."

Sawchuk was silent as she processed the information, then she shrugged. "I'm curious how you got the weapon on the plane, though."

"I didn't fly commercial from Vancouver."

"Forget I asked," she said, handing something over to him. He watched as she turned her hand over and opened her fist to reveal a palm full of 9mm cartridges.

He sighed, then took the bullets. "I thought it felt light," he said, retrieving the gun from his inside pocket and sliding out the empty magazine. "But how did you . . . forget it," he said, deciding he would rather not know how she had removed the gun from his pants without waking him.

"Don't worry," she said. "I won't tell anyone I disarmed you in your sleep."

"That's big of you."

"No problem. Tell you the truth," she said, "I feel better I'm with someone who might actually know how to use that thing, not some canapé-muncher from the State Department."

"I know how to use it, don't worry."

"Good, 'cause I have a bad feeling about this whole thing."

Matthews looked out the window as they followed the Alaska Highway's northwest trajectory, away from Whitehorse and toward the Coast Mountains of Kluane National Park and Alaska beyond. Though he said nothing, he shared Sawchuk's unease.

CHAPTER 22

Townsend looked through the screen into the clearing outside and noticed the change in light. Above the dense canopy of evergreen trees, the sun was coming up - time to get moving. He could feel Perry's steady breathing next to him in the silence, which he took as a good sign. Townsend hadn't had any sleep himself and though he was tired and chilled to the bone, a grim determination to make it to the highway outweighed all else. He knew there was a horse trail not far north of their current position that led down from the plateau all the way to the Alaska Highway where the walking would be easier.

He was about to rouse Perry from his sleep to start their journey when he heard a swishing sound that made him freeze. Straining to hear any other foreign sounds in the seconds that followed, he relaxed for a moment, until he heard the distinctive snap of a twig. Peering through the screen, he surveyed the downhill slope and, with the first hint of daylight filtering through the forest, he could just make out the rock shelter. He stared at it for several seconds, considering the possibility of a moose or a bear as he began to scan the area to the left of the shelter. Then he saw something moving to the right. His breath caught in his throat as he made out the distinctly human form creeping forward and, as the figure sharpened into focus, Townsend made out the extended rifle barrel trained on the shelter. A few seconds later, having confirmed that the shelter was empty, the man straightened and lowered his rifle as he surveyed the area around him, his gaze passing over the rise and the makeshift hideout as it continued in an arc before returning in the opposite direction. Townsend felt the hairs on the back of his neck stand up and his breathing stop altogether as the man seemed to stare directly at the uprooted tree for a few seconds before moving on.

He can't see us . . .

Relief flooded his system as Townsend watched the man walk off in the opposite direction. But the elation was short lived and the stranger was soon back, this time to examine the ground at the foot of the hill. If they had left a trampled bush or a footprint in the dark the night before . . .

Townsend quietly positioned himself behind the stock of the rifle, his finger on the trigger. He could try and take the shot now – downhill at a hundred and fifty yards was a pretty good range – but if he missed, he would give away their location and be down to one bullet. More importantly, he would have to move Perry's shoulder an inch or two in order to line up the shot properly and risk waking him. Suddenly, the man below turned and headed off to the east.

As Townsend sat there in the calm that followed his adrenaline surge, he took stock of the situation. If there had been any doubt about whether they had given this murderer the slip, it was gone now, and they would have to be on their guard every step of the way. Knowing which direction the killer was headed was an advantage and it reaffirmed Townsend's plan to head north, instead of the direct route east to the highway. The horse trail was farther north than they needed to go, but once they reached it, their progress would be faster, and the detour would hopefully create some separation from their pursuer. There was always a chance they would encounter him on the open trail, but it seemed the best plan overall. Glancing at Perry's placid features as he slept, Townsend wondered if the other man would have the strength for the still-considerable hike to safety. One way or another, they had to make it to the highway that morning - there was no way they were spending another night in the bush with a cold-blooded killer stalking them. He prodded Perry gently until he stirred, his sleepy eyes fixing on Townsend's index finger across his lips.

"It's all right," Townsend whispered. "We're gonna get moving again, but we have to be quiet. We had some company."

Perry blinked. "The rock shelter?"

Townsend nodded.

"Guess you were right not to spend the night there."

Townsend shrugged, thinking if they had, they would both be dead by now. Whether they would be anyway by the end of the day was still uncertain, but he didn't intend to go down without a fight. He gave Perry the best smile he could muster. "You okay to walk for a bit?"

"I'm not stopping 'til my feet hit pavement," Perry said, though his trademark Texan bravado seemed strained.

"Come on then." Townsend pushed back the cover and stood up, reaching out his hand to pull Perry up. "It's time to get the hell out of these woods."

CHAPTER 23

"That's Kluane Lake," Sawchuk said, pointing out a large body of water just west of the nose of the plane. "Burwash Landing's at the northwest point and, from there, we're about fifteen minutes out."

Matthews nodded. Their flight had been uneventful so far and whether she was actually licensed to fly or not, Sawchuk seemed at ease at the controls of the Cub. Despite his initial concerns over its appearance, the little plane and its rebuilt engine seemed more than up to the task and had provided a relatively smooth flight. Sawchuk had explained that, like Oyler's other plane, it had undergone some modifications and upgrades apart from the engine rebuild that allowed it to fly considerably farther and faster than the plane that had come off the assembly line in the eighties. It had begun to snow, a few squalls at first but then increasing to a steady flow of fat, white flakes.

"This gonna be a problem?" He pointed through the windshield.

"Naw," she said, with a shrug, adjusting their course northwest to align their flight path with the curve of the Alaska Highway below, visible sporadically through breaks in the white streaks of snow.

"I've got it put into the GPS, so visibility's not gonna be a problem, at least till we're landing."

"That's good to know," Matthews said, as they flew over the southern extremity of Kluane Lake. Continuing over the water, the snow thinned out and the ground below became visible again, revealing a range of mountains off to the west, rising gradually in elevation and stretching as far as the eye could see.

"That's Kluane National Park."

"Is that where they're hunting?"

She shook her head. "There's only a couple of draws for licences in the park – and they're expensive. Dale's turf is northeast of the park."

They continued in silence, apart from the steady buzz of the engine, as Matthews took in the spectacular view of the enormous park, its green valleys and snow-capped peaks untainted by any sign of human intervention. It wasn't something he was used to seeing and it was particularly spectacular from this vantage point.

"There," Sawchuk said, about ten minutes past Burwash Landing, pointing to a level plateau between several peaks. "The base camp's at the south end, but we go in from the north."

Matthews squinted to make out any sign of life, but they were still too far out. As Sawchuk flew the plane past the plateau and banked it into a turn, he could make out the main lodge, then the outbuildings.

"That looks like Dale's 180 down there," Sawchuk said and a second later, Matthews spotted the little blue and white plane, parked to the side of the lodge. It began snowing harder just as they were completing their turn and, as she straightened them up and started to descend into a final approach, the snow began to obscure their view of the lodge at the far end of the plateau. Matthews felt his heart jump to his throat as the landing gear slammed into the bumpy terrain at the north end, but Sawchuk seemed unperturbed and she kept the Cub on a straight line as it rolled along the natural runway, then up a gradual incline that slowed it further until it eventually came to a stop a hundred feet from the other plane.

"That's Dale's 180, all right." Sawchuk shut the engine down and when the propeller eventually stopped spinning and they took off their headsets, they were surrounded for the first time in an hour by total silence. Matthews pointed toward the lodge.

"No smoke from the chimney."

"Doesn't mean nobody's here," Sawchuk said, peering through the snow flying across the windshield as she unbuckled herself, reached for the rifle, and got out. Matthews drew his Beretta as they approached the other plane, confirmed that it was empty and then moved on to the lodge.

"I'll go around back," Sawchuk said. "Meet you in the middle."

Matthews nodded and crept up the front steps, standing to the side of the door as he checked the handle and found it unlocked. He pushed the door open and stepped inside, sweeping the interior of the open lodge with his gun, his eyes drawn immediately to a large stone fireplace to the right, over which hung a trio of massive horned animal heads, their eyes seeming to return his surprised look. A rough-hewn harvest table a dozen feet long stood in front of the fireplace and, as Matthews advanced, he saw something on the floor between the empty chairs. When he reached the table, he recognized the same blank stare he had seen from the wall-mounted trophies. He heard Sawchuk's voice from the other end of the lodge.

"Over here," he called out and a few seconds later, Sawchuk approached the table.

"Nothin' out back. Oh *shit!*" She froze as she spotted the motionless figure on the floor.

"Is this—"

She nodded as she joined Matthews on the far side of the table and they both stood over the body.

"It's Dale. Jesus, someone slit his throat." She put a hand over her mouth as she crouched down to inspect the body.

Matthews knelt next to her and examined the wound across Oyler's neck, running from ear to ear like a sinister smile. The dead man's shirt was also stained a blackish red over the abdomen.

"He was killed somewhere else," he said, noting the lack of blood on the floor. Seeing Sawchuk's expression, he added, "He would have bled out in seconds, if it's any consolation."

"It's not," she said, her face ashen. "And when I find the piece of shit who did this, he's gonna wish he was never born."

"Come on." He stood and put his hand on her shoulder and led her gently away. "Let's check the other buildings."

They spent the next five minutes confirming that the rest of the cabins and corrals were empty, before returning to the main lodge. They were approaching it from the opposite side this time and Matthews paused as something caught his eye.

"What?" Sawchuk said, sensing his sudden vigilance and following as he walked off to the right of the front steps and down a gentle, snow-covered slope. They both stood in silence over a patch of ground at the bottom of the slope where the dusting of snow was disturbed. There were reddish-brown smears all around the area and sitting off to one side was a mangled hunk of plastic and metal.

"What happened here?" Matthews leaned down for a closer inspection, while Sawchuk seemed more interested in the tracks leading off into the trees.

"This looks like a satellite communicator," Matthews said, holding up the damaged device.

"From Perry's bodyguard?"

"Most likely." He pointed to the trail. "Do you know where that leads?"

Sawchuk nodded, scanning the treeline. "Nowhere special, but I'm more interested in these," she said, turning her attention to the tracks in the snow. “Looks like they’re from a grizz. They’re pretty fresh too, so we probably shouldn’t be standing around out here.”

“A grizzly bear? It would attack like that?”

“This time of year? Yup, though this guy might have been dead already. The grizz’d just drag him into the woods and bury him, for later.”

Matthews looked at the bloodstains and the large prints to one side of the path of flattened snow, imagining the scene as a shiver ran down his spine. “I hope he was already dead, whoever he was.”

“Come on.” Sawchuk gestured to the Cub. “I’ve got to call this in first, then we can go find your Mr. Perry.”

CHAPTER 24

Townsend was waiting at the widening of the makeshift trail when Perry caught up to him, his breathing heavy.

"You all right?" Townsend asked, handing him a flask of water.

Perry nodded, though he had been lagging farther and farther behind as the morning wore on. He took a long drink before handing it back. "Thanks."

"Better?" Townsend asked, eliciting a determined nod from Perry as he looked back up the trail in the direction they had just come from, then scanned the path ahead. They had reached the horse trail and had been heading east for about an hour and, while they were more exposed than in the woods, the going was definitely easier and the knowledge that this trail would eventually deliver them to the Alaska Highway was more than enough motivation to keep them moving. That, and the certainty that somewhere in the surrounding woods lurked the maniac who had killed Garcia and, almost certainly, Oyler. Townsend had described the early morning appearance of their pursuer at the rock shelter as they walked the trail, both men quietly hoping that the woods lining the sides of the trail were large enough to occupy the killer until they could flag down a car on the highway and get back to safety.

"We should probably keep moving."

Perry grimaced and shook his head. "Go on alone."

"What are you talking about?"

"I'm just slowing you down. You should go on ahead and get help."

"I'm not leaving you here Richard, so forget it. This hunt was my idea, remember, and I'm not leaving you behind, so don't eve—"

"This . . . whatever this is . . ." Perry said, still looking down at his feet. "It's my fault."

"You keep saying that, but I don't understand how any of this is your fault. Is there something you're not telling me?"

"There was a man in Vancouver," Perry said.

"What man?"

"I should have listened to him. I just didn't want it to be true." Perry stopped and looked up at Townsend, who was standing stock still. "What is it?"

"Do you hear that?" Townsend was holding up a hand.

Perry's first reaction was to scan their immediate surroundings for someone emerging with a rifle aimed at them, but he could tell from Townsend's expression that it was something else that had drawn his attention. He listened keenly for a moment before the silence was suddenly broken by a distinctly mechanical sound. They both stood listening until it was clear that what they were hearing was the steadily growing hum of an aircraft engine.

"It's a plane," Townsend said. "It could be headed to base camp."

"It's gotta be the cavalry."

"But how would they know?"

"Had to be Garcia," Perry said. "He must have managed to make a distress call on the sat messenger. God only knows how."

They listened as the sound of the engine grew nearer, then the timbre changed and a few seconds later, it was gone.

"It must have landed," Perry said, the excitement evident in his voice.

Townsend nodded. "It had to have landed at base camp. The Plateau's the only strip of even ground long enough to set it down for miles."

Perry looked up the trail. "We should head back up."

Townsend frowned. "I don't know. We might be better off pushing on to the highway. Whoever's after us will have heard the plane, too."

"We've gotta be miles still from the highway." Perry looked down the trail to the east, desperation creeping into his voice. "Surely it would be quicker to head back to base camp. We might even meet up with whoever's on that plane if they head this way. Besides, we need to warn them this bastard's somewhere in these woods."

Townsend ran a finger over his top lip, seeming to consider their options. "All right," he finally said. "But it's gonna be tough sledding uphill."

"If you're worried about whether I can make it," Perry said, forcing a look of grim determination onto his face that he hoped made him look better than he felt, "don't be. I'm fine."

They were only fifteen minutes into the hike back up the trail when Perry's pace slowed.

"You sure you're okay, Richard?"

"Fine," Perry said, through ragged breathing.

"You don't look fine. Hang on." Townsend dug in his jacket and came out with a foil-wrapped granola bar. He opened it and handed it to Perry, who had taken the opportunity to sit on a tree stump. He made a half-hearted effort at waving off the food, but Townsend wasn't taking no for an answer and Perry eventually accepted it.

"You just need a shot of energy and you'll be fine," Townsend said, standing over him.

Perry was too busy chewing to respond and, just as he looked up to speak, he heard a dull thud, then watched a pink mist explode from the side of Townsend's head, followed by the delayed report of a gunshot echoing from above their position. He sat frozen in place as he watched Townsend's lifeless body crumple before him. It wasn't until the sound of the body hitting the ground shocked Perry back to reality and he lunged off the stump for the cover of the nearby trees, looking behind him as he scrambled downhill on a line parallel to the horse path, hoping the trees would offer some cover. He had been moving for thirty seconds or more – plenty of time for the shooter to reload and take aim – and yet the woods around him were silent, which encouraged him to keep moving on the same trajectory, away from where the shot had come from. He tried to put the gruesome image of his dead friend out of his mind as he dug deep for the energy to press on and increase his pace, telling himself that he could still make it. He looked back again for an instant and when he turned around, he froze at the sight of a tall, blond-haired man blocking his path, a rifle trained at chest level.

"This is far enough."

Perry's eyes darted left and right, looking for cover, but that only caused the other man to lean in closer behind the rifle.

"Do you want to die?"

"Who . . . *are* you?" Perry said into the deathly silence as the other man came closer, lowered the rifle, and pointed it downhill.

"Move."

CHAPTER 25

Matthews and Sawchuk were on their way to the Cub to contact Whitehorse when they heard it. They stopped dead and looked around, Matthews scanning from one end of the plateau to the other, while Sawchuk's eyes remained fixed on a point at the northwest end. There was no question in either of their minds that what they had heard just seconds before was the distinctive report of a rifle.

"Hunters?" Matthews said, breaking the silence, as Sawchuk continued to scan the trees at the north end of the plateau. She shook her head.

"This is Dale's turf, and everybody knows it," she said. "If he had a private hunt going on up here, no one would dare, for fear of getting an ass full of buckshot." She looked at Matthews, a smile flickering on her face, but it was gone as soon as it had appeared as she looked away again and went quiet.

"I'm sorry. I know Dale meant a lot to you."

"You have no idea." She glanced back toward the lodge. "I still can't believe that's him in there."

They stood in silence for a moment before he spoke again. "I guess we have to assume that whoever killed him took his rifle."

"Probably a .303 – Dale's favourite. Come on," she said, slinging the 7mm back over her shoulder.

"What do you mean, come on?"

"That shot came from the northeast." She gestured to the woods on the down slope of the northern end of the plateau. "There's a horse trail a few clicks up that Townsend would know about. They must have been headed to the highway and heard the plane."

"But we landed twenty minutes ago. Why would they wait so long to signal their location?"

Sawchuk's grim expression needed no response, as another possibility dawned on him. "We'd better hurry," she said, setting off toward the north end of the plateau. It occurred to him, as he followed her, that he would have no idea from which direction the echoing gunshot had come – how could she be so sure?

"What about checking in?"

She looked back at the plane, torn between a desire to get to the other end of the plateau as soon as possible and the need to follow protocol. "Let's make it quick," she finally said, turning and closing the last twenty feet to the Cub and yanking the cockpit door open. She put on the pilot's headset and flicked a switch, a frown clouding her face as she flicked the same switch repeatedly.

"What's the matter?"

She tugged the headset off and tossed it onto the pilot's seat. "Damn thing doesn't work."

"What do you mean, it doesn't work?" he said, as she stepped down from the Cub. "It worked this morning."

"The person-to-person worked," she said, with a sigh. "But I didn't file a flight plan before we left, so I didn't need to use the tower communication function. Maybe that's why Dale hasn't been flying the Cub lately." She gestured to the other plane. "We'll just use the radio in the 180," she said, setting off with Matthews in tow. When she reached the Cessna and opened the door, her frown turned to a dark scowl.

"What the *fuck*?"

Matthews looked past her into the cockpit at the empty slot in the dash where the radio should have been.

"The GPS is gone too."

"You don't have one of those satellite things?" Matthews asked, but from her expression, he knew the answer.

"I loaned mine to my dad. I didn't think we'd need one, but I wasn't expecting the Cub's radio to be out."

"So, we have *no* way of contacting anyone?"

Sawchuk's cheeks coloured. "Not unless you want to send smoke signals. Come on, we're wasting time."

"But how are we—"

"And put that thing away," she said, looking at the phone he had taken from his pocket, out of habit more than a realistic expectation that it would actually work in these surroundings. "I already told you, it's useless up here."

"What about the planes?" he said, looking back at the two aircraft, parked a hundred feet from one another. "In case someone manages to circle back."

Sawchuk dug in her pocket and pulled out two sets of keys. "If he does, he won't be flying out of here."

They set off at a jog, the uneven terrain below their feet preventing a sprint.

"How far's the highway from here?" Matthews asked after a few minutes, breathless already and wishing he had kept up his cardio routine after moving to Ottawa.

"About ten or fifteen clicks," she replied, her voice betraying no sign of duress as they reached the end of the plateau and she clambered up onto the rocks, maintaining course along the edge of the trees. "The shot we heard was from a lot closer than that, though."

"There's some boot prints," Matthews said, stopping and crouching to inspect one full print of a size ten or eleven boot tread.

"Probably our perp," Sawchuk said. "Townsend would have kept along the rocks to avoid leaving prints, but we'll probably come across some of theirs, too. Nobody's perfect." She watched him as he caught his breath. "You're not gonna crap out on me, are you?"

"I'm good," he said, trying to keep the annoyance from his voice. Out here in the middle of nowhere and with no communications, he was already a fish out of water – completely dependent on Sawchuk to lead him to Perry. The least he could do was keep up.

CHAPTER 26

"Here is good," Bosko said, looking around. They had been walking downhill for a good twenty minutes and Perry was winded from the pace.

"I guess this means he was telling the truth," Perry muttered to himself, as Bosko grinned and gestured for him to sit on a nearby fallen trunk. Perry felt as though someone had sucked the life from him and he had to put his hand out to stop himself from toppling over the back of the stump as he took the weight off his legs and sat awkwardly. His mind had transported him back to the soft leather chairs in the corner of the luxurious hotel lobby in Vancouver where he had first known something was wrong, or should have. He had sensed that the former WPI scientist was telling the truth when he had warned that lives were at stake, and yet Perry had allowed himself to ignore the warning – to construct whatever artifice necessary to avoid what was staring him in the face. Worse, he had actively concealed information and involved one of his oldest and best friends, breaking the sacred bond of trust in the process. What would his old college roommate think of him when he learned the truth? Was it weakness or just the comfort of old age, and an unwillingness to part with the trappings that came with it that had made him jettison his integrity? Whatever the reason, it was inexcusable, and he almost welcomed the reckoning that was coming.

"What did he give you?" Bosko asked, waving the end of the rifle at Perry, who barely heard the question as a deep sense of shame overcame him. His breathing became shallower as the image of John Townsend's ruined corpse lying at his feet entered his mind, followed by one of Garcia's lifeless body. If only he could convert the rage he felt into energy, maybe he could overpower the man looming over him.

"I will find it anyway but if you tell me, I make it quick for you. Otherwise—"

"Go to hell," Perry said, his voice a whispered rasp. He tensed for an assault as the other man took a step forward, but it was soon clear that a search of Perry's pockets was the focus for now. Sensing an opportunity, Perry summoned his courage and managed a convincing scowl as he looked up at the blond man. "You'll never leave these woods alive. Pretty soon, there'll be an army of people in here, scouring the place. You heard the plane, right?" he added, with a bitter laugh. "That's just the advance team."

The blond man continued his search, twisting Perry back and forth to thoroughly examine the pockets and linings of his clothes and the inside of his boots. Then he stood, let out a sigh, and spat on the ground before looking back toward the plateau, a lop-sided grin on his face. "I hope they will be sending someone good, yes?"

"You have no fucking idea."

"You think you frighten me?" The blond man took a step closer, then set the rifle down on the forest floor by his feet. Perry watched as he straightened up again, the grin now a sinister grimace as an odd-looking knife appeared from nowhere in his left hand. "You should be frightened instead."

Perry stared at the thick blade that extended from between the middle fingers of the other man's hand, its sharp steel glinting in the light as he fought back the fear that bubbled in his chest.

"What do you want from me?"

Bosko stood over him in silence for a while, then pulled some rope out of his pocket and gestured for Perry to stand. Unable to find the strength to resist, he obeyed and allowed his hands to be bound behind his back.

"Over there," the blond man ordered, shoving Perry toward a stand of Yukon birch just off the horse trail. In his weakened condition, Perry's legs gave out and he stumbled onto the ground, looking up to see his captor scowling at him as he got back on his feet and staggered on to the trees. Once there, Bosko ordered him to sit and tied his hands to the base of the largest trunk.

"Now," Bosko said, squatting down in front of him. "You tell me something."

Perry looked at him up close; he had made a career out of taking the measure of his opponents and he had developed a keen instinct for weakness. But this man's eyes showed no trace of humanity, let alone weakness. It was like staring into the eyes of a circling great white.

"I don't know what you're expecting me to say and even if I did, I wouldn't tell you a damn thing." Perry's bravado was undermined by an involuntary shiver as he broke off eye contact and stared down at the ground in front of him.

Bosko gave a snort. "You are cold, yes? We have ten minutes, maybe fifteen, before men from the plane come." Bosko ran his fingers lovingly along the edge of the knife blade. "Is up to you how you spend this time, but I can make ten minutes *very* long for you."

"Go to hell," Perry spat again.

Bosko let out a guttural laugh. “You talk like tough man, but you are weak. All businessmen like you are weak. You think money is power.”

As Perry stared at him and processed the statement, something dawned on him. “You don’t know who I am, do you?”

“You are VIP, big fucking deal,” Bosko said, but Perry detected a hint of uncertainty in the other man’s eyes for the first time. “Whoever you are,” Bosko continued, crouching down, “The men I deal with are harder . . . much harder. Perry was considering another retort when the other man’s wrist shot out and sank the razor-sharp blade into the flesh of Perry’s upper arm and flooded his nerve endings with a searing pain.

CHAPTER 27

Matthews heard the distant crack of a twig and stopped, waiting until he was satisfied that the sound had come from Sawchuk. She had been taking frequent detours into the woods as they descended the horse trail, just in case Perry and Townsend – or whoever was pursuing them – had decided to try to conceal themselves by following a creek bed that ran parallel to the trail. She emerged a few feet to his right a moment later and shook her head before continuing on. They had been on the trail for about fifteen minutes and though he had no objective evidence to support it, he had the feeling they were closing in. He tightened his grip on the Beretta, the bare fingers of his right hand oblivious to the cold as he and Sawchuk pressed on in silence.

"I'll try the creek bed for a change," Matthews said after a few more minutes of walking, ducking into the trees as Sawchuk gave him an odd look – half acknowledgement and half surprise that he would leave the relative ease of the open trail. The light was dim in the trees, filtered out by the millions of evergreen boughs around him. He reached the creek bed in a matter of seconds – it was less than thirty feet from the trail, though completely obscured by the forest. He followed it down for a few minutes and was making his way back out to the trail when he stumbled over something and almost fell headlong into a big spruce. Looking back, his breath caught in his throat as he made out the unmistakable shape of a human body.

Crouching down for a closer inspection, he recognized John Townsend's face from the photos he had seen at the RCMP detachment in Whitehorse. The hair on the right side of Townsend's head was matted with blood, and he soon found the entry wound just in front of his left ear. He was about to call out for Sawchuk when he heard a rustle behind him, accompanied by a guttural and unfamiliar sound that he knew wasn't good. Turning slowly, he found himself staring at an enormous bear about twenty feet away. He froze in place, not because he thought that was the prescribed response, but because he simply couldn't move. As he racked his brain for an answer to the question of whether to stay still or run while he still had the chance, the grizzly – even Matthews could recognize the distinctive hump at the shoulders – suddenly reared up and let out a roar that seemed to shake the trees around him. As the bear dropped back down on its front paws and began to charge, Matthews raised his Beretta and aimed at the massive creature's head, squeezing off three rounds in succession that he thought had hit the target dead on, but the colossal grey-brown mass kept coming. He kept firing as he backpedalled, then tripped over a tree root, causing his next two shots to go high and wide.

As he pulled himself up on his elbows, the bear was within ten feet and still charging. Bracing himself for a futile defence, he heard an ear-splitting crack followed by a dull thump, and when he opened his eyes, the bear seemed to have been staggered by some unseen force. Matthews was scrambling backward on the ground when a second crack rang out from behind him and, this time, the massive beast came to a full stop, its head lolling to one side. The bear seemed suspended like a marionette for a moment. Then it slumped and fell over onto the forest floor, the ground shaking as the razor-sharp claws of one of its forepaws came to rest just inches from Matthews's feet.

Matthews turned and saw Sawchuk standing twenty feet back, in the process of ejecting shells and reloading, until the rifle was primed again and pointed at the motionless lump on the ground.

"That's a big grizz," she said, matter of fact, as she walked up next to Matthews and looked the bear over, satisfied that it was dead. "He's old, too – dangerous combination. Probably the same one that dragged away whoever was outside the lodge up at base camp." She gestured toward the plateau. "Good thing I had my 180-grain shells, or you'd be shit out of luck."

"Thanks," he said, when he had regained the ability to speak. It was a few seconds before his rattled brain recalled how he had come to be face to face with the grizzly in the first place. "Townsend's dead."

Sawchuk stood there for a moment, no trace of acknowledgement in her face. "What are you talking about?"

"Back there," he said, gesturing beyond the fallen bear. He gathered himself and stood, giving the bear a considerable berth as he walked past. "I stumbled over him. He's been shot – I assume it was the shot we heard."

Sawchuk followed, then knelt in silence next to Townsend's body, examining his face for a moment. "No sign of Perry?"

Matthews shrugged as he got to his feet. "I didn't get a chance to look before that thing showed up," he said, pointing to the dead bear. They did a quick search of the surrounding area but found nothing.

"Goddammit," Sawchuk said, as they returned to Townsend's body. "He's gotta be close, but we'll have warned him off, now," she added, gesturing back to the bear and referring to the multiple shots that would have been heard for miles around in the thin mountain air.

"He could have a vehicle stashed down by the highway," Matthews said. "Or maybe he's just planning on carjacking someone. Either way, he must have Perry and we know where he's headed." Sawchuk was still staring at Townsend's body. "We've got to press on, Lee."

"He would have heard our plane," she said, without looking up.

"So?"

"So, maybe he doubled back. The base camp's a lot closer than the highway, even if it is uphill."

Matthews shook his head and set off down the horse trail, calling out to her after a few seconds. "Look," he said, pointing to some broken branches and a partial boot print by the side of the trail. If he was hoping these signs would be convincing enough for her, he was disappointed.

"I don't know." She stared at the ground for a second, then took a few steps farther along the trail, examining the trees and brush on the side. "I want this prick as much as you do, believe me. I'm just not so sure . . . there's nothing else down here. He could have made those marks on purpose, to throw us off his trail."

"We could split up," Matthews said. "But either way, we have to hurry."

Sawchuk frowned, then gave a reluctant nod. "I'll head back up to the base camp. You follow the trail until you hit the highway. You can't get lost."

"Two quick shots if you find something, then we meet in the middle."

Sawchuk nodded. "Although I'd prefer one shot, right between this fucker's eyes."

"Be careful," he said, checking the magazine of his gun and noting that he still had seven rounds left in the fifteen-round clip. He looked up to see something between a smile and a smirk on Sawchuk's face.

"I'm in my backyard, city slicker. You're the one needs to be careful. And try to stay away from grizzlies," she added, looking at his gun with disdain. "That thing'll only piss 'em off."

CHAPTER 28

The man who had rented the pickup under the name of Piotr Bosko stood over Perry and looked up toward the plateau. He had definitely heard multiple shots from two different weapons and from the sound of it, they were close – a kilometre away, maybe less. Whether they were hunters who just happened to be in the area or men sent specifically after him or the man at his feet didn't matter. He looked down at Perry, who was breathing heavily and looking like he might pass out at any moment, the right sleeve of his jacket stained a dark shade of rust. There would be no time for what he had originally planned, but Bosko was no stranger to improvisation. Brandishing his knife, Bosko swung it down as Perry tried to twist away, the blade tearing through the tough fabric of Perry's sleeve. Bosko cut all the way around Perry's upper arm, then tore the blood-soaked sleeve away.

"What are you—"

"Quiet," Bosko growled, waving the knife in front of Perry's face, before taking a few steps farther into the woods, away from the trail.

Perry looked around in desperation. Wherever his captor had gone, he knew he would return soon and he also knew the end was near. He tugged at the rope securing his wrists to the tree behind him and, although there was some play, he wasn't getting them free, not in his weakened condition. Feeling around behind his back, he managed to unclasp the metal strap on his watch, slide it under the rope, and get hold of it with his left hand. Repositioning himself, he strained and found he was able to reach the bark of the tree nearest to his hands. Pressing the edge of the metal clasp into the smooth, soft bark, he closed his eyes and visualized the shape of the letters as he worked quickly and deliberately, until he heard the sound of Bosko's footsteps and had to drop the watch into the leaves at the base of the trees, resuming his original position. In doing so, he was sitting directly in front of the largest birch, obscuring its trunk from the other man's view.

"Who did you tell?" Bosko said, standing over him, breathing heavily now as he brandished the knife. Perry took the question as further confirmation of what he already knew and instead of fear at the sight of the knife in his face, he felt nothing but regret and shame. He drew a ragged breath and took comfort from the fact that he was so weak and dizzy that he would barely feel whatever his killer had in store for him.

"They'll get you eventually, asshole," he managed to say.

"Not so elegant, for last words," Bosko muttered, bearing down on Perry with the blade protruding through the middle fingers of his left hand, the same lopsided grimace below those dark, gleaming eyes.

As soon as he made it back to base camp, Bosko headed straight to the two planes parked next to each other near the main lodge. He climbed into the Cessna that he and Oyler had flown up in and, seeing the ignition switch barren of keys, he crawled under the dashboard on the pilot's side and searched for the ignition wires. When he located them, he disconnected and then reconnected them, causing the engine to come to life. Once the plane's engine was running, he jumped out and popped the engine cover on the Cub parked nearby, ripping out hoses and wires until he was satisfied that it was disabled. Tossing the hoses into the running Cessna, he climbed into the cockpit and strapped himself in as he revved the engine up to rolling speed.

Testing the controls as he directed the plane to the far end of the plateau, he turned the nose to point south, revved the engine again and then released the brake, causing it to lurch forward. He had taken some rudimentary flight training in the army and, though some of the Cessna's controls were foreign to him, the fundamentals were the same. He had also watched Oyler carefully on the flight in, knowing the guide wouldn't be making the return trip. He reached for the beads normally wrapped around his right wrist and swore when he realized they were missing. For a moment, he worried that they had fallen off near the dead American but quickly dismissed the risk of anyone finding them as immaterial. He was more annoyed at himself for losing a talisman that had brought him good fortune since he had acquired them from a Chechen guerrilla leader he had encountered on a raiding party in the hills south of Grozny. Bosko had been caught dead to rights until the Chechen's Kalashnikov – a rifle known for its reliability – had jammed, allowing Bosko to take the man down with a knife.

He swore again as he revved up the engine, thinking the Chechen was long gone and he was still here, beads or no beads. He gritted his teeth and, as the plane picked up speed and bounced along the rough terrain, he kept an eye on the rapidly disappearing runway ahead. He could feel the momentum of the gentle downward slope and realized that he had its added depth to make up in order to clear the trees ahead. Steeling himself as they approached, he waited until the last possible moment to pull up hard on the control wheel. The nose of the little plane came up, seemed to hesitate then caught some lift and climbed, its wheels skimming the tips of the trees at the southern end of the runway. As the plateau fell away beneath him, he allowed himself a satisfied grin. The job hadn't gone quite as he had planned, but it wouldn't be the first time he'd had to adapt to changing circumstances and with whomever was still down on the plateau unable to use the disabled Cub, he had a considerable head start. He continued on his northerly heading, his little plane the only man-made thing in the sky or on the ground as far as the eye could see.

CHAPTER 29

Though he didn't realize it, Matthews was less than ten kilometres from the Alaska Highway when he heard the distinctive buzz of a plane. He stood frozen in place as he considered the various possibilities.

Good news first . . .

It could be a team from Whitehorse who had figured out where they were, in which case he and Sawchuk would have reinforcements. The alternative was that Bosko, or whatever his real name was, had gotten away. He didn't think even Sawchuk could have reached the base camp yet, but the fact that he hadn't heard the agreed-upon two gunshots was troubling. She must have seen or heard the plane, as he had . . .

As the noise of the engine grew to a roar overhead, he looked up and saw the blue and white Cessna, on a northwest climb from the plateau. He briefly considered taking a few shots at it – it didn't seem that high – but then abandoned the plan. He couldn't be sure who was in it and the chances of disabling it with a 9mm bullet at this range were next to impossible anyway. Looking back up the trail he had just come down, he sighed. The prospect of the uphill climb soon became irrelevant as a far more unsettling possibility formed in his mind and he took off up the trail at a run. What if Sawchuk *had* reached the plateau?

Sawchuk was almost back up to the base camp when she heard the plane's engine. She couldn't see the plateau yet but there was no mistaking the sound of Dale Oyler's Cessna 180. She swore and picked up her pace, determined to reach the top of the trail, if only to catch a glimpse of the plane's heading before it was too late. She called up the image of John Townsend's lifeless face to spur her on, her legs pumping like pistons as she gained ground. Then something caught her eye among the branches just off the trail – a piece of stained fabric hanging from a branch five feet off the ground. It looked like part of a coat sleeve and it was partially soaked in blood, the tan fabric stained rusty-brown. Her senses on high alert, she glanced around and took a few steps in the direction of the creek bed, then stopped dead. She could see something beyond the evergreen boughs, at the base of a stand of white birch trees – something that didn't belong out there, in the middle of nature. She kept walking, slowly but deliberately, until she knew without a doubt what she was looking at. She pulled her rifle off her shoulder and pointed it up into the sky and fired off two shots in rapid succession. Then she ran out to the trail to try and get a look at the plane, but it was too late – the Cessna was nowhere to be seen and the sound of its engine had faded into the distance. Pausing long enough to catch her breath for a moment, she prepared herself for what awaited her back in the woods.

CHAPTER 30

Matthews's heart was pounding and his legs throbbed as he continued his progress up the trail, Sawchuk's signal shots having intensified his pace. By the time he spotted her sitting on a rock at the edge of the horse trail, he was ready to collapse, but he could tell by her posture that the news was not good.

"You're not gonna like it," was all she said, as she got to her feet and pointed into the woods. They didn't speak as they walked the twenty feet through the trees to the clearing and the stand of birch trees, at the base of which lay Richard Perry's slumped body. His head lolled forward and his hands were tied behind his back, holding his motionless body in an awkward, half-upright position. His clothes were soaked in blood and, as Matthews came closer, he saw why – a gaping slash starting just under Perry's left ear and disappearing beneath his slumped chin.

"Jesus," he muttered.

"We've got to get back to the plane," Sawchuk said, gesturing toward the plateau.

Matthews stood there, staring at the body. "We can't just leave him here like this."

"We don't have a choice." When he didn't respond, she put her hand on his arm. "There's nothing you can do for him, Ben." The sound of his name and the touch of her hand brought him back to reality and he gave a grim nod. "The only way to make this right," she continued, "is to catch the piece of shit who did this."

He looked at her, then pulled out his phone, confirming what he already knew with a few swipes.

"I told you," she said quietly, "it won't—"

"How can there be no fucking service!"

"Come on," she said, turning and walking out toward the trail. Watching her leave, Matthews glanced back at Perry's body for a moment then sighed and followed her out.

The afternoon sky was darkening as they made their way up the trail, the few flurries turning to steady snow by the time they reached base camp. They went straight to the Cub but instead of reaching for the door to the cockpit, Sawchuk noticed the unfastened clasp on the engine cover and swung it open. She swore at the devastation inside.

"What is it?" Matthews said, looking over her shoulder.

"I'm no aviation mechanic," she replied, getting into the cockpit and turning the key in the ignition, to no avail. "But this thing isn't going anywhere."

She jumped down from the plane, swore again, and looked toward the sky. Matthews was absorbed in his own assessment of the situation, which was nothing short of disastrous. Both the former vice president and a former Canadian ambassador to the US were dead, along with a Secret Service bodyguard and their outfitter. The killer was rapidly widening his margin of escape as they stood there, in the middle of nowhere, with no form of communication and utterly helpless. It was a few hours at least down to the highway, probably longer if the snowfall got any heavier. He was already tired, bordering on exhausted, but it was how he was going to pick up Bosko's trail from here that concerned Matthews more. A close second was how he was going to break the news to Vanessa Ortiz.

"Come on," Sawchuk said, interrupting his internal discussion. "We'd better get going."

"To the highway?"

"It's the only option." She slid her little day pack off and dug around, pulling out a couple of energy bars. "Here. Eat one of these."

He took the bar and put it in his pocket as they began walking the now familiar path north to the horse trail, eventually ducking into the trees to avoid the increasingly intense snowfall. Even with the partial cover of the trees, he and Sawchuk looked like a pair of snowmen by the time they reached the start of the trail. But instead of the big white fluffy flakes from a Christmas card scene, the snow was a fine powder that felt like Styrofoam underfoot. The temperature had been dropping all afternoon and now, as daylight gave way to darkness, it seemed even colder.

"I told you you should have switched pants," Sawchuk said, as they took a break for a sip of water before hitting the eastbound trail. She was looking at his thin Brooks Brothers gabardines, encrusted in snow and torn at one knee. He brushed them off and shrugged, unwilling to admit that she had been right. Luckily, the parka he had borrowed was warm and long enough to cover his upper thighs.

"How long do you figure, to get to the highway?"

She shrugged. "Normally, it's only a few hours. But if this keeps up," she added, looking skyward, "it's gonna take a little longer. Storms up here come in quick and they can be unpredictable."

They took the trail down and the farther they went, the harder the snow began to fall. After about an hour, the wind picked up and forced them back into the trees. Even along the creek bed the wind and snow lashed their faces as they navigated the snowy ground, making their progress painfully slow. They had been walking along the bed for a couple of hours when the path they had been following seemed to disappear into a ravine. Sawchuk stopped and wiped the accumulated snow from her face and the front of her wool hat.

"We can't follow it any more from here. We have to go back out to the trail."

Matthews nodded, though he knew that the conditions would be even worse out in the open. Sure enough, when they left the shelter of the trees, the trail was barely recognizable. The ground was covered in a white blanket and, between the wind and the heavy snowfall, visibility was almost non-existent.

"This way," Sawchuk said, but her tone was slightly less confident than usual. Matthews stayed close behind her as they trudged through the heavy snow, their progress hampered by drifts several feet deep in places. After a few minutes, she turned and said something, her voice lost in the howling wind.

"What?" he yelled.

She started to speak, then pulled him by the arm until they were back in the trees.

"It'll take forever to make it to the highway at this rate," she said, her breathing heavy. "And there's a real risk of getting lost in this – I can barely see a foot in front of me."

"What time is it?" he asked, as they took a breather, their backs turned to the wind as they huddled by a large fir.

"Just after nine p.m."

"Is anyone even gonna be on the highway at night in this weather?"

She brushed snow from her eyes and shook her head. "Probably not."

"So, what do we do?"

They stood in silence and Matthews turned to look toward the trail, the wind lashing his face and driving snow pricking his eyes. He was prepared to endure whatever it took to get to the highway, but getting lost or dying from exposure wasn't going to help anyone. He could tell that Sawchuk was going through the same thought process, and he sensed that if there was any reasonable chance at all of pressing on and making it, she wouldn't have left the trail in the first place. Her irritation at being forced to stop was also palpable.

"Maybe we should shelter here," he finally said. "Especially if we're just going to be stuck sitting by the highway anyway." Sawchuk took one final glance toward the trail, then a look of grim resignation settled on her face as she slipped the rifle and backpack off her shoulders.

"We'll make a lean-to right there." She pointed to a little ledge about twenty feet down the slope of the ravine.

"A what?"

"Here." She handed him a Leatherman knife. "Cut off some thick boughs that we can thread into a screen. I'll look after the frame. We'll need some firewood, too."

They went about their work in silence, and when Matthews returned with a pile of boughs fifteen minutes later, he was shocked to find Sawchuk putting the finishing touches on a six-by-four-foot frame of small trunks, complete with two thinner, criss-crossed strips of wood.

"How did you cut those?"

She shrugged and gestured to what looked vaguely like a hacksaw on the ground. "Collapsible saw. I never go anywhere without it. Is that all you got?"

Matthews followed her eyes to the pile of boughs he had dropped at his feet.

"What do you mean?" he said, though he couldn't help but question his own productivity, given what she had managed to achieve in the same time it had taken him to collect his now sad-looking pile.

"Just . . . Forget it. I'll get some more. You start threading these into the frame."

"No." Matthews waved her off. "I'll do it," he said, heading back to the trees before she could respond. He worked as quickly as he could and by the time he returned, she had more than half of the frame completed.

"That oughta do it," she said, looking at the product of his labour in a way that made him feel like a sixth grader being complimented on a mediocre science project. When the last of the boughs had been threaded into the frame, they leaned it against the rock overhang, creating a partially enclosed area that was sheltered from the swirling wind and snow.

"Tie it down to that," she said, tossing him some string and pointing to the nearest tree as she set about piling dry boughs and sticks in the middle of the floor. As he was finishing his knot, he heard crackling and turned to see that Sawchuk had already nursed her tidy pile into an impressive blaze. She cracked some larger pieces of deadfall over her knee and tossed them on, then spread the unused boughs on the floor before sitting down. Sliding off his leather mittens, Matthews sat next to her. As the flames licked before them, he felt real warmth for the first time all day.

"You grab a few winks if you want," Sawchuk said, taking a bite of an energy bar. Matthews shook his head and listened to the crackling of the fire as Sawchuk chewed.

"Where do you think he went?" he finally asked.

"You said you saw the plane heading north."

He nodded. "But what's north of here?"

"Alaska's northwest," she said, poking a large branch with the toe of her boot to stop it from falling out of the fire. "But I'm not sure he'd have enough fuel and crossing into US airspace is risky."

They both stared at the fire for a while before she spoke again.

"I should have checked that damn radio before we left Dale's place. We could have had reinforcements up here hours ago."

"It wouldn't have made any difference," Matthews said, tossing another piece of wood on the fire and watching as the flames danced around it, licking at the loose bark. Neither of them spoke as they warmed themselves in front of the fire.

"How long have you been in Canada?" she asked, breaking the silence.

"A few weeks. I was in Ottawa for a bit before coming out to Vancouver. Funny thing is," he said, rearranging an errant branch with a stick, "I was supposed to be in London right now."

"London, England?"

"Yup."

"How'd you end up going from London to Ottawa?" she asked.

"It's kind of a long story – one that I don't want to get into, to be honest."

"You brought it up."

He sighed. "Let's just say I fucked up and leave it at that, okay?"

"Everyone fucks up once in a while," Sawchuk said. "I've got no problem with that, but I don't like not knowing who I'm working with and you seem to have a few too many secrets."

Matthews sighed. "I didn't *lie* to you about who I work for, I just withheld some of the details because they weren't relevant."

"Now you sound like a lawyer."

"Now you're just being mean. Look, if it makes you feel any better, the work I came out to Vancouver for is a collaborative effort with your folks."

"You mean CSIS? What kind of work? Counter-intelligence?" She waited for him to respond and when he didn't she gave a little snort. "You really have a hard time with the truth, don't you? Or is it that you'd have to kill me if you told me?"

He turned and saw the twitch of a smile at the corner of her mouth.

"Well, now that you mention it . . ."

"Good luck!" she said, and it was his turn to smile.

"You probably have a collapsible shotgun tucked up your sleeve," he said. "Unless you prefer to use the saw, that is."

"You don't want to find out."

"How about you," he said, tossing another branch into the flames. "Have you always lived in the Yukon?"

"Spent a few years down South for school and RCMP training and couldn't wait to get back," she said, leaning forward to warm her hands over the flames, her thigh nudging his in the close quarters. "Sorry."

"No problem," he said, thinking that he really didn't mind – the contact had triggered a warm glow deep within him that was much more pleasant than any fire, despite the idea of there being anything more than cool professionalism between them being laughable. Apart from the inappropriateness of mixing work and romance, there was also the fact that they were polar opposites in almost every way – he also got the distinct impression that she considered him something of a lightweight, an impression that especially stung in light of recent events.

"When you say *down South*," he said, abandoning a train of thought that was heading toward a spiral. "You mean where, exactly?"

She laughed. "Anything south of the 60th parallel. In my case, mostly Regina and Vancouver, but I had a short stint in Ottawa. I actually didn't hate Ottawa, except for all the politics."

"Armstrong made it sound like your dad was some kind of legend around here. Is he why you became a cop?"

She nodded. "He tried talking me out of it, but he knew there was no point. I was made for this. How about you – were your folks in law enforcement?"

Matthews hesitated, but for some reason, he decided to tell the truth. "My uncle was a cop and when I was young, that was all I wanted to be. My father didn't think I had what it takes."

"Probably just trying to protect you."

"Yeah," Matthews said. "Guess he wasn't wrong . . . about the dangers, I mean. My uncle was killed in the line of duty when I was in college."

"Sorry to hear that."

"Thanks. He's the reason I changed my focus to law enforcement and being at Georgetown, there was kind of a natural path to the Agency."

"I went to Washington for a conference a few years ago," she said. "It was nice, but too hot for me."

He smiled. "It's sure a lot different from the view from the plane today. I just wish I was here under different circumstances."

They went quiet for a long time, both staring into the dancing flames.

"Do you really have no idea who this guy is?" she eventually asked.

Matthews shook his head. "I wish I did. None of it makes any sense."

"It's gotta be politically motivated, right?" she said. "Something connected to Perry's time in office?"

Silence returned for a while, as they both sifted through their mental archives. Sawchuk was a bit younger than Matthews but not by much, which meant that they would both have barely been in grade school at the time Perry was in office. From what Matthews could recall of Richard Perry, he had been second banana to a Republican president who had gone on to make his mark in Iraq.

"Was John Townsend known for being particularly pro-war?" he asked.

"Not that I know of. I think he was known for NAFTA, mostly. He was a trade lawyer before they made him ambassador."

"I'm just wondering what political beef someone would have against both the US and Canada."

"Good question," Sawchuk said. "And why now? After all these years?"

"I don't know. But I'm sure as hell gonna find out." He turned to face her, as she continued to stare straight ahead, warming her hands over the fire. "You said you knew Townsend?"

She nodded. "When Townsend first came up here – must be ten years back – Dad took him on his first hunt and had him over for dinner."

"What was he like?"

"He was a politician, for sure," she said, with a trace of a smile. "But he seemed pretty genuine and whatever his politics, he didn't deserve that," she added, gesturing toward the trail, where Townsend's body lay several kilometres north of their current position, collecting a layer of snow.

"Neither did Perry," Matthews said, "though I never met the man . . . in life."

She asked, "Are you gonna be in shit, when we make contact?"

He let out a grim chuckle. "Well, let's see. I went off the grid and managed to get both of them killed, not to mention the bodyguard and Dale Oyler."

"Dale and the bodyguard were dead before we even got here, so I don't think they can blame you for that."

"Just a former vice president and ambassador," he said. "In that case, I'm sure it'll be back slaps all around."

Sawchuk took another branch of deadfall and laid it on top of the flames. "Well, at least we were in the ballpark – if everyone else hadn't gone up to Mayo, we might have caught this bastard by now. But we're *gonna* get him. That much I can guarantee."

"They say the Mounties always get their man."

"If I have to track this fucker to the ends of the earth, I will. I owe it to Dale, if for no other reason."

Matthews nodded as they stared into the fire, both of them struggling to maintain the manufactured optimism. Wherever Bosko was by now, it seemed too far away.

CHAPTER 31

It was pitch black by the time Bosko made it back to the Alaska Highway. After taking off from the Kluane Plateau and heading north for long enough to be out of sight, he had swung the Cessna southwest in a wide arc. The snow had gradually petered out as he made his way south. He had been able to chart his course by following the Alaska Highway, which he had picked up around Haines Junction. He used the highway as a reference point on his map of Northern British Columbia and Yukon. He had steered well clear of Whitehorse and might have been over British Columbia as he made his way east, but he was pretty sure the big body of water he had spotted in the fading light was Teslin Lake, which meant he was straddling the Yukon–British Columbia border.

He had originally been thinking of landing on a deserted stretch of highway, but then he had spotted the cleared strip on the northern side of the lake and taken a chance. The landing had been a bit rough but there was more than enough room to bring the plane to a stop. He had driven it straight into the bush, where it would be difficult to spot from the air. It was getting dark by the time he landed anyway and if things went as planned, it wouldn't matter if they found the plane in the morning.

The hike around the lake had taken longer than he had expected, and he was glad when he finally reached the highway, though it was barren and unlit. He knew someone would come by eventually, so he started walking east along the shoulder of the highway. After fifteen minutes, he turned at the distinct sound of an engine, then saw the beam of headlights over the hill. Stepping out into the road as the headlights approached, he shielded his eyes and began to wave. The vehicle slowed and he watched as a weathered pickup came to rest a few feet ahead of him on the shoulder. As Bosko approached, the driver's window came down to reveal an overweight man in his late forties with a grubby toque on his head and a few days' worth of grey stubble on his face.

"You want a ride?"

"If you have room, yes please."

The driver looked him over before asking: "Where you headed?"

"Vancouver."

"Well," he said, seeming to come to some internal conclusion. "I'll take you as far as Fort Nelson if you want. You can probably hitch a ride to Vancouver from there."

"Thanks," Bosko said, walking around to the passenger side door and opening it, the rusted hinges creaking in protest.

"What are you doing all the way out here, anyway?"

Bosko grinned. "I get a ride to Teslin from Whitehorse, then I walk for a while." He watched as the other man put the truck in drive and it moved back onto the highway. "I forget there are not many cars on this road."

"That's a cool accent you got there. Where you from?"

"Czech Republic."

"You're a long way from home, pal."

"Yes, I love the outdoors and it is a dream to come here one day."

"Well, I'm glad someone likes it," the driver said with a chuckle. "I'm Clay, by the way. Clay Fenwick."

Bosko took the man's extended hand and shook it. "Jaroslav Danko," he said, recalling the surname of a Czech policeman he had killed with his bare hands in a side street near the Charles Bridge in Prague.

Bosko glanced around the inside of the truck, which looked to be about twenty years old. It stank of body odour, stale cigarette smoke, and barbecue sauce, and the floor was littered with old food wrappers. Despite appearances, the ride was relatively smooth and the engine seemed to have no trouble producing a steady rumble.

"What do you do in Fort Nelson, Clay?"

"Oil and gas," he said. "I been spendin' the summers in Whitehorse for the past ten years or so. Had a woman lived up there for a while. She moved on but I decided to stay. Winters are too hard for me now, though."

"You don't like the cold weather, yes?" Bosko nodded.

"It ain't the cold. Shit, Fort Nelson's just as goddamned cold. No, it's the light. You mind?" Fenwick had already popped a rolled cigarette into his mouth and was in the process of lighting up with the coil lighter from the truck's ashtray.

"Of course," Bosko said.

"How long were you in Whitehorse, then?" Fenwick exhaled a thick cloud of smoke.

"Just a week. I meet a friend and we do a trip along the river. We also go to Dawson City," he said, reciting some of the options listed in the brochures he had seen in town and out at Oyler's lodge.

"A river trip? I'm surprised they took you out this late."

"It was just short trip," Bosko said, glancing at the gas gauge and noting it indicated three-quarters of a tank. "How long to Fort Nelson?"

"From here, six or seven hours, dependin' on the weather."

Bosko looked out into the darkness ahead. Beyond the beam of the headlights, he saw virtually nothing, but the stars were visible in the cold night sky. "Looks clear."

Fenwick laughed and blew out another cloud of acrid smoke. "Here, sure, but we're goin' up in the mountains. You never know what's gonna be waitin' for you up there and the roads aren't great in bad weather. I usually stop in Liard if the goin' gets too bad."

Bosko nodded. He didn't know where Liard was, but it didn't matter for now. Fenwick turned a knob on the dash and the radio began to emit a few bars of country music, competing with a pronounced mechanical hum and a crackle of static.

"You like country?"

"Sure." Bosko smiled and looked out the window again into the dark. It had now been almost fifteen minutes since he had been picked up and they hadn't encountered a single other vehicle. This was going to be too easy. He allowed Fenwick to do most of the talking, interjecting a few words now and then to keep his talkative host assured of his interest. After about ninety minutes of driving, he adjusted himself in his seat.

"This . . . Liard," he said. "This is hotel?"

Fenwick nodded. "There's a lodge there."

"You have reservation?"

Fenwick laughed and lit another cigarette. "It ain't a reservation kind of place. There's a restaurant there and there's some rooms upstairs. If they're available and you want one, you can stay. If it's full, the owner'll let you sleep in the barn."

"Okay," Bosko said with a smile, as he shifted in his seat again.

"Everything okay?"

"Is nothing."

"You want to make a pit stop?" Fenwick glanced over and saw his passenger's confusion. "I mean, do you want me to pull over for a bathroom break?"

Bosko nodded. "Bathroom break. Yes . . . please."

"No worries. My teeth are floatin' too. I was gonna pull over at Rancheria but that's another half hour." Fenwick slowed the truck and pulled over onto the shoulder, leaving the engine running and the headlights on. "This is as good a place as any," he said, opening the driver's side door and stepping out.

Bosko smiled as he looked outside. They were surrounded by forest on either side of the highway and though he knew there were thousands of kilometres of deserted road ahead and behind them, there was nothing but darkness beyond the beam of the headlights.

"I agree, is perfect," he said, as he watched Fenwick walk down into the roadside ditch, plant his legs, and fumble with his zipper. Bosko almost felt bad for the man as he slid the knife out of the sheath in the left sleeve of his jacket, pushed open the creaking passenger door and stepped out into the frigid night.

CHAPTER 32

The light was just coming up behind them when Matthews first saw the Alaska Highway in the distance. They had left the shelter a couple of hours before, when the snow had tapered off. Sawchuk's estimate of the time it would take them to reach their destination had been dead on.

"There it is," he said, as she came up behind him at the crest of the hill. The snow had been light when they had started out, then slowed, and stopped altogether about an hour later. The view of the valley cradling the highway and the mountains beyond was spectacular, not least because the snow-covered canvas before them was bathed in the red-orange glow of the rising sun. It was unlike anything Matthews had ever seen before, with nothing but mountains and trees all the way to the horizon – apart from the highway itself, stretching north and south as far as the eye could see. It looked deserted, but they still had a good half an hour's hike to reach it.

"I just hope someone comes by soon," he said, as Sawchuk set off down the hill. "What's the nearest town, anyway?"

"Nearest place with a phone and internet's Burwash Landing," she called over her shoulder. "About a half hour's driv—"

He watched in horror as her right foot slid out from under her, pitching her sideways as her body hung for what seemed like eternity before gravity took it over a nearby ledge.

"Lee!" he yelled, trying in vain to reach her before she went over, but she was gone. He reached the ledge in time to see her tumbling over the rock and undergrowth toward the edge of a much larger drop, into a ravine a hundred feet or more below.

"Lee!" he called out again, scrambling down the steep incline after her, desperately searching for something - anything - that would stop her progress toward what would certainly be a fatal fall. He lost his footing for a moment but caught himself from tipping over and, when he looked up, he saw that Sawchuk had come to rest by the trunk of a large fir, inches from the edge of the ravine. His initial relief turned to panic as he noticed she wasn't moving.

"Lee! Are you all ri—"

"Goddamn black ice," she said, with a groan as she sat up and dusted the snow off her jacket. "Jeez," she said, looking over the nearby ravine. "That was close."

"Are you okay?" he said, reaching her and taking her arm as she began to stand.

"I'm fine," she said, shrugging off his help, but halfway to her feet, her right leg gave out and she cried out in pain.

"What is it?"

"It's my ankle. Shit! I must have twisted it."

"Hang on," he said, as she tried to stand again. "Just sit down for a sec so we can have a look and make sure it's not broken."

"What are you, a doctor now, too? It's fine. It's just twisted."

He watched as she straightened gingerly, grabbing onto a tree for support instead of his outstretched hand. She took a breath then tried to hobble up the slope, collapsing after a few steps.

"Lee, just wait."

"It's nothing," she snapped. "I'm fine."

"You're not fine," Matthews said. "You can't walk on a busted ankle."

"I told you, it's not busted," she said, then tried moving again. This time, she couldn't manage a single step before collapsing on the ground. "Shit, shit, *shit*!"

He sat next to her in silence while she caught her breath.

"You go on," she finally said.

"What are you talking about?"

"It's obvious isn't it?" she said. "I can't walk and we need to get to that highway ASAP, so you go on and make contact. You can send someone back for me."

Matthews shook his head. "No way."

"What, are you afraid of getting lost? You can see the highway – even you couldn't get lost from here."

He ignored the jab. "What are we, a mile or so from the highway?"

Sawchuk sighed and tilted her head back. "I don't know, yeah, a couple of clicks. But there's no wa—"

"Come on," he said, gesturing for her to get up.

"What do you mean, come on?"

"I'll carry you."

"You're not carrying me anywhere. I'll only slow you down and you're not gonna make it five hundred feet in this terrain with the extra weight, let alone a couple of kilometres."

"I'm not leaving you here, so you're either walking or I'm carrying you. Which is it gonna be?"

"I told you, I—"

"We're wasting time," he said, then reached out his hand. She stared at it for a few seconds, let out another sigh, and then gritted her teeth and let him pull her up.

It was over an hour later when Matthews stepped up onto the snow-covered, stone-chip pavement of the highway and let out a deep breath.

"We made it," he said, as Sawchuk slid off his back and sat awkwardly while he knelt down to examine tire tracks on the roadway, partially covered by a dusting of snow.

"Someone'll be by before too long," Sawchuk said, seeming to sense Matthews's concern. "After last night's bad weather, there'll be plenty of folks eager to get back on the road, believe me."

He nodded and sat on the shoulder, leaning back with his hands behind him to look up at the sky as he caught his breath. He had underestimated the effort of a two-kilometre hike over terrain of varying severity with Sawchuk either on his back or over his shoulder. "I don't think I've ever seen a sun that's quite that colour."

"Yeah," Sawchuk said, shielding her eyes as she looked to the east.

Matthews ran a hand over his two days of scruff, then glanced down at his dress pants – incongruous next to the scuffed leather boots, even with tears in both knees – and imagined he was quite a sight. It occurred to him as Sawchuk stood and balanced herself on her left leg that she presented just the opposite image, despite having spent the same amount of time in the rough as him. Her bulky, flannel-lined jeans, heavy coat, and well-worn boots were far from a *Vogue* cover, but she had a certain look that was difficult to ignore. Maybe it had more to do with her height and the long blond hair protruding from her black woollen hat, or maybe it was her attitude. Whatever it was, he couldn't help thinking of Caroline, and what she would make of his attraction to a woman in workboots.

"How's the ankle?"

"It's still pretty sore," she said, as she began to rotate her right foot slowly in both directions. "But the range of motion's getting better."

"I guess you were right about it not being broken," he said. She nodded and continued to focus on rotating her ankle in silence as Matthews scanned the highway in both directions. He might have appreciated the exquisite scenery more if it didn't seem so desolate.

"Well," she finally said, without looking at him. "I s'pose I should thank you . . . for helping me."

"Forget it," he said, amused at her obvious discomfort.

"No, I – what's up with you?" Sawchuk said, having suddenly turned and noticed an expression he didn't realize he was wearing.

"Nothing, I was just thinking, if the people back in DC could see me now."

She looked at him for a moment, her eyes slightly narrowed, though he thought he detected a hint of playfulness. "Glad you can still laugh about it."

"You're right. I'm totally fucked."

"Not if we find this guy first."

"It's not looking so good," he said, glancing up and down the highway, but she had moved off, hopping toward the centre of the road.

"You hear that?"

"What?" He stood and dusted the snow from the back of his coat as his ears picked up the low grumble of an engine and he saw the unmistakable shape of a truck appearing in the distance.

As luck would have it, the old-timer who had picked them up on the highway had a cellphone, so Matthews and Sawchuk were able to brief their respective superiors right away. Rather than waste time heading back to Whitehorse, Sawchuk had wrangled a plane ride from one of her father's hunting buddies in Burwash Landing, so that by the time she and Matthews were back up on the Kluane Plateau, an RCMP plane was waiting for them and more reinforcements were on the way. It didn't help that most of the available planes and ground personnel had been sent to scour the hunting grounds around Mayo, four hundred kilometres or so to the northeast, and Matthews had been surprised to learn that no one had seen fit to allocate a least a few resources to the plateau. Obviously, John Townsend's carefully placed miscues about the location of their hunt had worked a little too well.

While Sawchuk updated her colleagues and reluctantly accepted some first aid for her ankle, Matthews spoke with Special Agent Croft, in charge of the US side of the hastily assembled FBI–RCMP operation in Whitehorse. Croft had been unapologetic about his decision to focus on Mayo, which – at least in the FBI man's opinion – the evidence suggested was Perry's most likely location, and Matthews hadn't felt it was the right moment to press. As with his initial de-brief to Vanessa Ortiz on the drive to Burwash Landing, Matthews found the weight of the news he was delivering almost overwhelming – a former vice president, not to mention a former Canadian ambassador, had been murdered. He tried not to dwell on the fact that it had happened on his watch, though objectively, it was hard to see how he could have prevented it given the circumstances. And while he sensed a great deal of anger at the other end of the phone by the time Croft ended the call, it seemed to be directed at the killer, for now at least. Matthews had felt particularly helpless relaying the last known position of the man known only as Piotr Bosko – headed north in a bush plane, almost fifteen hours ago.

Fifteen hours . . .

In the vastness of the environment all around them, it seemed like a lifetime, but there were only so many options for escape. Entering US airspace was too risky, which meant Bosko would have had to turn south at some point. As Sawchuk spoke on a phone paired to an inReach satellite communicator, her RCMP counterparts in Whitehorse worked to set up roadblocks and send out BOLOs on the man calling himself Bosko. Once they had tasked a team to track all possible escape options, the next priority was getting back to the bodies of Richard Perry and John Townsend. Assuming animals hadn't made off with the remains already, their locations represented crime scenes with potentially valuable information about the killer. Two crime scene crews – one from Whitehorse and a second from Juneau, Alaska – were already en route.

First, Matthews and Sawchuk joined the two Mounties to search the woods near where Garcia's body had been dumped. It took a while, in the surprisingly thick layer of fresh snow and with Sawchuk's ankle restricted by a walking boot that one of the Mounties had found in the back of the RCMP plane, but they eventually found the body, dragged under some deadfall and partially buried in leaves and other undergrowth the grizzly had been able to find before setting off again. They were trying to determine how much damage the bear had done when they heard the buzz of an aircraft engine and hurried back out of the woods in time to see the little plane headed toward the northern end of the plateau. As it came in for landing, Matthews spotted a second plane, still high up and off to the southeast.

"Looks like they sent a full crew," Sawchuk remarked, as a third plane came into view in the distance, just as the first bounced its way to the end of the runway and approached the lodge. A crew of technicians disembarked and unloaded their gear, and Matthews watched as Sawchuk had an exchange with the man in the co-pilot's seat. She brought him over a few minutes later, as Matthews was telling one of the crime scene technicians where to find Garcia and Oyler's bodies.

"This is Sergeant Daley," Sawchuk said, pointing to the man she had been talking to by the plane. "He's gonna stay with this team and work the crime scenes here."

"Ben Matthews, US State Department." He stuck out his hand and ignored the sideways look from Sawchuk.

"That's the second team of technicians," she said, pointing to the second plane taxiing toward them. "They're out of Juneau. We're going to take them up to Perry and Townsend."

"How far are the vics from here?" Daley asked.

"About an hour's hike."

"You must be exhausted, Lee," Daley said, glancing down to the walking boot. "You want to switch places? I don't mind."

"I'm good," she said, with a wave. "Just make sure a grizz doesn't make off with one of these techs."

She gestured to Matthews and started hobbling toward the second plane, leaning close to him as its propeller came to rest. "Why'd you bullshit Daley with that State Department crap?"

He shrugged. "That's my official title. Just because you blew my cover doesn't mean everyone has to know. I'd appreciate it if you kept it to yourself, by the way."

"Whatever," she said. "Come on, let's help these guys get unloaded so we can get them to the scene, and we can get the hell off this mountain."

Matthews stood at the edge of the perimeter the crime scene technicians had established around Perry's body, thinking how out of place the vivid yellow tape seemed up there. Despite a bright sun high in the sky, the air remained cold and the snow crisp underfoot, which at least made the technicians' work easier. He watched as one of them conducted a painstaking grid search to the right of the stand of birch trees, to which Perry's body was still tied, in exactly the same position they had left it the day before. Sawchuk was a kilometre or so away with the other team, detailing the scene around Townsend's body. He gripped the 7mm rifle she had given him back at base camp – she had taken a .303 from one of her colleagues on the third plane – and scanned the surrounding woods, thinking back to the moment he had realized his Beretta was as about as effective against an adult grizzly as a popgun. If she hadn't been there . . .

The sight of her standing there, looking down that rifle barrel with half of her full bottom lip pinched between her teeth and ready to take out whatever came through the trees next brought a smile to his face, which vanished as his scan of the woods ended and he found himself looking at Perry's drooping head again.

The fact that neither Perry's nor Townsend's body had been disturbed by wildlife was a relief and a surprise – the killer's careful placement of the blood-soaked strip of Perry's coat sleeve nearby and high enough in the tree to catch the breeze was no coincidence and would likely have attracted a hungry animal or two if Sawchuk hadn't found it first. Not that it was any easier to look at Perry's body now. The killer had slit a helpless man's throat, and as Matthews stood there, anger welled inside him.

"You're gonna want to see this."

He looked to the technician standing over Perry's body, then made his way carefully in from the perimeter and crouched to get a look at the spot where the other man was pointing. He didn't see anything at first, but as he examined the bark of the largest of the three trees, next to where Perry's wrists were still trussed, he made out some markings in the bark.

"Is that what I think it is?"

"It looks like he was able to scratch out a message." The technician held up an evidence bag containing the Rolex he had found beneath the snow and leaves at the base of the trees. "There's bark on the clasp of the strap."

"I can't make it out . . ." Matthews crouched farther down and twisted his neck to get closer to the engraving on the bark. "That looks like a four. *4 dat—*" he said, frowning and leaning even closer to make it out in the dim light.

"Is that '*days*'?" The technician had leaned in and was shining a Maglite on the trunk of the birch.

"I think you're right." The excitement was audible in Matthews's voice as the prospect of a viable clue grew. "*Four days to . . . step . . .* something."

"It looks like a '*v*'."

"Maybe he meant 'five'. *Four days to step five*?"

They both stared at the trunk for a while.

"Damned if I know what that means." Matthews stared at the carving as the technician straightened and resumed his inspection. As he racked his brain trying to put the cryptic message into some meaningful context, Matthews looked at the position of Perry's body and tried to imagine the effort it must have taken to carve the words behind his back, unable to see whether he was creating anything intelligible as his killer lurked nearby. However incomprehensible it seemed to Matthews right now, Perry had obviously felt it important enough to record the message – likely one of his last living acts – and Matthews knew it would reveal something about the killer eventually. He took out the satellite communicator the RCMP team had brought up and relayed the text back to the FBI in Whitehorse, who would get the analysts working on it right away.

The photographer came over from the other edge of the perimeter and the technician directed him to the engraving and instructed him to get close-ups. As the camera clicked away, Matthews turned at the sound of footsteps and saw the team from the other scene arriving, including the medical examiner who had been flown up from Vancouver, with Sawchuk leading the way. The ME walked up to Perry's body and began talking to the photographer.

"You done up there?" Matthews asked Sawchuk, who gave a nod. "Find anything?"

"Not that I could see." She shook her head. "How about down here?"

"Looks like he carved a message into the bark of the tree behind him," he said, as the ME began his examination.

Sawchuk perked up. "Well, what's it say?"

"It looks like: *Four days to step five*."

"What does that mean?"

"I don't know, but I'm gonna find out," Matthews said, as one of the crime scene technicians approached with something in a clear evidence bag.

"I think I found something."

"What's that?" Matthews said, taking the bag. It took him a moment to recognize a string of black beads with a fabric tassel by the clasp.

"They were in the snow back there," the technician said, gesturing toward the horse trail. "They look like some kind of prayer beads."

Matthews frowned as he examined the beads up close, showed them to Sawchuk, then handed the bag to the photographer. "Make sure you get some good close-ups to send to the analysts."

They discussed the possible interpretation of the carving and the prayer beads for a few minutes, and then the ME called for Perry's body to be moved onto the litter for transport back to the base camp. He asked one of the technicians to roll Perry's body onto its side to examine the back before giving a nod to indicate that the full body survey was complete.

"Cause of death is pretty obvious," the ME said, walking over to Matthews and Sawchuk as he removed his gloves. "The laceration severed the carotid artery. It would have been quick."

Matthews shook his head. "If you're looking to cheer me up, don't bother."

The ME gave a grim nod. "Based on the blood spatter, it looks like the killer turned him to the side before making the cut, presumably to avoid what would have been a significant spray. He also used an extremely sharp blade."

"So, he knew what he was doing," Matthews said.

"That's for you to determine. There's also a laceration to the victim's right upper arm and part of his sleeve is missing, but I understand you found that?" He turned to Sawchuk.

"The perp hung it nearby," she said. "Likely to attract a bear or a wolf – anything that might disturb the scene."

"Are you thinking that was the only reason for slashing his arm?" Matthews asked.

"You mean, was he tortured?" Sawchuk said. "It's possible, but I still think the perp was hoping to attract something that would . . . get rid of as much evidence as possible."

They stood in silence for a moment, then the ME gestured to Perry's body. "I remember him. He took a lot of heat for being on the ticket with Campbell," he said, referring to the president Perry had served. "A lot of people wanted him to run for the leadership, but he never did. He seemed like a decent person, as far as politicians go." He paused and looked back at Matthews and Sawchuk. "Whatever his politics, this is not the ending he deserved."

CHAPTER 33

"You clean up nice."

Matthews looked up over his shoulder at the familiar voice and saw Sawchuk standing there, her heavy plaid coat and jeans replaced with a light blue sweater and khakis. Matthews had spent ten minutes in a store next to the hotel that the American team had taken over assembling a new outfit, his suit pants having not been quite up to the rigours of the Yukon wilderness. The result was a pair of dark jeans and a black V-neck, as well as a pair of hiking shoes he wouldn't normally have gone near, but were the best of the available options in size thirteen. He hadn't had time for a shave, but the five minutes under steaming hot water had been more than enough to re-energize him. He had gone straight back to the RCMP detachment, where a large conference room had been converted into an operations centre for the hastily assembled US–Canadian manhunt for the man allegedly named Piotr Bosko. Matthews noticed a light citrus scent as Sawchuk leaned over his shoulder and looked at the monitor.

"CCTV?"

He nodded. "No sign of him at the airport, which figures. We've been through all the manifests for the past few days and everyone checks out. Same with the bus lines."

"So, you're sticking around, then?" she said.

"What do you mean?"

"I mean," she said, lowering her voice despite the absence of anyone else in the room. "I thought you might be returning to your . . . other work."

"Turns out I'm staying right where I am," he said, though the same thought had crossed his mind before his most recent conversation with Ortiz, who was adamant that he remain involved. At first, he wasn't sure why, but he knew Ortiz hadn't gotten to where she was without being both politically astute and opportunistic. It didn't take him long to figure out that she saw another in a string of recent Secret Service bungles as a chance to convince the powers that be that the Agency was better placed to manage the personal protection function, not to mention the large budget allocated for the work. "Sorry to disappoint you," he added.

"I wasn't saying . . . Forget it," she said, then pointed at the screen. "That's the Main Street footage?"

"Yeah. Nothing there so far either, or from the cameras up by the Gold Rush Inn. Marcie's reviewing all the footage we can get." Matthews gestured to the next room, where Marcie Kilpatrick had been stationed after giving a description of the man who had shown up at Oyler's lodge the day before the outfitter had disappeared. The clerk at the rental agency had already been through the same exercise. There had been no usable prints from the rented truck and the fake ID had led nowhere, at least so far.

"I saw the composite," Sawchuk said, referring to the sketch that had been developed based on the descriptions provided. "How are you holding up?" she asked, taking a seat next to him.

"Not bad. That shower did me a world of good. You got any good coffee around here?"

She nodded. "I was just gonna get some myself. I'll hook you up." She paused, noticing him leaning in closer to the monitor. "What is it?"

"How do I back this up a few seconds?" he asked the IT technician who had just walked into the room. He rewound the footage with a few clicks of the mouse and when Matthews resumed control of the video, he advanced the footage of the east end of Main Street for a few seconds before hitting pause.

"There." He pointed to the screen.

"Who's that?" Sawchuk leaned in closer.

"Can I enlarge this?"

The technician played with the mouse for a few seconds and the onscreen image transformed until it was slightly larger. "That's about as good as it'll get. Any bigger and it gets really grainy."

"That's fine," Matthews said, getting up. "Where's Special Agent Croft?" he asked Sawchuk.

"I think he's meeting with the crime scene techs," she said, following him to the door. "Why?"

"I've got to go to Vancouver," Matthews said, lowering his voice.

"What are you talking about? Why?"

He took her by the arm and led into the empty office next door. "I told you I was in Vancouver when I got word that Perry was missing," he began, as she looked at him with a confused expression. "I was looking into a consular case – the death of a US citizen – and the guy on the monitor in there," he gestured to the conference room they had just left, "was on the lobby camera footage at the victim's hotel. I'm sure of it."

"But . . . you can't even see the guy's face," Sawchuk said. "I guess it's a distinctive hat, but it's just a hat."

"It's not just the hat. This guy's got the same style of jacket, hair colour, and build," Matthews continued, ignoring Sawchuk's incredulity. "I also spoke to an eyewitness who said he heard the suspect in the Vancouver homicide say something in a strange language."

"You mean Polish?"

"Eastern European probably, maybe Polish. Either way, this is no coincidence and there's not much I can do from here, anyway. The analysts are still working on the carved message and as far as I can tell, there's not much in the way of forensics from any of the crime scenes up on the Plateau to go on."

Sawchuk frowned. "Is there something else you're not telling me - related to the counter-intelligence work you were doing in Vancouver, maybe? Because otherwise, I've gotta say, it sounds pretty thin."

Matthews hesitated, then closed the door to the office. "I was looking into anti-Sikh extremists in Vancouver when I stumbled on the consular case I mentioned, and the victim just happened to be Sikh."

Sawchuk seemed to process the information. "But what does that have to do with Richard Perry?"

"Part of Perry's brief as VP was to foster relations with emerging economies, including India."

"I still don't see how—"

"Some of the recent anti-Sikh activity may be state-sponsored, and Perry maintained a close connection to the Indian Foreign Minister long after they were both out of office. Perry has been to India several times in the past five years. There's something there, I just know it."

"Well," Sawchuk said, after a pause, "I suppose it could be something."

"It's a lot better than anything else we've got right now," Matthews persisted. "And I have no intention of sitting on my ass and hoping our guy turns up at a roadblock. I need to do *something*."

Sawchuk's eyes flashed. "You think I don't? You seem to forget I'm a lot more personally invested in this than you are, so don't even thin—"

She stopped as the office door swung open and Sawchuk's boss stood in the open doorway.

"Oh, there you are. Any news?"

Matthews explained the image they had found and his intention to go to Vancouver to investigate, omitting the counter-intelligence angle. If Sergeant Armstrong thought it was dubious, he hid it well as he glanced at his watch. "We've got a Lear headed to Vancouver in about thirty minutes. You can hitch a ride if you want."

"I'd like to go along," Sawchuk said, surprising them both.

Armstrong shook his head. "I need you here, Lee. Especially if we need to go back up to the Plateau."

Matthews looked on uncomfortably. Ditching Sawchuk now didn't seem right, but he wasn't sure what he could do to help.

"You're forgetting that I'm the only one who's actually seen him," Sawchuk said. "Other than Marcie and the rental clerk."

Armstrong frowned. "What are you talking about?"

"I saw the perp . . . through my scope."

"If you were close enough to see him through the scope," Armstrong said, his eyes narrowing. "Why didn't you take a shot at him?"

"I tried to but my rifle jammed. By the time I cleared it, he had reached the plane and taken off."

Armstrong turned to Matthews.

"I wasn't with her at the time," he said, with a shrug. "We had split up to cover off both possible escape routes. I could sure use her help though, especially if she can make a positive ID," he added, avoiding eye contact with Sawchuk. "I'm also concerned about the timeline."

Armstrong was frowning again. "You mean the reference to four days." He seemed to consider it for a moment, then he turned to Sawchuk and shrugged. "All right, but I don't want any of your cowboy shit, Lee, I mean it. I want regular updates and you'll have to be ready to get back here on short notice."

She nodded and looked to Matthews. "Come on. We'd better get to the airport."

They hurried outside and jumped into an RCMP vehicle. As she started the engine, she gave him a sideways glance. "What, you think you're the only one who can bullshit?"

He smiled and shook his head but said nothing. As the truck climbed up the highway and out of the city toward the airport, Sawchuk spoke again.

"I guess I should thank you," she said, keeping her eyes on the road.

"I haven't forgotten that grizzly. Plus, now you're gonna have to tell me what cowboy shit Armstrong was talking about."

CHAPTER 34

Bosko sat on the bed in a motel room in Prince George, watching the local television station's coverage of the manhunt established to find whoever had killed a former US vice president in the Canadian North. Fighting back the urge to put his fist through the screen, he hurled the remote at the wall instead, unsure whether he was angrier at his employer or himself. He had been tasked with liquidating a wealthy pharmaceutical executive and, given the short notice and the money on offer, he hadn't bothered to ask for more than the name and photo he had been given, which was of a silver-haired man in his sixties or seventies. He had much more background on Dhillon – a trouble-making scientist who had to be silenced – and he also knew the two men had attended the same conference in Vancouver. So Bosko had taken the opportunity to try and extract whatever additional information he could that might provide some assurance to his employer before executing his assignment up on the plateau. It had seemed a clever means of garnering a bonus at the time, but now it just highlighted his miscalculation. He had murdered a former American vice president!

The search for Perry's killer would be relentless and Bosko knew the Americans would never stop.

He had made it out of the Yukon in time to avoid roadblocks and had switched cars in northern British Columbia, so he was confident that he was safe enough for now in the fleabag on the outskirts of town. His original plan had been to fly back from the hunting lodge and drive the rented pickup south, ditching it somewhere in northern Alberta before anyone knew Perry was missing, let alone dead. From there, he had planned to backtrack to Vancouver to collect the balance of his fee. But someone had come for him – he didn't know who, or how they had known – and the unexpected company up on the plateau had thrown his plans to make his victim disappear without a trace impossible. It was all the more unfortunate given this particular victim's high profile and the extra attention his death would attract. If he could make it to Vancouver, Bosko knew, his chances were still good – the port offered plenty of options if he decided to make a run for it, or he could lay low for a while after he collected his money.

He ran his hand through his newly dark hair – he had picked up some black hair dye and a pair of glasses that, combined with a change of clothes, did a good job of altering his overall appearance. Walking over to the window, he pulled back the curtain and glanced out over the parking lot outside, sparsely populated with dented pickups and a couple of old-model sedans. Satisfied that there was nothing or no one out of place outside, he picked up a cellphone and sat in the rickety chair. The phone was one of several pre-paids he had picked up a week before in Vancouver and he dialled the number from memory, waiting for several long rings before someone answered.

"It's me," Bosko said. There was no acknowledgement at the other end, just the sound of breathing. "You didn't tell me who he was."

More silence, before the gravelly voice finally vibrated through the phone. "Yuri didn't tell you?" Bosko couldn't resist a grim smile before the other man continued, his tone indicating the matter was not up for discussion. "It changes nothing. You completed the work."

"I had to rent a vehicle locally. My picture—"

"I didn't think I was dealing with an amateur."

Bosko bristled at the slight. "The price just went up."

"You're in no position to make demands. Have you seen the news lately? He was supposed to disappear, no loose ends."

"His identity was important to know," Bosko countered. This time, the silence extended for a good ten seconds before the gravelly voice returned on the line.

"Did you learn anything else?"

"He had nothing on him. I asked if he had told anyone else about Dhillon, but there was no time to be sure."

"Unfortunate. Where are you?"

Bosko held back the urge to laugh at the question. "Safe, for now."

"I'll consider an increase in your fee," the other man said, after another pause. "In the meantime, can you make it to Vancouver?"

"Yes."

"Very well. We'll set up transport from there. Someone will check back in a couple of hours with an update for you."

Bosko ended the call and tossed the phone on the bed, then returned to the window and peeked out from behind the curtain. He was pretty sure the people at the other end of the line lacked the capability to trace a call from a prepaid burner, but he made it a practice never to underestimate. He had been very useful to them over the years, and he had completed the mission, albeit with more attention than he would have liked, and even his increased fee was pocket money for these people.

Still . . .

He checked the full clip in his semi-automatic and sat on the bed so he was facing the door. If they were stupid enough to try anything, he would be ready.

CHAPTER 35

Matthews and Sawchuk sat in the back of a cab as it worked its way toward downtown Vancouver. They had spent the past ten minutes climbing a hill that took them past hedge after hedge, punctuated by doorways and gates that grew in size – and, undoubtedly, value – the closer they got to Metro Vancouver. At the peak of the hill, the sun came out and the city below came into view, with the waters of Vancouver Harbour in the foreground and the mountains in the distance. Sawchuk put down the window.

"I'm roasting back here," she said, the eighteen degrees Celsius being quite a contrast from the blowing snow and subzero temperatures they had experienced just twenty-four hours earlier. Matthews was inclined to agree and the cab's stuffy interior made him miss the clean, Northern air. He plucked his phone from his pocket and scrolled through some messages before finding the number he was looking for and dialling it.

"Is this Sergeant Lam? It's Ben Matthews . . . yeah. Listen, I was wondering if I could ask you a few follow-up questions about the matter we were dealing with the other day." Matthews could tell

Sawchuk was listening casually as he continued his call. "Yes, I'll be there in about fifteen."

"I suppose you're a member of the Vancouver PD, too," she said, after he had ended the call and tucked the phone back in his jacket pocket.

He ignored the jab. "That was the investigator I was working with on the Dhillon case." He had brought her up to speed on Gian Dhillon's death on the flight down, including the Vancouver Police Department's assessment that it was a random mugging gone wrong, but also the contrary eyewitness account of Travis Wolfe.

Ten minutes later, the cab deposited them in front of Vancouver PD's headquarters on Cambie Street and, after a short wait, the door opened and they were led into the conference room where Detective Lam was poring over the contents of the Vancouver PD's file on Gian Dhillon, laid out on the table in front of him.

"Detective Lam," Matthews said, with a smile as he walked into the room, but Lam seemed much more interested in Sawchuk, who stepped past Matthews and introduced herself.

"Does somebody want to tell me what the fuck is going on?" Lam said, sitting back in his chair as Matthews and Sawchuk took a seat. "I mean, one minute, you're here digging around the Dhillon homicide. Now, it's the murders up North."

"We think they're connected," Matthews said, explaining the CCTV images from Whitehorse and Dhillon's Vancouver hotel.

"So, you think there's a connection based on some guy wearing the same hat?"

"It's more than that," Matthews said, a little sharply. "I had the photo from Bosko's driver's licence sent to some analysts, who came up with a couple of hits for the date range in Vancouver."

"Where?" Lam asked.

"You know where the Pan Pacific Hotel is?"

Matthews, Sawchuk, and Lam were seated at a table in a conference room at the Pan Pacific Hotel, where the head of security had connected a large monitor to a laptop. Compared to the limited number of views at Gian Dhillon's hotel, the coverage at the Pan Pacific was extensive. They had been working their way through the lobby CCTV from the thirteenth of September and were twenty minutes into it when Matthews pointed to the screen.

"There. Can you blow that up?"

"I can try."

The security head played around with the image dimensions and quality for a few seconds, until they were looking at a close-up of the familiar flat cap, but also a partial profile of its wearer – an imposing figure with close-cropped blond hair. He was clean shaven but only part of one cheek and ear and the man's nose were visible in profile. It appeared that he was wearing a dark jacket with a collar. It wasn't much to go on, but it was the most they had so far.

"We're going to need all the views for that date," Matthews said.

The security head let out a loud breath. "That's gonna be a lot of video."

"And I need to speak to the front desk staff, too. Right away."

The security chief consulted a schedule, then gestured to the hall. "Two of the girls out there now were working that day. You can start with them. The others are off today but I can get you their contact info."

Lam looked to the monitor. "I'll start reviewing these if you two want to go talk to them." Matthews nodded at Sawchuk and headed for the door, pausing in the hall and looking back in. "Can I get a colour print of that?" he asked, pointing to the monitor.

Armed with the printout of the image of the man in the flat cap, Matthews and Sawchuk made their way out to the reception area. The first clerk didn't remember anyone fitting the description in the image and, after a few questions, Matthews could tell she wasn't going to be much help. The second woman frowned as she looked at the picture.

"I do think I remember this guy," she said. "He was sitting over there." She pointed to an arrangement of chairs and sofas on the far side if the lobby. It occurred to Matthews that it was the perfect vantage point for surveying the entire lobby.

"Did you talk to him?" Sawchuk asked.

She shook her head. "It was too busy. There was a convention on that day, it was crazy. The only reason this guy sticks in my mind was he was there for quite a while."

"Do you remember if he was talking to anyone else, or just sitting alone?"

"Not really," she said. "Sorry, I know that's not much help to you."

"Anything you can tell us is helpful, believe me," Sawchuk said.

The clerk shrugged. "I think he was alone. I don't recall seeing him with anyone else."

"You mentioned you were busy with a conference?"

"A big pharmaceutical convention. Over a thousand people, a lot of them were guests here at the hotel as well, and there was a problem with some of the bookings." She sighed. "It was actually a bit of a nightmare."

They asked a few more questions and were wrapping up when Lam appeared from the rear of the lobby.

"Thanks for your time," Matthews said, turning to meet Lam halfway. "What's up?"

"I think I found another image of our guy. No hat, but a big guy with blond hair, brush cut, and the same jacket."

"Where's the image from?" Sawchuk asked, as they returned to the security office.

"Seventh-floor lobby." Lam sat behind the computer and set up the video. He hit Enter and the video began playing. In it, a tall, blond man wearing a dark jacket and pants got off the elevator after a well-dressed couple and seemed to linger in the hallway for a while, before making his way slowly down the hall.

"What's on the seventh floor?" Matthew asked the security chief, who was looking on.

"That's the Gold Floor," he said. "Better rooms, plus a business lounge. You need keycard access from the elevator."

Matthews nodded, pointing to the screen. "Unless you follow someone else up to the floor."

The security head said nothing as they all kept their eyes on the screen, which showed a man in a hotel uniform approaching the blond man. After a brief exchange, the latter returned to the elevator and Lam paused the video. "The inside of the elevator's a different feed," he said, looking to the security chief, who was tapping away at the keyboard of another computer.

"I'm working on it."

"Was that one of your staff who spoke with the blond guy?" Matthews asked.

"I'm pretty sure that was Carlos. He's in the hotel today. I'll get him in."

"We'll need the names of all of the guests staying in the hotel that day," Lam said. "Starting with the seventh floor."

"Even if this is the same guy." Sawchuk pointed to the image frozen on the monitor. "I still don't get the connection."

"Call it a hunch," Matthews said quietly. "Besides, we don't have much else to go on, do we?"

She shook her head. "The girl out front mentioned a convention. Maybe it had something to do with that?"

Matthews paused, then nodded slowly. Two minutes later, they were back out at the front desk talking to the same receptionist.

"You mentioned a big convention on the thirteenth of September," he asked. "Pharmaceutical companies or something?"

"Hang on a sec." She began shuffling through a file folder. "I think we still have the posters back here." She plucked a sheet of paper from the folder and handed it to Matthews. It was an eleven-by-seventeen-inch colour poster, in the centre of which was written in big bold letters:

> Wellstead Pharmaceuticals International
> Annual General Meeting, September 13–14.

The company logo was at the top of the poster and there were other corporate logos in smaller font across the bottom.

"This looks familiar," Sawchuk said, pointing to the Wellstead logo.

Matthews nodded his agreement, thinking he had definitely seen it before.

"WPI's a pretty big company," the clerk said.

Matthews was staring at her. "What'd you call it?"

"WPI," the woman replied, looking puzzled.

"WPI," Matthews repeated, remembering Cathy Dhillon first saying the name. "Short for Wellstead Pharmaceuticals International," he added, as if to himself, before racing back to the security office as Sawchuk and Lam exchanged puzzled looks.

"Can you pull up the video of the seventh floor again?" Matthews said, as the security head looked up from the document on his desk.

"What are we looking for?"

Matthews didn't answer, focused on pulling up an image on his phone, which he set on the desk.

"Him," he said, pointing to the little screen, as Sawchuk and Lam re-entered the room. "Focus on the hour before and after the guy in the hat shows up."

The security head clicked around with his mouse for a few seconds and images appeared on two large monitors in front of him. On the left was the view of the seventh-floor hallway leading away from the elevators. On the right, the monitor displayed six separate views from inside each of the elevators that accessed the seventh floor. The video had only been running for a few minutes when Sawchuk's hand shot out to point at the left screen.

"There!"

As the four of them leaned in for a closer look, the security head looked up at Matthews.

"Who is that, anyway?"

Matthews turned to Sawchuk. "That's Gian Dhillon."

CHAPTER 36

Bosko walked the aisles of the discount grocery store around the corner from his motel, plucking some essentials from the shelves and putting them into his cart: bread, cheese, chocolate, and water. He could have used a bottle of vodka but he couldn't find the section with liquor and he didn't want to ask. Turning a corner and noticing a security camera hanging from a wall over the dairy case, he tugged his hat down and made his way to the checkout. He pulled some bills out of his pocket and avoided eye contact with the cashier as she ran his items through.

"They say the snow's comin'," she said, as the total came up on the display and he passed over two twenties.

"Yes," he said, making a shivering motion with his arms and shoulders.

"They've already had plenty up North."

"Really?"

She took the money and waited for the machine to display the required change, then selected some coins from the cash register and handed them back.

"There you go," she said, giving him a thoughtful glance. "Say, you're not related to Bob Lemieux, are you?"

He shook his head and pocketed the change. "No, I'm sorry," he said, picking up the plastic bags of his things as another customer arrived behind him.

"Just that you look so much like him, is all. Have a nice evening."

"You also," he said, hurrying toward the exit and cursing his luck. As he walked back to the motel, he swore under his breath, angry at himself for his decision to leave the room at all. He had some energy bars that would have sustained him until tomorrow. It was an unacceptable lack of discipline and a sign that he was getting soft. As a child, he had gone days without food and there were plenty of times in the army when food would have been his last concern, even if he were literally starving. Still, he thought, as he reached his motel room and locked the door behind him, he would soon be long gone from this place, and if the chatty clerk did happen to come forward with a description of him, it wouldn't make any difference. He slid back the curtain and peered out into the parking lot again at the same assortment of vehicles. Returning to the bed, the shrill, electronic sound of his phone pierced the silence. He resisted the urge to snatch it up and waited for a few rings before answering with a calm voice.

"Yes?"

"Your fee has doubled."

Bosko noticed the absence of the gravelly voice and knew he was speaking to the same man who had tasked him in Vancouver. "Why the fuck you don't tell me?"

"I didn't know either," the other man said, making only a half-hearted effort to dress up the lie. "Can you make the meeting point tomorrow?"

"Yes," Bosko said, biting back his anger. He had negotiated his rendezvous as far north of Vancouver as possible, but the small town of 100 Mile House was still three or four hundred kilometres south of his current location in Prince George, and he knew the police would be looking for him. The highway seemed the only realistic option, but he knew there would be roadblocks.

"I don't have to tell you to be care—"

"Just make sure you have money and way out."

"It's already arranged."

Yuri used a different phone for his next call, and he wondered if it was too late as three rings stretched to four. Then the familiar gravelly voice came on the line and Yuri quickly brought him up to speed.

"How did he sound?"

"Angry," Yuri said.

"Enough to do something stupid?"

"You want me to make sure, boss?"

"No."

The man with the gravelly voice tossed the phone onto the bed, then stepped out onto the rooftop patio. At the railing, he looked out over Park Avenue, listening to the sound of distant sirens, then watched the passersby on the sidewalk below as he pondered his situation. The man making his way back to Vancouver had been both useful and loyal over the years, and he possessed a skill set that would be difficult to replace. But he would never have dreamed of trying to renegotiate his fee five years ago. He was a dangerous man to begin with, but if he started thinking that he could offer his services to the highest bidder without any fear of consequences . . .

Still, the main objective had been achieved and, in three days, the investment made so long ago would bear fruit on a scale that was beyond imagining back then. There would be plenty of time after that for revisiting many old arrangements that had run their course.

CHAPTER 37

Matthews sat in the Vancouver PD's conference room at Cambie Street, with Sawchuk next to him and Lam on the opposite side of the table.

"And you're sure Gian Dhillon worked for WPI?" Lam said.

Matthews nodded. "That's what his widow said."

"So," Sawchuk said, "we have Mr. Flat Cap on CCTV in Whitehorse two days before Perry and Townsend were killed, and we think it's the same guy who's on video at both Gian Dhillon's hotel and at the Pan Pacific, where WPI was having its annual general meeting."

"And where Gian Dhillon also happens to be on the hotel's CCTV," Matthews said.

"If this *is* the same guy," he added, pointing to the paused image from the Pan Pacific's seventh-floor hallway camera on the screen, "It'd be a hell of a coincidence, don't you think? And I know you don't think Dhillon's death was some random mugging gone wrong, any more than I do."

Lam said nothing for a moment, which was as good as an answer to Matthews. "So, what's the connection?" he finally asked.

"I don't know, but it's up to us to figure it out, and quick. Those fucking prayer beads have got everyone thinking it's terrorism. Something related to Perry's tenure as VP."

Lam looked puzzled. "What prayer beads?"

Matthews got up and walked over to the conference room and shut the door. "There was a tasbih – a string of Muslim prayer beads – found near Perry's body. It's been kept under wraps so far, so please keep it to yourself."

Lam nodded. "Of course."

Sawchuk was frowning. "So, they're thinking it's terrorism based on some prayer beads? Pretty racist, no?"

"Not everyone at the FBI got the memo on diversity," Matthews said. "Though Richard Perry was second fiddle to a president whose foreign policy didn't make him many friends in certain parts of the Arab world, to be fair."

"Could the beads be a decoy?" Sawchuk asked.

"Maybe, and if they are, they're working pretty damn well, considering the current focus of the investigation." Matthews shook his head. "I *know* Perry's murder is related to Dhillon's somehow, but I can't even raise it without an ID, or even a better image of this guy," he said, pointing to the monitor. "Or something concrete connecting Perry and Dhillon."

"So then we find something." Sawchuk reached for the other laptop and opened the browser, typing "Wellstead Pharmaceuticals" into the search field. A list of results popped up and she selected one near the top, waiting as it loaded and the information appeared on the screen. "Whoa. This is a monster. It had sixty *billion* in revenue last year." She added Dhillon's name as a cross-reference and scanned the results. "It'd take a month to sift through all this."

"We don't have a month," Matthews said. "We have two days."

Sawchuk shrugged. "Then I guess we'd better get started."

It was eleven p.m. by the time Matthews and Sawchuk returned to their hotel.

"I don't know about you, but I could use a beer," he said, passing the lobby bar.

Sawchuk didn't need much convincing and they were soon seated at the empty end of the bar. There were a few patrons scattered around, but it was a pretty quiet night. One of the two big screen televisions behind the bar was showing highlights of a Canucks pre-season game, the other a cable news program that was covering a category three hurricane approaching the eastern seaboard.

"What'll you have?"

"One of those." Sawchuk pointed to a large blue-and-white tap.

Matthews looked at the unfamiliar logo. "Is it local?"

"Pretty much. It's not bad."

"Two Kokanees," Matthews said, as the bartender arrived. "It's on me," he added. "The least I can do."

Sawchuk smiled. She was putting on a brave face, but Matthews could tell she was exhausted. They both were. They had spent a few hours researching WPI but they were no further ahead in making a connection between Perry and Dhillon, or explaining why Dhillon would have been at WPI's annual general meeting. Matthews's attempts to make a meaningful connection between Richard Perry and Gian Dhillon based on anti-Sikh extremism had been just as fruitless. He had learned more details of Perry's travels to India in the past few years, and while he had spent some time in the Punjab region, he had also visited the Taj Mahal and Mumbai, making the trips seem more like vacations than anything else.

"Can we be sure it's *not* terrorism?" Sawchuk said.

He sighed, then turned to her, confirming that there was no one within earshot. "We can't be sure of anything at this point, but those prayer beads certainly don't fit with the kind of terrorism I was looking into in Vancouver. I'm starting to wonder if there really is a connection between Dhillon and Perry after all. As for anti-US terrorism," he continued, keeping an eye on the bartender as he poured their beers at the opposite end of the bar. "We devote so much in resources to intel on that front that I have to think we would have had some kind of warning about something like this, plus it doesn't fit the MO of any of the main players. The problem is," Matthews added, his expression darkening, "it's an easy fit for some, and we're running out of time to try and change their minds. We only have two days before whatever Perry was warning us about in his message is supposed to happen."

"Well," Sawchuk said, "money's always a good motive and there's certainly enough of it at WPI."

Matthews nodded. "What did you say the CEO made last year?"

"It's not entirely clear, but according to one blog I read, his compensation package might be a hundred million this year. Something to do with a big contract for their latest vaccine."

They were silent as the bartender returned with their beers.

"Cheers," he said, tapping his glass off hers and taking a sip.

"What about Perry's carved message," she said. "Your analysts turn anything up?"

"Just every conceivable combination of letters and numbers, none of which makes any sense to anyone."

"It is an odd message," she said, taking another sip. "Maybe we just need to consider it with fresh eyes. We could probably both use a few hours' sleep."

"It has been a hell of a couple of days, hasn't it? How's your ankle by the way?" he asked, looking down and noticing that she had ditched the walking boot.

"It's pretty good," she said. "Still a bit stiff, but nothing a Tensor bandage and some Tylenol can't handle. I guess I have you to thank for not letting me make it worse," she added, raising her glass.

He smiled and lifted his own glass with mock solemnity. "If we're doing thank-you toasts, I should mention your excellent aim, without which I wouldn't be sitting here tonight."

Sawchuk tapped her glass off his and took a sip, then let out a little laugh. "That grizz sure did look like he wanted to take a bite out of you."

"I thought I was a goner, honestly."

"We should probably toast Perry and Townsend too, no?" she said, after their smiles had faded.

He nodded. "Let's not forget Mateo Garcia and Dale Oyler."

They tapped glasses again and drank.

"Do you know if Garcia had a family?" she asked, after a silence that had grown awkward.

"Single, thankfully. What about Oyler?"

"No family. Dale was kinda notorious for never settling down. I'm sure he had plenty of lady friends who'll be sad he's gone, though."

Matthews sipped his beer and nodded, glancing up at the television screen and noticing the banner across the top: *Condolences Flooding In for Former Vice President*. He motioned to the screen and Sawchuk followed his eyes.

"They don't even mention Townsend."

"It's a US network," he said with a shrug.

They both watched as clips of various world leaders, both current and from Perry's time in office, expressed their condolences and offered support in bringing his killer to justice.

"Could you turn that up a bit?" Matthews asked the bartender, pointing to the screen. Glancing around toward the other end of the bar, where no one seemed to be paying much attention to either screen, he picked up the remote and punched the volume up a few notches, just as the President of the United States took the podium at the White House and made a brief statement, which was followed by snippets from various prime ministers, ambassadors, statesmen, and executives. Matthews almost choked on his beer when he saw the name under the image of a burly, grey-haired man in his sixties: *Walter Tate, CEO, Wellstead Pharmaceuticals International.*

"What the fuck?" Sawchuk was pointing at the screen.

They watched in silence as the image changed to a panel of political talking heads who began discussing Perry's vice presidency and his life in the world of business after he had left office. A blond anchor mentioned Perry's positions on the boards of several corporations and charities, as well as his being a much sought-after consultant. As a group on the other side of the bar broke into laughter, Matthews grabbed the remote and turned up the volume again. He and Sawchuk listened intently as the panel dissected Perry's politics and theorized about possible motives for his murder, terrorism being the only serious contender. As the news show moved on to coverage of the approaching hurricane, Matthews turned down the volume, set the remote back on the bar, and looked at Sawchuk.

"I think we just found our connection."

"There's something odd about this whole WPI angle, for sure," she said. "But is this enough to get your people on side?"

Matthews shook his head and downed the rest of his beer. "There's a briefing tomorrow at oh-six hundred. I need to flag this to Croft right away to be sure it makes it onto the agenda, but we'll need to flesh it out before the call." He stood and plucked some bills from his pocket and set them on the bar. "We've got about five hours. You focus on Walter Tate, and I'll look for any evidence of a link between Perry and WPI."

CHAPTER 38

Walter Tate was on the phone when his assistant opened the door of his cavernous office and edged herself inside, hugging the door as if ready to use it as a shield. Her employer's expression when he noticed her was of little comfort, but she gritted her teeth and stayed put.

"I'm going to have to get back to you," Tate said. "Yeah, whatever," he added, hanging up the phone. "What?"

"I know you don't like being disturbed, sir, but—"

"But what?"

"It's Mr. Kester, sir. He says it's urgent."

Tate grunted and then made a gesture of grudging acquiescence. Jake Kester was Tate's troubleshooter and whatever bullshit title he actually held, that's what he did - he solved problems, whether by legal means or otherwise. He also knew when to and when not to interrupt his boss, so Tate knew it must be important.

"Send him in."

The assistant breathed a sigh of relief and slid around the door, replaced a few seconds later by Kester's six-foot-three frame. He shut the door behind him and walked over toward Tate's desk.

"We may have a problem, sir."

"What problem?"

"Someone's been asking about Gian Dhillon."

"What? Who's asking?"

"Head office got a call yesterday, from someone on the task force—"

"Why the fuck am I only hearing about this now?"

"I just heard myself," Kester said. "It doesn't sound like they know anything, and all they got out of HR was that he worked for WPI as a scientist and that he retired last year."

Tate frowned and rubbed his upper lip with a thick finger. "This is bad," he said. "Really bad. If they start digging into Dhillon's death, it's only a matter of time before they . . ." He trailed off, deep in thought for a few seconds, then he punched a button on his phone.

"What time is Sanderson flying to Boston," he barked.

"I think he's en route to the airport now, sir."

"He can fly commercial," Tate said. "I need the jet. And get in touch with my wife, tell her I'm going to New York a day early for something urgent. I'll call her later."

"Yes, sir."

Tate punched the button again and looked across the desk at Kester. "You're coming with me," he said, standing and reaching for his suit jacket on a nearby rack. "We have to get out in front of this."

CHAPTER 39

Matthews sighed and looked at the clock. It was almost three a.m. and, so far, he had little to show for his research. He glanced over at Sawchuk, who was typing on her laptop.

"Any luck?"

She pushed her chair back and shook her head, then stretched her arms overhead. "I could use some fresh air," she said, walking over to the patio door that led out onto a little concrete balcony overlooking West Georgia Street. She slid the door open and stepped outside, Matthews following her out into the cool night air. It was distinctly warmer than the past few nights but still refreshing compared to the overheated hotel room.

"I don't know about you," he said, as they both leaned on the railing. "But what I've found so far isn't going to get me very far at tomorrow's briefing. I can't find anything on Gian Dhillon apart from his name popping up in some obscure scientific publications. Tate obviously knew Perry enough to offer condolences, but the only connection I could find is that Perry did some consulting work for WPI."

"That's hardly a revelation," Sawchuk said. "Perry was on the books as a consultant for a lot of different companies. It's kind of standard operating procedure for political bigwigs after they leave office."

Matthews nodded. "And from everything I've seen, WPI's squeaky clean. Their main business seems to be supplying vaccines to governments worldwide, and if you believe their own PR, they're the planet's saviour. Even the objective stuff seems to acknowledge their medicine has saved a lot of lives – not to mention making them a ton of money in the process."

Sawchuk nodded. "Pretty much the same with Walter Tate. One article suggested he's a bit rough around the edges for Big Pharma, but there's no real dirt."

"What do you mean, rough around the edges?" Matthews asked, as an ambulance roared by on the street below and switched on its siren, the electronic wail cutting through the stillness of the night.

"He's a former real estate developer. Most of these CEOs have science backgrounds, even if it ends up being all about the money."

"Anything shady?" Sawchuk asked.

"Not that I can find. He's supposed to be a self-made, rags-to-riches type of guy."

"Well, we know he's made a pile of cash, and it looks like they've practically cornered the vaccine market this year."

"Their 'super-vaccine'," Sawchuk said, nodding. She relayed the information she had found online, about a vaccine that was effective against a wide range of COVID-19 and flu strains and being marketed as a cheaper alternative to its competitors because of its broader application. "There's a lot about it on the WPI website. You think it could be related to Perry, somehow?"

Matthews shrugged. "He's not on the board of WPI, or best buds with Walter Tate, but yet Tate's on TV paying tribute to him. There has to be some kind of relationship, but I can't find any evidence of it." He took a deep breath of the fresh air and looked toward the harbour. Canada Place and the Pan Pacific Hotel were both lit up like Christmas trees, in stark contrast to the black void of Vancouver Harbour, the lights of North Vancouver twinkling in the distance on the other side. It had been a while since he had been on the West Coast – a conference in San Francisco a couple of years ago – but there was something about it that seemed foreign. It occurred to him that the conference was where he had first met Caroline. The memory of that encounter put the ghost of a smile on his face, until the blare of a car horn broke the spell and brought him back to reality.

"What happened to you?"

He turned to see not Caroline, but Lee Sawchuk, standing next to him. Her face was half cast in shadows, but the dim light only made the delicate structure of her cheekbones and lips more pronounced. After a moment, he realized he was staring and abruptly leaned back from the rail.

"What . . . what do you mean?"

"When we were up on the Plateau, you said you fucked up and your posting got changed. I was just wondering what happened." He hesitated long enough for her to let out a sigh and shake her head. "Forget I asked."

"No," he said, thinking it was a fair question from someone who had gone out on a limb – at least partly for him, though likely more so for Oyler. "I can't get too deep into details, but it was an assassination attempt on a couple of MIT students."

"My God, did they—"

"No one was killed. We intercepted some communications that led us to a handler, and then to the assassin himself, but not before he had seriously injured one of the students. Her name was Rania, and I can't seem to get her out of my head."

Sawchuk didn't say anything for a moment, then broke the silence. "But by definition, an assassination attempt in which no one is killed is a failure, isn't it?"

Matthews let out a laugh. "Too bad it wasn't you writing the post-mortem report on the operation. The people who did were a little more critical."

"Of what?"

He paused before answering. "The suggestion was that we were – that *I* was, actually – too slow in extracting the necessary intel from the handler. It was dressed up in the usual bureaucratic bullshit: *Failed to employ all necessary means commensurate with the urgency of the situation* – or words to that effect – but the meaning was clear enough. I was too soft on the handler, and I almost cost one of the students her life."

Sawchuk sniffed. "Funny how it's the people writing those reports who have the least knowledge of how things actually happen on the front lines. Shit, you wouldn't be doing anything worthwhile at all if you didn't have at least a couple of black marks in your file."

He smiled. "I take it you have a few of your own?"

"Hell, yes. Insubordination, failure to respect the chain of command. In other words: *Refused to listen to assholes*."

"What about the cowboy stuff Armstrong was talking about?"

She sighed. "More of the same shit. Blaming me for a partner who couldn't keep up. Don't get me wrong, I'll take a bullet for my partner but they've gotta carry their own water and I'm not letting a perp get away if they can't. Doesn't mean I'm not a damn good cop."

He nodded. "I've seen enough first-hand evidence of that, for sure."

They were silent for a moment, leaning on the railing, and looking out over the city. "My dad always says focus on the police work and let the paperwork take care of itself," she finally said, adding "and he's the best cop I know."

As a siren wailed from the street below, they followed the flashing lights until they disappeared, then Matthews began tapping the railing with his finger. "I just can't shake this feeling that they're all connected," he said. "Dhillon, Perry, Tate. They have to be."

"I can't either," she said, and despite the lack of any objective proof to support her statement, he found it and her smile strangely comforting. "And my hunches are usually pretty good."

He let out a little chuckle. "It's hard to believe we were building a lean-to and huddling by a fire so we wouldn't freeze to death just twenty-four hours ago."

"You held up pretty good, for a Cheechako."

"Armstrong used that word too. Said it meant southerner," he said with a puzzled look.

"It's the opposite of a Sourdough," she said, grinning.

"If that's supposed to be clearer to me, it didn't work."

It was her turn to laugh. "A Cheechako's a newcomer to the Yukon. A Sourdough's someone who's spent at least a full year. What part of the States are you from, anyway?"

"I was born in North Carolina."

"Figures," she said, with a smirk.

"What's that supposed to mean?"

"Nothing, just that I can see why the cold might not agree with you."

"You mean you think I'm a wimp."

She held up a hand. "Not saying I handle the heat any better."

He was thinking of a quip to respond with but noticed she had gone quiet. There was a pregnant pause as they both looked out over the twinkling lights of the city. "What is it?"

She shook her head. "I'm just thinking about this Bosko guy. He seemed awfully at home up there on the Kluane Plateau and he told the car rental clerk – and Marcie too, as I recall – that he was Polish." She stopped and continued to stare out into the night.

"What are you getting at?"

"What were US–Russian relations like when Richard Perry was in office?"

"You think our perp's Russian?"

"It would explain the accent and his familiarity operating in the North. And I know you're thinking those prayer beads are a decoy, but what if they're legit? Maybe this guy's from one of the former Soviet republics. Some of them have significant Muslim populations, don't they?"

Matthews shrugged. "The Cold War was just coming to an end in the early years of Perry's term, but there was plenty of tension. Still is."

"It doesn't explain why whoever it is would wait all this time before getting revenge, though," Sawchuk said. "If this whole thing really is somehow related to Perry's time in office."

They went back inside and when he saw it was almost three-thirty, Matthews let out a sigh. "I don't think I'm gonna find anything conclusive between now and six, and I'll need some sleep if I'm gonna have any chance of convincing Croft to turn his attention to WPI."

"Good idea. I'm bagged too."

"You want to swing by at quarter-to?"

"Good night," she said, on her way out. He walked toward the door and listened for her footsteps outside in the hall. For a moment, there was silence and he imagined her standing there, mulling over the same thought he was, then he heard the sound of her moving off to her room. He leaned back against the door for a long moment, then set the alarm on his phone and collapsed onto the bed.

CHAPTER 40

The Lincoln Navigator slid along to the end of the alley and stopped in front of a service entrance, where an imposing man clad in black leather stood guard. Kester got out of the back seat and, after a brief exchange, he waved to the vehicle and Walter Tate emerged. They both followed the other man through the entrance and waited halfway down a dimly lit hall as he rapped twice on a door. It opened a few seconds later with a creak to reveal more leather-clad muscle – this guy larger and meaner-looking than the first, giving Tate and Kester a once-over before stepping aside. Entering the room, Tate headed straight for the table in the corner, where a large man sat smoking a cigar. Kester stood against the wall, between the table and the door and surveyed the little room. It smelled of ingrained smoke and liquor and, from the dull noises coming from the other side of the wall, it sounded like they were in the back room of a restaurant or a club of some kind.

"Long time, Walter, since you come to see your old friend." The deep timbre of the heavyset man's gravelly voice reverberated in the small space.

"We've got problems, Sasha."

The other man grinned and drew on his cigar. "It must be bad, for you to come in person. But you always worry too much."

"I'm not fucking around. This is really serious. Someone's been asking questions about Dhillon."

Again, there was only a thin smile from across the table. No sign of concern, much less alarm. "Let them ask," Sasha said, blowing out a cloud of pungent smoke.

"I would, except it's the FBI who's asking."

In the silence that followed, the big man's cigar smoke hung over the table, then the smile returned.

"Walter, Walter." Sasha had returned his focus to his cigar, balancing it on the side of the ashtray in front of him. He shook his head and his long, grey-streaked black hair flopped from side to side. "You worry about nothing."

"It's not nothing," Tate said. "If we're not careful, these questions are going to lead somewhere we don't like." His subconscious was telling him to stop, but he couldn't help himself as he took in Sasha's patronizing smirk. "When I told you his travel plans, it was on the understanding that you wouldn't d—"

"Who the fuck you think you are!" Sasha roared, his enormous fist crashing on the tabletop and sending ash and sparks from the cigar onto the floor. "You come here and tell me what to do?"

"I'm just saying," Tate ventured carefully, after a pause. "It's the fucking *FBI*," he added, unsure of the reaction his latest words might provoke and thinking this was precisely why he despised these face-to-face meetings. He could feel sweat trickling down the middle of his back as he waited in silence.

"This Dhillon, he worked for you, no? And is *my* fault you don't control him?"

Tate didn't respond, preparing himself for another violent outburst, but there was no movement whatsoever from Sasha. His smirk had returned, and he looked as though he was enjoying some inside joke as he spread his hands in a gesture of peace.

"Walter, I always tell you, you have to keep your head." He wagged his thick forefinger in Tate's direction and though he was smiling, there was violence in the gesture. "How many times I tell you?" he said, glancing at the two men by the door. Tate followed his gaze and swallowed hard as the two bodyguards gave him a malevolent stare. Kester was a pretty tough customer, but he was no match for these two – if it came to that.

"You see?" Sasha continued, picking up his cigar again and waving it toward the larger of the two leather-clad men. "You are even making Yuri uncomfortable."

"I'm just saying, we need to be careful."

"We have a very big day ahead of us, no?"

Tate nodded. "Of course, that's why—"

"Shh," Sasha drew the front edge of his flattened hand across his own throat in a rapid motion that made Tate wish he would go back to wagging his finger. "You are not losing your nerve, are you? It would be a shame to do something stupid now. In two days, my friend, we will have so much money that none of this will matter. Now, that is a happy ending, yes?"

Tate gulped again and nodded. "Yes, but—"

"And don't forget, Walter," he said, lowering his voice to a deep rumble as he leaned across the table. "I *own* you."

Tate waited for the other man to straighten again, then he nodded. "I know, Sasha. I haven't forgotten. I'll do whatever you want."

Sasha was shaking his head now, but the smile was back on his face. "You disappoint me, Walter. Do you really think this is first time I have to deal with FBI?"

"I'm sorry. I just kind of freaked out."

"You did right thing, to come tell me – face to face, like the old times. And maybe I will call on you to help."

Tate felt the weight of Sasha's hand as it landed on his shoulder like a cinder block, but it was nothing compared to his discomfort at the prospect of being coerced into whatever help Sasha had in mind.

"Um . . . what can I do?" Tate said, immediately wishing he hadn't.

"Who knows? You have so many resources, Walter. You have a property near Vancouver, yes?"

"Well, yes I . . . suppose," he stammered, wondering how his chalet in Whistler had come to Sasha's attention, much less become part of his plan. "I'll do what I can, of course."

"Of course you will," Sasha said, as he stubbed his cigar out and gestured to the men at the door, then took one of Tate's hands in his. "But for now you must go about your business. Everything as usual, yes?"

"Yes."

"You have business reason to be in New York?"

Tate nodded. "A meeting with our insurer first thing tomorrow. I fly back in the afternoon."

"Good," Sasha said as he delivered a slap on the back that propelled Tate toward the door, where one of the bodyguards waited to take them back out through the dingy hallway, the larger of the two staying behind in response to a nod from his boss.

"I need you to make some inquiries, Yuri," Sasha said, after Tate and Kester had gone. "It seems maybe our friend in law enforcement forget their obligation to us. You need to remind them."

Bosko was sitting on the bed cleaning his gun, a twenty-four-hour news channel on in the background with coverage alternating between the fast-approaching hurricane and the Perry murder. When his cellphone rang, he peeked out from behind the curtains before taking the call.

"Yes?"

"I decided to adjust your fee . . . upward." Bosko said nothing, waiting for the catch he knew would follow but the next words took him by surprise. "It's an even million."

Now Bosko was speechless, but his greed only momentarily obscured the red flag that went up at the mention of such a spike in compensation. "What are the new terms?"

"Someone has been making inquiries about our scientist friend in Vancouver."

Bosko's mind was whirring. First, the silver-haired VIP up North turns out to be a former vice president, now someone was poking around Dhillon's death. He had taken Dhillon's wallet and phone to make it look like a mugging and he thought he had disposed of them carefully, but now he began to second-guess himself.

"You told me there were no loose ends, so I believe you. These inquiries are . . . unfocused so far, but we need them to stop before they get any further." There was a pause as neither man spoke, then the deep voice returned. "I just sent you photos of the two individuals involved. Officially, they're both part of the FBI task force, though he's CIA, posing as State Department, and she's RCMP, so you must be careful."

Bosko put the call on speaker and pulled up the pictures of a blond woman and a dark-haired man, both in their early thirties.

"An attractive couple, don't you think? Apparently, they're inseparable, which you may be able to use to your advantage. Maybe an accident – the kind that doesn't attract too much attention – but the important thing is to silence them, for good."

Bosko's confidence returned as he caught sight of the banner across the top of the television screen: *Perry murder likely an act of terrorism.*

"Where are they?"

"Vancouver."

There was a pause as Bosko digested the information. "This was not part of plan. I had my orders and I carried them out."

"And this isn't the Red Army – things change. Do we have a problem?"

"I will take care of this," he added quickly.

"Good."

Bosko listened as the line went dead. This was a significant detour from his original plans and the risk was higher. Then again, so was the payday. He stared at the two photos – an attractive pair indeed, but they would be less attractive when he was done with them.

CHAPTER 41

Matthews stepped out of the shower at five-thirty a.m. to the sound of his phone pinging with an incoming email. He was still focused on the message when he heard a knock at his door and opened it to find Sawchuk standing there with a tray of coffee and muffins.

"I guess I'm a little early." Her eyes darted up and down before settling on his.

"Come on in." He stood back from the door, suddenly conscious that all he was wearing was the towel cinched around his waist. "It looks like we're both early."

"What do you mean?"

"I just got a message that the call's been delayed by an hour."

They both stood in the narrow entrance to the room, his hair still wet. "You want me to come back in an hour?" she said.

Matthews shrugged. "You're here now, you might as well stick around." He stepped aside but she didn't move, other than to place the paper tray on the nearby table as she glanced at the beads of water on his chest, then down to the towel. "I'll just throw on some clothes," he said, gesturing to the closet.

"You know," Sawchuk said, stepping between him and the closet. "I never got to thank you for carrying me out to the highway."

"It's . . . you would have done the same for me."

Sawchuk didn't reply but smiled and pressed herself against him, lifting her mouth toward his. "You're not very good at reading between the lines," she whispered, adding before their lips locked, "for a spy."

They were both catching their breath when he pulled himself up onto an elbow.

"I'm really starting to like Canada," he said with a grin, as he traced his finger down her neck and over her silver choker and its delicate pendant – her only jewellery. "That's beautiful."

She took the pendant between her thumb and forefinger and turned it around to show him the engraved side. "My mom gave it to me, a few years ago." She seemed to be about to say more when her phone went off. "I'd better get that."

He took the opportunity to find his clothes and, a minute later, Sawchuk had wound up her call.

"That was Whitehorse RCMP. They found a body by the side of the Alaska Highway, near Teslin."

"Related?"

"An oil and gas worker from Fort Nelson," she said. "Guy called Clay Fenwick. I'm guessing they're gonna find Dale's Cessna tucked away not too far from wherever they found this poor bastard," she added, reaching for her jeans.

"Where's Teslin, anyway?"

"It's near the BC border."

"So he definitely headed south, after all," Matthews said, recalling that the last time he had seen Oyler's plane with the killer at the controls, it was headed north.

Sawchuk nodded. "Probably to Vancouver. Only place he wouldn't stick out like a sore thumb."

Matthews checked his phone and was surprised to see that this information hadn't been sent to him yet. "How long ago did they find out about the body?"

Sawchuk sipped her coffee and shrugged. "About a half an hour, according to the Whitehorse detachment. They would have briefed the FBI by now."

"I'm sure they did," he said, with a snort. "Too bad Croft decided not to let me know." Sawchuk glanced at her watch and looked at him, snapping him out of the growing anger that was obscuring all other thoughts. "I know," he said. "The briefing. Let's go see what else they haven't told me."

Arriving at the Vancouver PD's building on Cambie Street, Matthews and Sawchuk joined a dozen other cops and agents in the large conference room, dialling in to a task force briefing that was being chaired by someone in Washington named Max Worthington. After a quick round table, Worthington launched into a shortlist of groups with motives for the killings, based on the analysis coming out of the FBI's counterterrorism section. Matthews and Sawchuk listened as one official after another, both American and Canadian, listed the reasons why a particular extremist group should be at the top of their list. They also learned that there had been several raids in the past twelve hours that had swept up a large swath of people who were now being interrogated. The more Matthews listened, the more he sensed that terrorism was a foregone conclusion as the motive. He had to admit, listening to the various analysts and their dissection of what Perry – and the president he had served – had done in office, it sounded pretty convincing. His mind was whirring when he realized the saucer phone in the middle of the conference room table had gone silent and Sawchuk was staring at him.

"You there Matthews?" The sound of the voice of Special Agent Croft jolted him back to reality. "I thought there was something you wanted to raise, but if—"

"I was just wondering if we're looking at Perry's connection to WPI at all," Matthews said, prompting an ominous silence, both from the phone and in the conference room, but he carried on undeterred. "Wellstead Pharmaceuticals. Perry's done some consulting for them."

"How's this relevant?" Worthington asked in a clipped voice, his question confirming that Croft hadn't bothered to brief the task force chair with the summary that Matthews had provided the night before, of the possible connection between Gian Dhillon's death and that of Perry and Townsend.

"We're looking into a possible link between the murder last week of a former WPI employee and Perry's killer."

After a pause, Worthington's voice cut through the silence, his tone even sharper. "What link?"

"A man fitting the general description of Gian Dhillon's killer – Dhillon's the former WPI scientist who was killed in Vancouver last week – is on some of the CCTV footage from Whitehorse, though—"

"Though what?"

"It's not a conclusive match, but the guy's wearing the same hat in several of the images." Matthews paused and he could tell from the faces around the table that he had fallen considerably short of the convincing argument he had been hoping to mount.

"You're telling me you want me to waste valuable resources on this based on a fucking *hat*?" Croft chimed in, his tone even more dismissive than Worthington's.

"There's an eyewitness to the Dhillon murder, sir," Matthews pressed on, unwilling to give up. "He says the killer spoke a foreign language – Polish, or maybe Russian – and we know Perry's killer was using a Polish identity and spoke with an accent."

"You said *we* a minute ago," Worthington said. "Who else shares this theory of yours?"

"Sergeant Lee Sawchuk, sir," Sawchuk said, without hesitation. "RCMP, Yukon."

"All due respect," Croft said, his voice conveying anything but, "I'm not ready to change our focus based on some half-baked conspiracy theory, even if Sergeant . . . what did you say your name wa—"

"It's Sawchuk," Matthews jumped in. "And if it wasn't for her, we'd still be looking for Perry's body and we'd be doing it a few hundred miles in the wrong direction."

"All right, all right," Worthington said. "We're all on the same team. I agree we owe a debt of gratitude to Sergeant Sawchuk for tracking the perp up North and locating Perry's body, but I also don't see enough here to change our focus at this time."

"There is something else that might be worth looking into, though," Croft said. "A report out of the LA Field Office. Are you on the line, Ridley?"

There was a loud beep indicating someone new on the line. "This is Special Agent Ridley, Los Angeles. Sorry to jump in late but we've had a development here."

"Go ahead, Ridley," Worthington said.

"We've been interrogating members of a cell we rolled up yesterday and it looks like they were planning a fairly significant hack to some government sites – both state and federal, and LAX as well."

"What's the relevance to Perry?" Worthington sounded skeptical.

"Two things," Ridley said. "The first is the timing – they were set to launch the virus tomorrow, which lines up with the four-day window we're working with based on the message at the crime scene."

"It does." Worthington's tone had softened. "What's the second thing?"

"Two of the cell members work for a software company in Palo Alto called Emergence. They develop software for government applications, and we think that's how they were planning on introducing the virus – through one of their software applications. Richard Perry was on the board of Emergence. We're still looking into it, but it's possible he could have stumbled onto the plot."

"What sort of damage are we talking about?" Worthington asked. "If the hack had been successful?"

"LAX would be crippled, for one thing. They were targeting IRS and state vital statistics data as well," Ridley continued. "Depending on how deep it went, we could be talking about a major information breach – identity theft, general chaos, not to mention a huge ransom demand to restore the lost data . . . you get the picture."

Matthews was barely listening as Ridley added more details about the plot they had unearthed. He had no doubt that it was legitimate, but it wasn't what Perry had warned about in his message – he just knew it. Worse, it was sure to draw everyone's focus and he could forget about raising the WPI connection again. If they weren't listening before, they certainly wouldn't be now.

After the meeting concluded, Matthews walked out into the hall, avoiding the eyes of the others as he headed for the front door. Sawchuk followed and caught up with him in the stairwell.

"I guess we have to keep looking," she said.

He stopped halfway to the ground floor. "Did you not hear them in there? They're not going to consider *anything* other than the terrorist angle."

"So you're just going to give up?"

Matthews stood there, one hand on the railing as he considered her earnest expression. Whatever the others thought, he knew she thought he was right – she believed in him.

"Can you get in touch with someone in Whitehorse and find out more about this body they found at Teslin Lake?"

"Sure."

“I’m going back to the hotel,” he said. “It’s only a matter of time before they have me looking into West Coast terrorist cells if I stick around here.”

“I’ll make a couple of calls and meet you there.” She hesitated, as though she was going to say something more, then she turned and headed back up the stairs.

CHAPTER 42

Bosko sat on the motel room bed considering his options. He had to get moving, but the question was how to get to 100 Mile House undetected. Public transportation was out of the question, as was hitchhiking. He had spotted an older model Ford at the rear of a parking lot that looked like it hadn't moved in quite a while, and he hadn't seen any security cameras in the area, so hot-wiring it was an option. But even if no one reported it stolen, he would have a hard time getting it through a roadblock with a California driver's licence. Then again, staying put for too long was just as dangerous.

He checked his watch and got up, walking over to the window and pulling back the curtain to glance out over the motel parking lot. It was quiet, as usual. Looking toward the highway in the distance, flanked by a vast swath of forest, his mind turned to the drive up less than a week ago, the isolation reminding him of his home. There were good memories: of playing for endless hours in the Siberian wilderness with his friends, of hunting with his father in the hills near Kuznetsovo, or of enjoying a warm fire on a bitter night. But darker memories were never far behind.

He was brought back to the present by the sound of the anchor on the television news talking about the death of Richard Perry. He watched for a moment, tuning it out as it transitioned from the news of his death to what Perry had achieved in life; Bosko was disgusted by the accolades for someone for whom life had been so easy. He thought of his own success despite everything he had overcome: Running away from his alcoholic and abusive father all the way to Krasnoyarsk, where he had stowed away on a train that had eventually delivered him to Moscow. Those first few nights of his introduction to the big city had been the hardest, trying to keep away from both the police and the various gangs that claimed the area near Kiyevsky Railway Station as their home turf. But he had learned to fight and to kill, skills that had been useful when he enlisted in the army at fifteen.

Even in training, he had stood out from his peers, not only for his ruthlessness and endurance, but also his facility with a rifle. The next thing he knew, he was in Chechnya, where he was given free rein to deploy the most bloodthirsty tactics against his enemies. Men like Richard Perry could never fathom such an existence, let alone compete with someone who had been forged by them, and Bosko had no fear of the men tasked with finding him now. Let them try, he thought, and let them die.

He started at a noise outside and walked over to the window, carefully drawing back the curtain and looking out onto the parking lot again. A blue van was idling by the motel's end unit, a white plume of exhaust rising in the cold morning air. He scanned the rest of the lot and, seeing it was vacant, he grabbed his duffel off the end of the bed and headed to the door. Stepping outside, he saw a figure come around to the back of the van, open the door, and toss a bag into the back before slamming the door shut. As the figure turned side on, he saw a long braid of hair coming out of the back of the baseball hat and realized he was looking at a woman. Glancing around and confirming that they were alone in the parking lot, he pulled a tattered map out of his pocket and continued toward the blue van.

"Can you help me?" he called out, pointing to the map with a perplexed look on his face. If she felt ill at ease, the woman didn't show it. If anything, she seemed amused.

"You lost?"

"Not anymore," he said, closing the gap between them and pulling the gun from his inside pocket and pointing it at her as the colour drained from her face and her eyes grew wide.

CHAPTER 43

Matthews had only been back in his room for fifteen minutes when he heard pounding on the door. When he opened it, he found Sawchuk standing there, breathing hard.

"What's the matter?"

She pushed past him and closed the door. "I talked to the RCMP in Whitehorse five minutes ago. They found Dale's Cessna on the other side of Teslin Lake."

Matthews nodded, unsure why Sawchuk was so excited about the news. They had both assumed that the dead body on the side of the road was no coincidence, and confirmation that it had in fact been Bosko's handiwork was of little help in locating him.

"So, it was our guy who killed Clay Fenwick," he said. "Likely for his car, but how does that help us?"

"They also found Fenwick's car – in Dawson Creek, in the lot of an abandoned warehouse."

Matthews went to his laptop and pulled up a map of British Columbia, tracing the highway down from Teslin Lake. By the scale of the map, Dawson Creek was a good distance away.

"What is that, five hundred miles south of Teslin Lake?"

Sawchuk frowned. "More like eight hundred. It's about twelve hundred kilometres."

"Shit," Matthews said, as he focused on the little dot indicating Dawson Creek on the map.

"What?"

"It's no coincidence he ditched the car here," he said, pointing to the dot, at the crossroads of two main highways.

"You mean he could be headed to Vancouver or Edmonton."

Matthews nodded. "And we need to know which one – fast."

Sawchuk ran a finger over her top lip. "I took a look at the list of tips called in over the last twenty-four hours, in response to the composite sketch we put out. I'm pretty sure I saw Grande Prairie on there somewhere."

"Where's that?"

"Alberta. About a hundred clicks from Dawson Creek." She stabbed an index finger halfway down the right-hand side of the onscreen map. "There."

Matthews stared at the screen for a moment, then looked at her. "How many calls are on the list?"

"I only saw the first screen . . . could be hundreds by now, with all of the media attention this is getting." She paused and let out a sigh. "Most of the callers are wing nuts or attention seekers, but the task force must be looking into them all, anyway."

"For sure they are," Matthews said. "But a second set of eyes – two sets, actually – wouldn't hurt."

Sawchuk shrugged. "I guess we could divide it up – you take Alberta and I'll take BC. The only half-decent sized Alberta town between Dawson Creek and Edmonton is Grand Prairie. If our guy was looking to get gas or food, that's where he would probably stop. The other places are so small that strangers stand out. I'll look into Prince George in case he's headed to Vancouver," she added.

"It's a bit out of the way, but you never know."

"Who's in control of the list?"

"Duncan."

Matthews recalled the young Vancouver cop who had dismissed Travis Wolfe's evidence. "Can you get him to email it to us? I'm afraid if we go back to the station we'll get dragged into the same wild goose chase everyone else is on."

"I'm pretty sure he'll send it to me."

"What makes you so sure?" he asked, but seeing her in the doorway, her figure framed by the light from the hall, Matthews just smiled. "Forget I asked."

It was mid-morning when Matthews's cellphone went off, interrupting his review of the list of callers from anywhere along the route to Edmonton. He glanced at the number and sensed it was bad news.

"Oh shit."

"What?" Sawchuk put her hand over the mouthpiece of her phone, as she sat on hold with the Kelowna RCMP.

"It's my boss."

"At the embassy?"

He shook his head. "DC."

"You gonna take it?" she asked, as the phone continued to ring.

He took a deep breath and hit the button to accept the call. "Matthews."

"What the hell's going on up there? I just got off the phone with the head of the task force and he says you've gone rogue. I told you, you're supposed to support and assist – be part of the team, remember?"

"I don't play with losers," Matthews shot back.

"You wanna tell me what that means?"

"It means the FBI's got everyone going full tilt on the terrorist angle, rounding up cells and looking for bogeymen wherever they can find them." Matthews paused. He had a good rapport with Vanessa Ortiz, who was no fan of the FBI – something he hoped to exploit at least for a while, before her long fuse burned out. When that happened though – look out.

"And where should they be looking instead?" Ortiz finally said.

"If I knew for sure, this op would be over, but I think it's related to the murder I was looking into in Vancouver."

"The one you had no business looking into in the first place?" she said, pausing before adding: "They said you raised the possibility of a connection to Wellstead Pharmaceuticals on the call this morning."

"That's who the victim in Vancouver – Gian Dhillon – used to work for, and guess who was on TV offering condolences for Richard Perry's dea—"

"WPI's CEO. I know, but it's a bit thin, isn't it? Counterterrorism's pretty convinced that the task force is on the right track and this hack that they discovered does fit with the timeline of Perry's warning."

"Come on Vanessa, some prayer beads don't mean shit on their own, and as for the hack, I'm not convinced that's what had Perry so concerned."

Ortiz hesitated before speaking. "Well, the connection you're making to WPI isn't exactly convincing, either."

"Convincing to who, Croft? He's part of the problem," Matthews said, walking out onto the balcony as Sawchuk began talking to her RCMP counterpart. He tried another tack. "What's the harm in my doing a little digging into the possible WPI connection?"

"This isn't the fucking Ben Matthews show, you know. The Agency's role in this is tenuous enough already. The last thing I need is for you to go chasing after some red herring. It's been raining shit on me all morning from people way above my pay grade."

"Since when do we alter our approach because of political pressure?"

"When we have no evidence, usually. And don't be so fucking naïve."

"So, what – you're telling me to toe the line?" Matthews said, knowing full well the reaction the statement would provoke, just as he knew that despite her bluster, Ortiz thought he might be onto something. If she didn't, she would have shipped him back to Ottawa at the first sign of trouble.

"I didn't say that. I'm not sure I have any more confidence in Croft than you do, but you need to at least appear to be co-operating." There was silence on the line for a moment, during which Matthews was trying to think of something – anything – to bolster his case. Finally, Ortiz spoke again. "I talked to the Secret Service and got Perry's schedule for the days before his hunt, including his time in Vancouver. Looks like he spent an hour at the Pan Pacific Hotel on September thirteenth."

"WPI's annual general meeting," Matthews said, wondering why he hadn't thought to check himself. "Do you know what time?"

"I'll send you the details, but follow up discreetly and play nice with your task force friends, or at least pretend to. You hear me?"

"Loud and clear," Matthews said, taking Ortiz's willingness to indulge him as a sign he still had a little bit of wiggle room – or maybe it was just more rope to hang himself with. "And thanks," he said, before realizing the line had gone dead.

Sawchuk was staring at her laptop screen when he came back inside.

"Everything okay?" she asked, looking up. Before he could answer, her phone went off again and she took the call as he returned to the little desk where his own laptop sat. He scrolled down through the tip list, feeling like he was trying to keep a sinking cruise ship afloat by bailing water with a toy bucket. He heard Sawchuk's tone change and began to listen to her end of the conversation.

"You think it's legit?" she said.

They exchanged looks, then she waved him over and pulled up the map of British Columbia on her screen and pointed to Prince George. "I'm gonna put you on speaker, if that's okay. I've got a colleague here . . . from the US State Department," she added. A moment later, a tinny male voice came through her cellphone speaker.

"Sergeant Dan Forbes, Prince George RCMP."

"You were saying," Sawchuk prompted, "A local cashier says she served a man matching the composite at a supermarket last night in Prince George?"

"That's right."

"And you believe her – I mean she's not some wacko."

"I get my groceries from her every week," Forbes said. "She's not nuts, and she says the guy reminded her of someone – something about his jawline. She said the only difference from the composite was this guy had dark hair, and he was wearing glasses."

Matthews and Sawchuk exchanged another look.

"Where's this supermarket?" Sawchuk asked.

"East side of town. I go there 'cause it's quiet and it's halfway between the detachment and my house."

"Are there any hotels nearby?"

There was a slight pause, then Forbes's voice returned. "There's a few motels. Lower end. We've had a few calls to some of them."

"Can you have someone go round them with the composite, to see if anyone fitting the description stayed there last night? You might want to mention that he could have dark hair and glasses now as well."

"I can do that. I'll call you if I get anything."

"Thanks. And Sergeant Forbes?"

"Yeah."

"This guy – if it's who we're after – he's to be considered armed and *extremely* dangerous. You don't go alone, and you don't take any chances. We clear?"

"Got it. I'll be in touch."

Sawchuk ended the call as Matthews looked at the map. "How far's Prince George from here? Can we drive there?"

"It's about eight hundred clicks," she said, shaking her head. "It's a short flight, though."

Matthews checked his watch, then reached for his jacket. "Come on."

The little regional jet bumped its way through the cloud cover and the green of the ground below came into view, fifty kilometres from Prince George. Sawchuk had found a commercial flight from the back seat of the cab on the way out to the Vancouver airport that would get them to Prince George a little over ninety minutes after getting off the phone with Forbes. She had also managed to get them pre-cleared at the airport or they never would have made it through security in time for boarding. As the plane finished its descent and hit the runway, Sawchuk whipped her phone out and checked for messages, spotting one from Forbes asking her to call right away. She hit the dial button and waited through three rings as the plane taxied to the gate.

"Forbes."

"It's Lee Sawchuk."

"I may have something," Forbes said. "A clerk at one of the motels in the vicinity of that supermarket says someone looking a lot like the composite might have stayed there last night."

"Has he checked out?"

"I don't know. The clerk said he hasn't seen him today, but check-out's not for another hour."

"Where are you?"

"I'm here, with the manager."

"We just landed. How far is the motel from the airport?"

"You're in Prince George?"

"Yeah, we lucked into a quick flight."

"I'll have you picked up. The hotel's only ten minutes from the airport."

Sawchuk nodded. "Okay, but promise me you'll just sit on the room until we get there."

"I'll be waiting."

She ended the call and looked at Matthews. "He may have stayed at a motel near the supermarket where the eyewitness works. Forbes is waiting for us there."

Matthews frowned. "He'll have left by now, though."

"Probably, but maybe he left something behind. We could get lucky."

Fifteen minutes later, they pulled up in front of the hotel office and met Forbes inside.

"He says the guy was in unit ten." Forbes gestured to the manager, who was looking worried.

"And you haven't seen him today?" Sawchuk asked, prompting the manager to shake his head.

"Did you see what he was driving?" Matthews looked out over the parking lot.

"He didn't fill in a plate number when he checked in," the manager said. "I'm not sure if the girl at the desk forgot, or maybe this guy didn't have a vehicle."

Matthews looked at the little plan of the L-shaped motel on the wall over the manager's desk. "He was in this unit?" he said, pointing to number ten. It was the last one, at the tip of the '*L*'. "Is there anyone in these other rooms?" he asked, pointing to numbers nine and eight, which were corner units, connecting with the main strip.

The manager checked a book on the counter and shook his head. "Eight and nine are empty. There was someone in seven, but they checked out early. Four and two were rented last night and they haven't checked out yet."

"We should get them out of there, just in case," Sawchuk said, as Forbes stepped away to take a call.

"I assume the rooms have phones?" Matthews asked.

"Well, yeah." The manager looked offended, but if he was going to say anything, he was pre-empted by Forbes's return.

"One of my constables just ran the plates of an abandoned car on the other side of town," Forbes said. "It was stolen out of Dawson Creek yesterday."

"It's him. It's got to be." Matthews turned to the manager. "Call the people in those rooms – tell them they need to come to the office. We don't want them to panic, but we need to get them out of there. Tell them there's a gas leak at the far end of the motel and they need to come to the office right away, as a precaution."

As the manager made the phone calls, Matthews, Sawchuk, and the two Mounties went over the logistics. Five minutes later, with the two bewildered-looking guests sitting in the back of the manager's office with cups of stale coffee in hand, they headed outside. Sawchuk and Forbes took the front door, while Matthews and the constable circled around the back. From his vantage point at the back, Matthews heard the sound of them knocking on the door, then silence as they used the master key to gain entry. Sawchuk's voice came through the side window of the unit.

"Clear!"

Coming around the front, Matthews walked in to find Forbes and Sawchuk going through the room. The comforter was a little rumpled, but the bed didn't look slept in. In fact, nothing seemed out of place.

"Crime scene's on its way," Forbes said, sliding his phone back in his pocket as Sawchuk got down on her knees and lifted the bed skirt.

"Nothing," she said.

"The bastard was here." Matthews looked around the room. "I can feel it in my bones. How long are your crime scene guys gonna be?"

"The detachment office is only ten minutes away," Forbes said, with a shrug. "Hell, everything's about ten minutes away in this town, more or less."

Matthews nodded. "Good, because no matter how careful this guy was, chances are he left a print or something in this room, and we need to find it as soon as possible."

CHAPTER 44

Matthews was on a heated call in the meeting room of the Prince George detachment as Sawchuk entered with a tray of coffees. When the call ended a few seconds later, she passed him a cup.

"Bad news?"

"Just Croft, calling to tear me a new one for leaving Vancouver without telling him. I'm surprised he gives a shit, since he doesn't seem to think anything I have to say is worth his valuable time."

"I don't think he's your biggest fan, that's for sure."

Matthews shook his head. "He accused me of being a loose cannon."

"Maybe he's got a point," Sawchuk said with a grin.

"He also said he told my boss I'm a distraction to the task force."

Sawchuk smile faded. "Could he get you kicked off?"

Matthews snorted. "Not likely, though I'm sure he went to Ortiz behind my back and tried."

"Your boss?"

He nodded. "Which would only piss her off. She doesn't like anyone telling her what to do. Least of all the FBI."

"Anything on prints?" Sawchuk asked, referring to the partial they had lifted from the underside of the flush handle in the bathroom of the motel room. The crime scene technicians had found the top surface of the handle clean, but whether Bosko had forgotten to wipe the underside, or only wiped off part of a particularly well-defined print, what remained was usable. The two women employed by the motel for cleaning the rooms had been ruled out immediately – the print was from a much larger finger, likely male – and both Sawchuk and Matthews were hopeful that the print might identify the killer.

He shook his head. "Nothing in either of the CPIC or FBI databases."

"So what, we're chasing a ghost?"

"I didn't say that," he added, lowering his voice and glancing over toward Forbes, who was on a call on the other side of the room.

"You're running it through one of your spook databases?" she whispered.

"Something like that," he said, as his phone pinged with an incoming email. "That might be the results now." He clicked open the message and scanned the contents of the attachment as Sawchuk sat by, growing more and more curious by the second.

"Well?"

"Well . . . Holy shit. You were right."

"Right about what?"

"He's Russian. Viktor Davydov. Ex-Spetsnaz sniper, dishonourably discharged, and believed to be freelancing for organized crime."

"You got something?" They looked up to see Forbes standing over them as they both hunched over the little screen.

"I'm gonna email you something and ask you to print it out right away."

Forbes shrugged. "Sure."

Ten minutes later, the three of them had been through their own printouts on Viktor Davydov and they had all forwarded copies to their respective superiors. Matthews had started with Ortiz, followed by Croft in Vancouver, which had led to the hastily arranged conference call that was currently taking place. The phone in the middle of Forbes's desk beeped every time a new caller joined until they were up to about twenty.

"So, we have our lead suspect," the task force head, Max Worthington, began. "Good work up in Prince George, by the way," he added, avoiding any mention of Matthews or Sawchuk specifically, or the fact that he had dismissed their input just hours earlier. "And he's a real piece of work. Former Russian special forces, including several rotations in Grozny between 2002 and 2005 as part of a guerrilla kill squad. This guy knows his way around weapons and he doesn't have any problem using them, either. He went private after the Russian army kicked him out for murdering two men in his own unit. He's been associated with a half dozen murders over the past few years – and those are just the ones we know of." Worthington paused to let the rest of the participants on the call soak in the information. "Bottom line is this guy should be considered armed and *very* dangerous."

"Any idea of his current location?" someone asked.

"We assume he's continuing south," Croft jumped in. "We think he must have left Prince George in the early hours, which means he could be in Vancouver by now. We're checking transportation routes and the border's on alert."

"So where does this leave us on motive?" Matthews asked. There was a pause where you could almost hear Croft talking himself out of something snide.

"It's one of two things," he began, his tone authoritative. "Either he's been contracted by a terrorist outfit, which means we keep our current strategy in place. The other is that it's related to the anti-Russian policies of Perry's administration. US–Russian relations weren't exactly cozy at the time, and there's any number of reasons why someone on the Russian side might be carrying a grudge."

"Thirty years is a long time to hold a grudge, no?" Matthews said, imagining the spike in blood pressure on the other end of the line.

"Well, it's a lot more likely than the WPI angle," Croft said, in a tone that bordered on scathing. "If you're still flogging that dead horse."

Matthews refused the bait, thinking they were at least all looking for the right person, even if their theories about who had hired him diverged. As the call continued and they mapped out a plan to close the net around the fugitive Davydov, Matthews considered what other clues the Russian's identity might reveal. Although nothing obvious stood out to him, he was unable to quell the feeling in his gut that Davydov's involvement didn't have anything to do with decades-old politics.

"So, what now?" Sawchuk said after the call had come to an end, but before Matthews could respond, her phone went off. He watched her face darken before she stood and walked out of the office, and he could hear her raised voice down the hall. He and Forbes exchanged a look and when one of the constables appeared at the door, Matthews stepped out into the hall. He could see Sawchuk outside, pacing back and forth in front of the detachment entrance with her phone at her ear and by the colour of her cheeks, he guessed she wasn't exchanging niceties with whoever was on the other end of the line. A minute later, she pushed the front door open with enough force to make it rock on its hinges.

"What's wrong?" Matthews said.

"I'm out, that's what's wrong."

"What are you talking about?"

"That was Armstrong. He wants me back in Vancouver in time to catch tonight's flight to Whitehorse."

"Why?"

"Because he's too much of a goddamn, by-the-book ass . . .," she trailed off and let out a sigh, visibly drained from arguing. "I told him to dock me a week's vacation if it makes him feel better, but he's got his mind made up."

"I guess he figures they don't need you to identify Davydov anymore," Matthews said, prompting a little grin from her, and he wondered whether Armstrong had believed her to begin with – that she had really had a first-hand look at Davydov up on the plateau – or had given her the benefit of the doubt so as to maintain her role at the heart of the pursuit. Anyone who knew Sawchuk probably knew that if she had gotten close enough to see Davydov through her scope, she would have put a hole in him.

"I could still use your help. Is there anything I can do?"

She shook her head. "It's probably better if you don't. Armstrong's already pretty steamed at me, and if he thinks I tried to use you to do an end run, it'll just make it worse." She paused and let out another sigh. "At least now that we've ID'd Davydov, it simplifies things."

"How?"

She looked at him, her eyes narrowed. "You're still convinced about the WPI angle?"

He paused, then sighed. "I don't know. I just can't help thinking we're missing something big."

Sawchuk walked over to the other side of the lobby and stared at the map of British Columbia and the wider Canadian North pinned to the wall. She placed her finger on the top left corner.

"You know, Russia's only a few hundred miles from the Kluane Plateau. I'm surprised he didn't just make a beeline for the Bering Sea. He'd be home free by now."

Matthews stared at the map, realizing that after Alaska, the next border actually did belong to Russia. It was difficult to imagine, being in North America and yet so close to a country that always seemed so far removed.

"But he's not gonna come as far as Prince George and then double back," Sawchuk said, "So wherever he's headed, it's somewhere to the south."

They had a quick de-brief of the call with Forbes, who promised to let them know if anything else came from the crime scene technicians at the motel room, but they all agreed there was probably little else to do for now.

"Well, I guess we'd better both get back to Vancouver," Matthews said. "Do you know when the next flight is?" he asked Forbes.

"I can get you a lift if you want. We've got a plane we use for local flights that's available. It'll take a little longer than a regional jet, but it sure beats the drive."

Matthews was sitting in the main conference room at the Cambie Street building, scouring the contents of a report on terrorist cells in Western Canada and the US Pacific Northwest, when he sensed someone behind him, turned, and saw Sawchuk standing there.

"How's it going?" she said.

He shrugged. "I really don't know. Davydov could be anywhere by now, and our chances of finding him once he gets out of the country are not good. And if he makes it back to Russia, we might as well forget it." He paused and glanced at his watch. "Are you heading out?"

"Just came to say goodbye."

He stood and put on his jacket. "I'll walk you out."

"Any luck on connecting Dhillon and Perry?" she said, as they reached the top of the stairs.

He shook his head. "Total dead end. I can't believe their both being at the Pan Pacific at the same time was a coincidence, and I don't care what the facial recognition software says, Davydov was there too – I just know it. Proving it, and making sense of the link is another thing. I'm still making calls, chasing whatever I can, but I'm on my own . . . really on my own, now. To be honest," he said, after a pause, "I'm starting to wonder if I'm not barking up the wrong tree. As much as I hate to admit it, maybe Worthington and Croft are right."

"I still think you're on the right track," Sawchuk said. "I wish I could stick around and help you prove it, and I'd give anything to be the one to collar the piece of shit who killed Dale."

"You're sure there's no way you coul—"

"My CO's adamant," she said, with a shake of her head. "Now he's saying he wants me back up on the Plateau tomorrow – they've got some kind of reconstruction team heading up there in the morning. Sounds like a waste of time, if you ask me."

"Well, I can see why he wants you back," Matthews said. They were silent as they reached the ground floor and walked out onto the sidewalk.

"Listen, Lee—"

She put up a hand but softened the gesture with a smile. "Let's not make this complicated, okay?"

"Sure . . . but I do want to thank you, and not just for saving my ass up on the Plateau."

She gave him an awkward wave. "It's no biggie, really. Try and stay out of the firing line, okay? And if you do find out anything more about Dhillon, or WPI, you'll let me know, right?"

"Of course."

"There's my ride to the airport," she said, pointing to a cruiser that had pulled up at the curb. She turned to him and they stood there awkwardly for a moment, then she leaned in and gave him a hug.

"Take care, Ben."

Feeling the warmth of her body, he held her tightly for a moment, then they parted.

"You too," he said, as he watched her get in the waiting car and close the door. He stood on the sidewalk as the car drove off, unable to move until it had disappeared from sight.

CHAPTER 45

Viktor Davydov scanned the road ahead as the blue van trundled along, continuing its journey south. Its driver gripped the wheel in terrified silence, her eyes darting back and forth between the road and the gun resting on her passenger's thigh, the barrel pointing at her midsection.

"I promise I won't say anything. Just take the va—"

"Quiet," Davydov snapped, the terseness in his voice borne of irritation at her whimpering. They had already been on the road for a few hours, and he was looking forward to being rid of both her and the van. He doubted anyone would be searching for either yet, and he had tossed her cellphone by the side of the road on the north side of Prince George before directing her to turn around and head south. "Just drive and don't worry. Take me where I want to go, and you will be free." He looked ahead through the windshield as she sought some kind of confirmation from his dark eyes. They narrowed at a flickering of light just over the crest of a hill a few kilometres away.

"Roadblock," he muttered, sliding off the passenger seat and crouching down behind the driver's seat. The interior of the van was open, but the cargo area behind the seats was so jammed with an assortment of plumbing parts, tools, and general bric-a-brac that he could easily conceal himself, as he had done when they had stopped for gas in Williams Lake.

"Are you sure?" she said, peering out through the windshield. "I don't see anything."

Hearing the tremor in her voice and concerned about the woman's mental state, he set about mitigating the risk in the little time that he had. "Listen to me." He poked her arm with the barrel of the gun, causing her to jump, and the van to wobble as she struggled to regain control. "Calm yourself!"

"I'm trying . . . I'm—"

"Just listen to me. The police will stop you," he said, leaning forward between the two front seats, the barrel of the gun just touching her side as she stared ahead. "You will show them your licence. You will say you are going to Vancouver to meet your friend, yes?"

She hesitated, then nodded quickly as he prodded her again with the gun. "Yes, I understand."

"You will say that your friend is sick, and you are in hurry to meet her," he added calmly, as she nodded again. "What is the name of your friend?" he said, in the same even tone.

"Wh-wh . . . what?"

"If they ask you a name, what you will say?"

"I . . . I don't know . . . Amy," she finally said, gripping the wheel in determination.

"Amy. Very good. Amy who?"

"Amy Sm . . . Amy Warren."

He nodded. "Where does Amy live?"

"In W-w-west Vancouver."

"Excellent. And what sickness does Amy in West Vancouver have?"

"Cancer."

"Very good." He patted her on the arm as they reached the crest of the hill and the roadblock ahead finally came into view, a handful of cars and a large SUV parked behind the barriers. "Remember," he said, showing her the gun one last time before slipping back behind the seat. "You are innocent and they will know it. Your fear is for your friend, Amy – it is easy to get through this. But if you don't," he added, his tone hitting a more sinister note. "I will kill the police first, then you, yes?"

She nodded repeatedly as he wedged himself between a large tool chest and a crate, arranging a tarp to cover his head. "Think of your friend Amy, in West Vancouver," he whispered, as she began to apply the brakes and gripped the steering wheel tight.

CHAPTER 46

"Agent Matthews."

Turning in response to the familiar voice, Matthews saw Sergeant Dave Lam leaning out of the doorway of an office he had just passed. Something about the look on the cop's face made Matthews instantly curious.

"I've got something you might be interested in."

Matthews followed him back into the office and over to a computer monitor on a desk in the corner. Lam pointed to the screen, which was centred by an image of an empty sidewalk that looked vaguely familiar.

"What's that?"

"That's the storefront of the convenience store at Main and East Cordova," Lam said, moving the mouse and clicking it a few times so that the image changed.

"Right." Matthews nodded. "Near where Dhillon was found. Now I recognize it."

"We already had the store's CCTV. This is from a business across the street. The owner was out of the country, and we just got a hold of the footage this morning. Watch." Lam clicked the mouse once more and set the video in motion as they watched in silence.

"What am I supposed to be seeing here?" Matthews said after several seconds of staring at the deserted sidewalk in front of the store.

"It's coming." Lam moved an index finger closer to the screen as a single figure emerged from the store and lingered near the entrance.

"Who's that?" Matthews said.

"Hang on," Lam said, as a second figure appeared from the opposite side of the screen. He clicked the mouse and the image froze.

"That's Dhillon," Matthews said, leaning in for a closer look.

"Right. Now check this out." Lam fiddled with the mouse again until the video restarted and Dhillon disappeared inside the store. When the first figure turned in the direction of the camera, Lam paused the video again and they both stared at the image of a man of uncertain age, dressed in tattered clothes, and wearing a baseball hat perched atop long, straggly blond hair.

"Who's that?" Matthews was pointing at the screen.

"If it's who I think it is, he's a small-time dealer and thief, not to mention a CI," Lam said. "Name's Shawn Hobbs."

"Do you know where to find him? He may be the last person who saw Dhillon alive."

"Yeah, I can find him," Lam said, as he restarted the video and Dhillon re-emerged from the store, just as the first figure seemed to decide to go back in. The two men collided, if only for a second, and Dhillon stepped back, looking surprised. Both men seemed eager to get away from each other, disappearing quickly beyond the camera's range in different directions.

"That's it," Lam said, clicking the video to a halt. "I've been through the rest of it and there's no more of either man and not much traffic in and out of the store – certainly no one who matches the description for our perp. There's also no view of the parking lot next door, where Dhillon is headed."

"Can you play that again?" Matthews pointed to the monitor. "The part where they bump into each other."

"Sure." Lam shrugged and started to replay the scene.

"There." Matthews pointed at the screen, as Lam froze the video again.

"What?"

"Play it again, at half speed, and can you enlarge it?"

Lam spent a few more seconds playing around with the image, then restarted it just before the moment when Dhillon emerged from the store. It was running at a quarter speed, and the size of the image had doubled. The quality was a little grainier as the video played but there was no mistaking what was displayed on the screen.

"Well, shit," Lam said, straightening up, as Matthews did the same. "You said you know where to find this guy?"

"Come on," Lam said, leading the way out of the office.

Fifteen minutes later, they were driving along East Hastings Street, in a part of town that looked more down at the heels the farther east they went.

"The mission's up here," Lam said, pointing out the window to a four-storey building at the next intersection.

"How far's this from the convenience store?" Matthews asked, as Lam took a left onto Princess Avenue and pulled the unmarked into a little lot a couple of hundred feet from the intersection.

"About four blocks."

They waited in the car, watching the front of the mission in their mirrors. A dozen people were gathered outside – some sitting, some standing. Matthews scanned the faces and was about to ask Lam if he recognized anyone when a man wearing a tattered jean jacket and a baseball hat emerged from the entrance to the mission. The clothing, hat, and long blond hair matched what they had just seen on the video.

"That's him," Lam said, as they continued to watch the man's progress down the steps and onto Princess Avenue, heading north. He waited until Hobbs had passed them on the opposite sidewalk and almost reached East Cordova before pulling the car out and driving up behind him. Lam and Matthews got out and, at the sound of the doors slamming shut, Hobbs turned to face them, his eyes flashing with recognition.

"Just want to talk, Shawn." Lam held out his hand in a gesture of peace. The young man glanced up the street, as though calculating whether he could get away clean, but Lam had closed the gap and was cutting off his escape to the north while Matthews stayed behind him to make sure he didn't bolt the other way.

"What the fuck, man? I didn't do nothin'."

"I know," Lam said, maintaining a smile as he took Hobbs by the arm, exerting just enough pressure to convey that he meant business. "Like I said, we just want a word, over here," he added, pulling him along the sidewalk toward the car.

"Who's your friend?" Hobbs glanced at Matthews.

"I'm askin' the questions, Shawn," Lam said, the friendliness gone from his tone as they reached the car and he shoved Hobbs back against the hood.

"He must be the good cop," Hobbs muttered.

Lam shrugged. "He's an interested observer, but you should worry about yourself, Shawn, not him."

"What are you talkin' about?"

"You jacked someone's phone in front of the convenience store at Main and Cordova last week."

Hobbs's eyes narrowed for a moment, then his mouth curled into a surly grin. "Are you fuckin' serious? You got nothin' better to do than—"

"You're on camera, asshole," Lam continued. "Not to mention probation, but that's not what worries me."

Hobbs's eyes narrowed again as he looked from Lam to Matthews, then back again. "You got nothin' on me, man. This is bullsh—"

"The guy you stole it from turned up dead," Lam added. "Less than fifty feet from where you're standing in the video." He had Hobbs's full attention now.

"I don't know nothin' about no dead guy," he said, shaking his head.

"Save it for the judge." Lam reached under his jacket for a set of cuffs. "But I'm pretty sure whatever happens, you're gonna be a guest of His Majesty for a while. You better hope no one finds out about your activities on the side when you're in remand," he added, glancing back down the street toward the mission, just out of sight.

"What the fuck do you want from me?"

"I want that phone, Shawn, and I want it now."

"I didn't take—"

"Stop fucking around." Lam poked a thick index finger into Hobbs's chest. "Just get me the phone and maybe we can see about making the rest of it go away."

Hobbs seemed to consider the offer for a few seconds before speaking. "I don't have it," he finally said, with a shrug.

"Who'd you sell it to?"

"I don't kn—" He stopped as Lam took a step closer, then sighed. "I sold it to Casper."

"Where do I find Casper?"

"He's around."

"Well, Shawn. You're gonna find him for us," Lam said, opening the back door and gesturing for Hobbs to get in, helping him overcome his obvious reluctance with a little shove and adding, just before slamming the door shut: “And you’d better pray he has that phone.”

CHAPTER 47

"Evenin' ma'am," the young constable said, as Alice Wright brought the blue van to a halt in front of him and put the window down.

"Hi. What's . . . what's going on?"

"We're just doing a spot check. Can you shut off the engine and give me your licence and registration, please?"

"Um, sure," she said, turning the engine off and fumbling in her purse for the documents and handing them over as the cop glanced into the van's interior.

"What's in the back?"

"Plumbing supplies, tools – that kind of stuff. It's my husband's van."

"Where you headed?"

"Vancouver."

"Work or pleasure?" the cop said, looking over the papers, then back at her. A slight frown appeared on his face. "Is everything okay?"

"It's . . . I'm going to Vancouver to see a friend. She's really sick . . . cancer."

"I'm sorry to hear that," the cop replied, continuing to watch her as she fought the tremble she felt on her bottom lip. "You mind if I have a look in the back?"

She was frozen for a moment. If she got out of the van, the man sitting inches behind her would start shooting. He had said the cop would die first. She stared at the young constable's earnest expression as it turned to puzzlement.

"Mrs. Wright?"

"It's . . . open. Go ahead," she finally said, as the cop glanced inside again then turned and walked to the back of the van while Wright gripped the wheel until her knuckles were white. She could almost feel the cold steel of the gun barrel pressing through the seat cushion into the small of her back.

Please don't find him . . .

She jumped at the squeak of the hinges as the constable opened the back door, then she glanced in the rear-view as he scanned the interior. She continued to watch in the mirror, averting her eyes from the space between the tool chest and the seat, where the man sat with a gun at the ready, concealed by a crumpled tarp. Surely, the cop would see him.

"Sorry about the mess," she said, trying to sound casual.

The cop said nothing as he continued to scan the interior of the van. He stepped back and her heart leapt, thinking he was done. But then he knelt on the bumper in order to lean farther inside the back of the van, moving a cardboard box to the side. Wright tried not to stare as he pushed the box aside and seemed to look right at the tarp. She couldn't bear it anymore and looked down at the steering wheel, squeezed her eyes shut, and waited for the end.

Please don't . . .

She jumped at the loud bang, but instead of the screaming and bloodshed she expected to follow, there was utter silence but for the sound of the cop's footsteps as he walked along the driver's side of the van.

"I hope your friend gets better," he said, handing her licence and registration back and giving her a nod.

"Thank you," she said, putting the documents back in her purse. A few seconds later, they were past the roadblock, continuing south, when the accented voice returned from the cargo area.

"Very good. You did very good."

The adrenaline rush of the past few minutes now gone, Wright felt an overwhelming sense of fatigue as she drove on, knowing that all she had done was delay the inevitable. Her fatigue morphed to a simmering anger at the man sitting behind her as the minutes passed in utter silence, but for the consistent hum of the old van's engine. She thought of his promise to let her go once he had reached his destination and allowed herself to hope for a moment, then remembered the look in those cold eyes when he had said the words.

He's going to kill you . . .

She drove on, her mind churning to come up with some viable means of escaping, but it seemed hopeless. As they hit a rut in the road, the van shuddered, and she noticed a rattle in the driver's door. Glancing down at the narrow storage pocket at the bottom of the door, she spotted one of her husband's screwdrivers. She was used to seeing the same brand of tool lying around the house, this one a Phillips with a shaft a good six inches in length. If she could only get her hands on it without her captor noticing.

"Pull over."

She jumped at the sound of his voice at her ear. Davydov had moved between the seats and was pointing to a sign for a rest stop up ahead, on the outskirts of the town of 100 Mile House. She slowed the van and put her indicator on and, a few seconds later, they were off the highway.

"Keep going," he said, pointing to a dirt road at the back of the deserted rest area, beyond an open gate.

"Where are we go—"

"Don't worry," he said, in response to the wobble in her voice as she proceeded past the gate and a faded sign indicating a private road. "I'll let you go, but I must have head start."

She nodded and shot a sideways glance at the screwdriver still in the driver's door as the road began a gentle uphill climb. She adjusted herself in the seat and used the motion to snatch up the screwdriver in her left hand, tucking it up her sleeve as her hand returned to the wheel, just as Davydov moved to the passenger seat, apparently unaware of her acquisition. They kept going for a few minutes, then he pointed to a turnaround cut into the bushes on the right side of the road up ahead.

"Stop there."

She pulled over and turned the engine off.

"What now?"

He gestured for her to get out. "Please move away from door," he said, pocketing the key from the ignition as she stepped out. He opened the passenger door and did the same, and as he came around the front of the van, she backed up across the road. For a moment, it looked like he was going to get in and drive off, but then he lunged at her. She was unaware of the knife concealed in his palm and focused instead on stabbing wildly at him with the screwdriver. As they collided, the screwdriver sank into his forearm, while his knife tore into her right flank.

"*Cyka!*" Davydov swore, pulling out the screwdriver that was lodged in his forearm. When he looked up, the woman was already in the woods, leaving behind a trail of blood on the gravel road. He followed her into the woods, losing sight of her for an instant as his eyes adjusted to the dim lighting in the heavy tree cover but soon spotted her pushing through the branches off to his left. He ran after her and was within a few feet when he heard a shriek and then a distant thrashing sound followed by a barely audible thud. He stopped himself just in time to see the ground fall away steeply into a ravine, and he scanned its bottom for a few seconds before he spotted her, three-quarters of the way down. She wasn't moving and he guessed that she was dead, but he couldn't be sure. He knew he had made solid connection with the knife, but not whether he had hit anything vital. It had to be a sixty-foot drop and quite steep. Still . . .

Muttering a curse, he began to climb down to finish her off, then heard the sound of an engine. He froze, looking back toward the road but the sound seemed to be coming from the other direction, and now it sounded like two engines – off-road vehicles maybe, and getting closer. He shot a glance down toward the woman's body, still motionless near the bottom of the ravine, and within sight of a well-travelled trail. When the buzz of the engines grew louder and headlights became visible through the trees, he made up his mind.

Davydov felt the car come to a stop and then the engine noise disappeared. A few seconds later, the false floor of the sedan's trunk was removed from above him, and he drew a deep breath of the cool night air. Even the dim glow from a nearby light pole seemed bright after the enveloping darkness of the last several hours.

"Good luck," was all the man standing by the trunk said as Davydov climbed out. Then he got back in the car and drove off, leaving Davydov to take in his surroundings – a parking lot behind a Chinese grocery store on East Pender Street with a delivery van to his right and a dumpster to his left. He watched as the car pulled out of the parking lot and disappeared. He had never seen the driver before, but he would recognize one of Yuri's men anywhere – they all looked and acted the same. The main thing was that the man had been at the rendezvous at the appointed time and provided Davydov with safe passage to Vancouver. The rest was up to him. He spent a few seconds thinking of the woman in the ravine but then dismissed her as a concern. Even if she wasn't dead, his work would be done and he would be long gone by the time anyone connected some woman at the bottom of the remote ravine with him.

He stretched and felt the pull of the bandage he had applied to his forearm and laughed. It would take more than a woman with a screwdriver to take him down, and he had taken care of the flesh wound with the car's first aid kit before setting out for Vancouver. Pain had never bothered him and he barely noticed the throb in his forearm, let alone the dull ache in his upper arm from the still-healing gunshot wound. He had endured far worse, and his training had taught him to harness pain and use it to his advantage – as a kind of fuel.

Leaving the parking lot and heading west, Davydov looked up at the sky, encouraged by the fact that it would soon be dark, making it easier to blend in with the Downtown East Side crowd. Spotting a used clothing store across the street, he waited for the lights to change and then crossed over, entered, and quickly scanned the racks. He selected a worn, oversized hoodie and a peaked hat that would conceal most of his face, then made his way to the cash, where a tattooed young woman took the money he slid across the counter without comment. Back out in front of the store, he pulled the hoodie on and slid the cap on his head. Assessing his reflection in the store window, he started walking. He would spend the next couple of hours in this neighbourhood before making his way west toward the hotel where his two targets were staying. He dug his hands into his pockets and set off down East Hastings as a police car rolled by, the officer in the passenger seat casually looking in his direction before turning his attention elsewhere. Davydov smiled as he kept walking.

CHAPTER 48

Matthews sat at the end of the conference room table, scanning the latest entries from the tip line. Apparently, Viktor Davydov had been spotted in Vancouver, Seattle, and Los Angeles in the past few hours, not to mention similar sightings from as far afield as Toronto, New York, and Washington, DC. Clearly, there were a lot of people out there with too much time on their hands. He leaned back in his chair and sighed, debating whether to step out for another dose of caffeine – he was actually beginning to crave the ubiquitous Canadian concoction in the white and red cup instead of his usual cappuccino. His plans were derailed by Sergeant Dave Lam's appearance at the door.

"Our friend Casper's in interview room two," he said, prompting Matthews to follow him out into the hall.

"What's he saying?" he asked, as Lam led the way upstairs to the interview rooms.

"Not much. I was waiting for you to get into it with him. We're checking pawn shops on the East Side in the meantime but no luck yet."

"You got any leverage with this guy?" Matthews asked as they stopped in front of a closed door marked with the number two.

"He's got a possession charge pending and he's on probation for theft under."

Matthews nodded, thinking it was something, at least. Lam opened the door and they both walked in to find Dwayne Ryder, a.k.a "Casper," sitting on one of the hard plastic chairs, his right leg jerking up and down. One look at his complexion solved the mystery of his nickname.

"Casper. This is the guy I was telling you about – he has some questions for you."

"Oh yeah?" He looked up at Matthews before his eyes darted to the door and then down to his hands.

"I told you already," he said, with a quick nod toward Lam. "I bought the phone on the up and up, man. How was I s'posed to know it was hot?"

"Maybe the fact that you only paid twenty bucks for it?" Lam gave a snide laugh. "That might have been your first clue, dickhead."

"Let's not worry about that," Matthews said. "We're more interested in finding out what you did with it *after* you bought it from Hobbs."

"I don't know . . . I think I sold it to some kid. Yeah, I remember now – gave him a great deal. Like I said, I didn't know it was—"

"Cut the shit, Casper," Lam said, giving him a not-so-gentle cuff across the back of the head.

"What the fuck!" Ryder was grabbing his head as though he'd been hit with an anvil. "That's police brutality, man. I got rights," he added, looking up at the camera hanging from the corner of the room.

"That's not turned on, asshole," Lam said. "And you have no rights. That phone is part of an international manhunt, so the usual rules are out the window." He paused and moved closer to Ryder, who tensed in preparation for another cuff. "I could shoot you and toss your worthless ass into the harbour and nobody would give a shit."

Matthews stood next to Lam and loomed over the increasingly anxious-looking Ryder. "I'm afraid he's right, Casper. The good news is, all you have to do is tell me where I can find that phone."

"What's the big deal about some frickin' Nokia anyway?"

Matthews and Lam exchanged glances.

"It wasn't an iPhone?"

Ryder shook his head. "If it was an iPhone, I could have . . ." He trailed off under the gaze of the two cops.

"You could have unloaded it right away," Lam completed his sentence.

"I didn't say that."

"Don't push your luck," Lam said, before turning to Matthews. "I thought you said Dhillon had an iPhone?" he whispered, as they stepped away from the table.

"He did." Matthews's mind was racing to make sense of the incongruity. Then he remembered his meeting with Dhillon's widow and what she had said about her husband's cellphone calls not appearing on their regular bill, suggesting that Dhillon had two phones.

"There was no other phone found at the crime scene, or at Dhillon's hotel, right?"

Lam shook his head. "Nope."

Matthews returned to Ryder, put his hands on the table and leaned in close, so they were face to face. "I'm only going to ask you this once more. Where's that fucking Nokia?"

"I'm telling you, I don't . . . I mean, I sold it!" Ryder's leg was jumping under the table again and Matthews was considering plucking him out of his chair and putting him up against the wall – or maybe through it – when his own phone went off.

"I gotta take this," he said, walking out of the interview room. He stared at the name on the screen and took a deep breath.

"Matthews."

"It's Croft."

"What's up?"

"You still working a possible connection between Perry's death and WPI?"

"Murder, actually, and no, not really. Who wants to know?"

"Relax, I'm not trying to fuck you over."

Matthews bit back the retort on the tip of his tongue. "So, why are you calling?"

"Walter Tate," Croft said. "We made some inquiries about Perry's consulting work for WPI."

Matthews hesitated, surprised that Croft had followed up on the Perry–WPI angle, given the contempt he had previously displayed for the line of inquiry.

"And?"

"And Tate said he wants to clarify the relationship between WPI and Perry. Basically, he's saying there wasn't one and he can provide proof, but he only wants to talk face to face. He doesn't want WPI dragged into some PR nightmare. He's in Vancouver and I'm supposed to meet him tonight."

Matthews's surprise turned to shock – first at Tate's wanting to say anything, second at Croft's willingness to share the information with him. "When?"

"Ten o'clock, near his hotel. He made it clear it's not an interview, just an informal chat. I was planning on going myself, but I've been dragged into something else."

"Where's he staying?"

Croft hesitated a moment. "The Fairmont, but he wants to meet offsite – a monument by the seawall, called the Komagata Maru Memorial. It's a few minutes' walk from the hotel."

"Why all the cloak and dagger?"

Croft snorted. "Scared to meet with him without your favourite Mountie there to protect you?"

"Just curious, that's all," Matthews said, thinking he could understand why the lobby of a five-star hotel might not be the best place for a discreet meeting. It was less clear to him how Croft knew that Sawchuk was no longer involved.

"You listen to what he has to say and report back to me," Croft said. "No one else. Understood? The last thing we need is Walter Tate suing us over some unfounded theoretical link between his company and Perry's death."

"Did he threaten legal action?"

"Not in so many words, but you know how these corporate assholes operate. For all I know, he'll be lawyering up for the meeting."

"All right. I'll hear him out."

"And remember, Matthews, this is strictly off the books – you mention it to *no* one for now. We'll decide what, if anything, to do with his information once we have it."

"Got it," Matthews said, encouraged by Croft's reference to the assessment of Tate's information being a collective exercise.

"And this doesn't mean I think your theory has any merit, by the way," Croft added, as though reading his mind.

"Don't worry, it never crossed my mind."

"And watch what information you provide to him," Croft said. "Tate strikes me as a slippery fuck. Just meet with him and report back – I should be free by eleven-thirty."

Matthews hung up the phone and considered the call. Perhaps Croft wasn't as stubbornly opposed to looking into the Perry–WPI angle as he had thought. He was halfway back to the interview room when he heard raised voices, and when he turned the corner, Lam was chest to chest with a burly man in his fifties dressed in an ill-fitting suit.

"You have no grounds to hold him, and you damn well know it," the man was saying. "I want to talk to my client, *immediately*."

Lam seemed to hesitate, then gave a shrug, and pointed to the door of the interview room. "Be my guest."

"Who's that?" Matthews said, after the man had entered the interview room.

"Legal Aid's finest," Lam said, with an eye roll.

"Like a public defender?"

"Yeah," Lam said. "And this particular one's a real pain in the ass. I'm probably going to have to cut Casper loose."

Matthews nodded, thinking the odds of Ryder actually divulging anything in a formal interview were slim to none anyway. "Let him go."

Lam gave him a sideways look, but any questions he had were pre-empted when the interview door swung open again and the lawyer emerged with his client in tow.

"Unless you're planning to charge my client with something," he said, pausing in front of Lam. "We'll be leaving now."

Lam exchanged a quick glance with Matthews, who gave a subtle nod as Dwayne Ryder hurried past, close behind his lawyer. It took every bit of Matthews's self-control not to react to the little smirk on Ryder's face as he walked past.

After ending the call with Matthews, Croft stared out the window of his hotel room, fighting back the bile rising from his stomach. He stared at the phone for a full minute, willing some intervention that would reveal another option, but he knew there was none, and he eventually gave in to a fate that had been sealed years before. If he had his time back, he would have done things differently . . . or would he? Looking out over Vancouver Harbour, he watched as a float plane revved up at the far west end, skipped along on the light chop, and then slowly lifted off. Once it had disappeared to the north, he turned his attention back to the prepaid phone, dialled another number, and waited for the voice on the other end of the line.

"Ten o'clock," was all he said, before ending the call, sliding the back off the phone and removing the SIM card, which he promptly flushed down the toilet.

CHAPTER 49

Matthews was in the back of a cab headed north on Princess Avenue when he spotted Dwayne Ryder on the opposite sidewalk, smoking a cigarette.

"Here's good," he said to the driver.

"It's still a couple of blocks to the mission."

"Right here's good," he repeated, reaching into his pocket for some bills and handing them forward, his eyes still on Ryder on the other side of the street, facing away from the cab. Matthews waved off the driver's question about change and crossed the street, taking up his pursuit from about fifty feet back. He had only been following him for a few minutes when Ryder took a right turn onto a side street and then walked up the front steps of a squat apartment building that looked like it had seen better days. Matthews hurried to close the gap and bounded up the steps before the entrance door swung shut.

"What the hell?" Ryder said, in response to the sight of Matthews squeezing through the door behind him.

"Hey, Casper," he said, with his brightest smile. "I'm glad I caught you."

Ryder shook his head and turned toward the stairs. "Man, I got nothin' to say to you."

"Does this look like it's voluntary?" Matthews said, raising his Beretta so that Ryder was looking down the barrel, his eyes wide as saucers. "I'm not Vancouver PD," Matthews said, "so I don't have to follow their rules, and I'm done fucking around. Come on." He grabbed the slighter man by the shoulder and shoved him toward the stairs, the gun pressed into the small of his back.

"All right, all right!" Ryder protested, as Matthews gave him another shove, propelling him up the steps until they were on the second floor. Ryder hesitated at the door, earning himself a blow to the side of the head with the butt of the gun. He was still rubbing behind his ear when they entered his apartment, a squalid, cramped hovel that stank of stale cigarette smoke and feet. As soon as the door was shut, Matthews grabbed Ryder by the front of his shirt and pinned him up against the wall.

"I want that Nokia you bought from Hobbs, and I want it *now*."

"Man, I don't got it."

Matthews held Ryder's gaze until the other man looked down – a sure tell that he was lying. The question was, how far was Matthews prepared to go to get the truth out of him?

"I think you do."

"You think what you want, but I haven't got shit."

It wasn't the words, but the slight smirk of self-assurance that accompanied them that set Matthews off as he pictured Rania Ahmed's battered face and the terror in the young scientist's eyes when he had finally reached her.

Not this time . . .

Tightening his grip on Ryder's shirt, he raised the gun and pressed it against the man's cheek.

"I'm gonna count to three," Matthews said, moving the gun to Ryder's mouth and tightening his hand around the other man's throat, holding him in place as he pushed the barrel between his teeth.

"You c-c-can't do this, man."

Matthews applied more pressure to the gun. "One."

"Thisss fucked up," Ryder mumbled, around the gun barrel.

"Two," Matthews continued, pressing the gun still farther into Ryder's mouth before yanking him like a rag doll onto the battered sofa, taking one of the threadbare cushions and putting it over Ryder's face, filtering muffled shouts. Matthews was starting to apply pressure to the trigger before he realized what he was doing and this time, it was Sawchuk's face that appeared in his mind's eye just before he stepped back in disgust, his pulse pounding in his ears.

Get a hold of yourself . . .

Ryder had tossed the filthy cushion aside and was gasping for breath, wild-eyed. "What the fuck, man!"

"Where's the damn phone?" Matthews said, regaining his composure. "If I have to tear this place apart and you with it, I'm gonna find it." He started moving toward the kitchen and suddenly changed course and turned toward the bathroom, turning to catch Ryder's expression as he did. For a career criminal, his poker face was shit.

Matthews found the FBI IT tech seconded to the Vancouver PD from the task force sitting behind a laptop in the main conference room at Cambie Street. He walked over and dropped a large Ziplock containing an assortment of phones on the tabletop. There were droplets of water on the outside of the bag.

The tech gave the bag a disinterested look. "What's this?"

"I'm pretty sure one of these belonged to a murder victim with ties to the Perry investigation. I need the call data on these SIM cards ASAP."

"Why's the bag wet?"

"You don't want to know, believe me," Matthews said, thinking that at least the inside of Ryder's toilet tank was cleaner than the bowl.

"There must be a dozen phones in here."

"So you'd better get started. Good news is, I'm only interested in the Nokias."

The technician sighed, then picked up the baggie by a corner. "Looks like there's five or six. I'll do what I can."

"Thank you."

"What's going on?" Lam had appeared at the door.

"Burners," Matthews said. "I'm hoping Dhillon's Nokia is in there."

Lam frowned. "Where did you get them?"

"From someone with a strong sense of civic duty," Matthews said, looking at the large-scale map of downtown Vancouver on the conference room wall, searching the harbourfront and locating the Komagatu Maru Memorial, at the eastern end of Cole Harbour Park.

"I have a hunch I shouldn't ask," Lam said, after a pause.

Matthews smiled. "Where would we be without our hunches?"

"On that note." Lam held up a sheet of paper. "This might be nothing, but a van turned up abandoned in 100 Mile House."

"Where?"

"A small town about five hundred clicks north of here, on the road to Prince George. The van was registered to a plumbing company there. When they contacted the owner," Lam continued, "he said he hasn't been in contact with his wife since early this morning. She was driving the van."

Matthews frowned and reached out for the sheet of paper containing details of the abandoned vehicle and some notes on the owner. "Any sign of the woman?"

Lam shook his head.

"I'll pass it on to the task force. Maybe it's connected."

Lam nodded. "Be my guest, although I kinda hope it isn't, cause if this was our guy, chances are the woman's dead.

CHAPTER 50

Sawchuk sat in the airport lounge, sipping a coffee as she waited for her delayed flight, half watching the news channel on the overhead screen. The hurricane scare was over – having been downgraded to a tropical storm by the time it hit the Atlantic coast. It had done a lot of damage in Haiti but that seemed to be of much less interest in the twenty seconds devoted to the storm, before coverage moved on to the manhunt for the killer of Richard Perry and John Townsend. More and more information about Viktor Davydov had seeped out and Sawchuk watched with interest for a while, until her frustration at no longer being directly involved in the chase won out and her attention drifted to the other passengers seated nearby. It was a rare flight to Whitehorse where she didn't know a few of her fellow travellers but, so far, she hadn't recognized anyone. She stretched her arms overhead and thought about having a good sleep in her own bed, after several days with only a few hours of shut-eye. A long, hot bath was also on the agenda.

Her mind wandered back to the possible connection between Gian Dhillon, WPI, and Perry's killer and she wondered, not for the first time, whether it was anything more than Matthews's overactive imagination – obsession, even. From the way things were playing out, she almost hoped he was wrong. Then again, Matthews had surprised her before – displaying a hardiness up on the Kluane Plateau that was at odds with his fancy clothes and suave looks – and she had to admit that she found his tenacity both intriguing and attractive. Her mind wandered further to the early morning encounter in his hotel room and she was content to relive it for a moment, until the sound of a distant cellphone ring brought her back to reality. She looked around and realized the sound was coming from her bag. Rummaging in the side pocket, she pulled out her phone and glanced at the number displayed on the little screen, feeling an undeniable surge of excitement as she took the call and heard the familiar voice.

"I wasn't sure if you'd be in the air," Matthews said.

"Flight was delayed. I've been sitting here for an hour."

"I wanted to ask you something about WPI."

"So, you're not giving up," she said, unable to resist the smile that teased the corners of her mouth.

"Actually, I'm meeting with Walter Tate in a couple of hours."

"Really? I'm surprised he'd agree to that."

"He called Croft to set it up. Says he wants to talk – off the record."

Sawchuk frowned. "Is this an official inquiry?"

She noticed Matthews hesitated a tick before answering. "Actually, it's anything but, considering we're meeting at some monument down by the seawall – the Komagata something or other."

"That's weird."

"Tate's afraid of bad publicity, apparently," Matthews said. "I guess he doesn't want to be seen in public with anyone connected to the Perry task force."

"You're hardly a public figure, though."

"He thought he was going to be meeting Croft, not me, and if anyone asks, I never mentioned the meeting to you. I'm just glad Croft decided to follow up."

"Yeah," Sawchuk said. "He didn't sound too convinced last time you brought it up, but I guess you changed his mind. And don't worry, I'll keep it to myself."

"Thanks."

"So," Sawchuk said, "what did you want to ask?"

"You mentioned something about Tate's compensation package, and I was wondering if you recall the source."

"There was a blogger," she said, trying to shut out the sound of a boarding announcement at a nearby gate. "He had an unusual name that I forget, but the blog's called *CEO Insider*. It's sort of a mix of financial news and gossip. There was some good information there, but I couldn't help thinking the guy was a bit of a conspiracy theorist. It was also clear he didn't like pharmaceutical companies much."

"I'm just trying to find out whatever I can before the meeting."

"Money's always a good point of focus."

There was a pause before Matthews spoke again. "Listen, Lee. Part of the reason I was calling—" he began, but she cut him off.

"Is this about that grizz again? You can stop thanking me for that. You would have done the same for me, or at least tried to. Besides, you're the one had to drag my sorry ass out of the bush in the end, so I guess we're square."

"I just," he said, but as she waited for more, she knew there was nothing else to say. "If there's ever anything I can do," he eventually said. "Well, you know where to find me."

"I'll consider myself one of the lucky few."

He laughed. "Take care, Lee."

"You too." She ended the call and tucked the phone back in her pocket, her spirits falling even farther as she caught the red banner next to her flight number, indicating a further delay. She glanced over toward the coffee shop on the other side of the waiting area, considering an overpriced sandwich, then decided against it. Most of the time they tasted like sawdust anyway. Stretching her long legs, she looked up at one of the overhead screens showing a hockey game, then to another, featuring a mixture of news and advertisements. She watched distractedly as an ad for a foot massager was followed by one for the flu shot. A miserable-looking, red-eyed actor was blowing her nose into one tissue after another over a banner across the bottom of the screen that read: *The average Canadian loses four days of work per year due to flu symptoms. Today's flu vaccine is highly effective – get the shot!* She kept watching the screen as the haggard looking woman morphed into a smiling, clear-eyed mother snapping on her skis before her and her photogenic nuclear family set off down the slopes.

Sawchuk smiled at the clichéd image – probably the result of hours of strategy and focus groups – but as she closed her tired eyes, the images stayed in her head, along with the messages: *Get the flu shot! An average of four days per year lost to flu . . . today's flu vaccine is highly effective . . .*

As she sat there and wished away the minutes, her mind began to subconsciously jumble the messages from the ad into various combinations. *Flu shot . . . four days . . . vaccine . . .* Catching her breath, she entered "FDA" into the browser on her phone and waited for the results to load, scanning through the numerous entries related to the US Food and Drug Administration, including its organization, size, and history looking for any reference to Richard Perry and finding none.

She clicked on the bio of the current director and skimmed it before entering his name into a new search box. More of the same information popped up and she was about to close the browser when the last entry at the bottom of the screen caught her attention: *FDA Head Daniel Holbrook laments the death of his old friend, Richard Perry.* As she read through the article, describing a long-time relationship between the two men that went back to their days as roommates at Yale, she felt a growing excitement, interrupted by the ringing of her phone and the appearance of Marcie Kilpatrick's name on the screen.

"Hey, Marcie. What's up?"

"You remember you asked me to check that name?"

Sawchuk's curiosity spiked at the reference to her request from the day before. "Yeah?"

"It wasn't in the computer, but Dale was still doing everything on paper up until a few years back, so I went through the paper records and there it was."

"There what was?" Sawchuk said.

"Dale took Walter Tate and two other fat cats on a grizzly hunt five years ago." After a long silence, Marcie asked, "You still there?"

"What? Yeah, I'm here," Sawchuk said, her mind spinning as the answer to a question that had always bothered her fell into place - how Davydov had known that Richard Perry would be using Dale Oyler as an outfitter. "Are you sure, Marcie?"

"I'm sure. I can send you a copy of the page if you wa—"

"That'd be good . . . Listen, Marcie, I've gotta go."

As she dialled Matthews's number and got a busy signal, the excitement she had previously felt turned to something else - it was pure fear.

She dialled his number again as she grabbed her bag off the floor and headed for the exit.

CHAPTER 51

It was about nine when Matthews checked his watch. He had spent the past hour in a borrowed office at Cambie Street doing some online research, including reading all of the CEO *Insider* posts related to WPI or Walter Tate. He was thinking it would soon be time to leave, to get in a little reconnaissance before the ten o'clock meeting, when his phone rang.

"Matthews."

"It's Lam. We found Alice Wright."

"Who's Alice Wright?"

"The woman with the van."

"The one stolen out of Prince George?" Matthews was all ears.

"Someone left her for dead at the bottom of a ravine," Lam continued. "She's gonna make it, but only 'cause some hunters on quads spotted her. Lucky they knew first aid."

"Where?"

"Just north of 100 Mile House."

"Is she saying anything?"

"She's still recovering," Lam said. "No one's had a chance to talk to her, but she's being transported to Vancouver General tonight. Maybe tomorrow we can try talking to her."

"Okay, thanks for the update."

Matthews had just put his phone down when the IT tech poked his head around the door.

"I got some of the data you were looking for."

"Luponio, right?" Matthews stood.

He nodded and led Matthews back to the conference room, where Luponio took a seat behind a laptop and brought up a screen that looked like a spreadsheet of some kind.

"These," he said, pointing to the top of the six-column chart, "are the accounts associated with the six Nokias. And these," he added, pointing to the rows below each phone, "are the calls to and from each account." Matthews saw that each row contained a ten-digit number and, while some of the accounts only had a few rows beneath them, others had dozens. "I've identified some of the numbers, but I'm still working on a lot of them. It takes time."

Matthews nodded, though he was thinking that was precisely what he didn't have. He skimmed through the names next to some of the numbers and none looked familiar. Then he saw something near the bottom of the screen that drew his attention, in the second-to-last row under the fifth phone's account.

"Does that say Pan Pacific Hotel?" he asked, squinting to make out the small font of the onscreen notes.

Luponio nodded. "Yup."

Matthews started searching the rest of the rows in column five and zeroed in on a particular prefix."2-0-6," he said. "That's Seattle, right?"

Luponio shrugged, opened a new page for his browser and a few keystrokes later, he was nodding. "Is that significant?"

Matthews pointed to the fifth column, where most of the numbers remained unidentified. "I need you to focus on this phone. Forget the rest. I need IDs for all the numbers in this column. How long will that take?"

Luponio was already busy clicking and typing, adjusting the criteria for his ongoing search. "It'll speed things up if I'm limited to one column, but it could still take some time. It depends . . . oh, look, here's another name under phone five."

Matthews leaned forward and read the name aloud, "Joseph Mwangi."

"Is that name familiar to you?"

Matthews shook his head. "Keep searching," he said, straightening up and patting Luponio on the shoulder. He walked over to a vacant laptop on the other side of the table and opened the web browser, entering Mwangi's name. After scanning the results for a few minutes, he sighed and took out his phone. He debated calling Vanessa Ortiz, then entered a Virginia number instead and waited for four interminable rings before a voice answered.

"Merlin. I didn't wake you up, did I?"

In the pause that followed, Matthews imagined the young forensic IT tech's expression as he sat behind a bank of computer monitors, where he frequently spent fifteen hours straight.

"What's up, Matthews?"

"I need some help with a name – Joseph Mwangi, anything and everything you can find in . . ." he paused and looked at his watch, "twenty minutes? It's important."

"Did Ortiz authorize this? I caught some serious shit going off the books last time."

"You bet," Matthews lied, waiting patiently through another pause. He knew the tech didn't believe him, but he also knew the hook was set – Merlin could never resist a challenge.

"Call you back on this line?"

"Thanks. I owe you big time."

"I'll add it to your list," the voice deadpanned, before the line went dead. Matthews looked over at Luponio, hard at work behind his laptop. "You want a Tim Horton's?"

Luponio looked over the top of the screen and nodded. "Why not."

Matthews was at the Tim Horton's down the street paying for his coffees when his phone went off. He saw the number and punched the accept button.

"Everything okay?" he asked, a little concerned that Merlin was calling back so soon, and wondering if he needed more background information.

"That depends."

"What do you mean?"

"You want the good news or the bad news first?"

"Just spit it out," Matthews said, taking the tray of coffees and heading for a table in the corner.

"I think I found your Dr. Mwangi. If it's the right one, he's on a slab in the Seattle morgue, while they try to figure out what to do with him."

Matthews took a moment to digest the information. "He's dead," he finally said, more to himself than as a question.

"Very. OD in his hotel room about a week ago. September twelfth, to be exact."

Matthews felt his heart rate spike a bit at the news. "Are you sure about the date?"

"Unless the Seattle PD got it wrong, yeah. They tend to be pretty careful about those kinds of details, though."

"All right, what do we know about this guy? Where was he from and why was he in Seattle?" Matthews was still stuck on the fact that Mwangi had died two days before Dhillon, and that they had both been in Seattle at the same time.

"I thought you might want to know that, so I took the liberty of doing a little digging. The guy's from Nairobi – that's in Kenya in case you didn't know," Merlin added with a little flourish. "He's an immunologist – that's an—"

"Merlin."

"Right. He worked all over Africa for various outfits, some for profit, but a lot of his work seems to have been volunteering, including a stint with Global Doctors."

"You have the names of the companies he worked for?"

"I think I have all of the paying ones," Merlin said, listing off a handful of corporate names that were unfamiliar to Matthews.

"What about the volunteer organizations?"

"Well, there's Global Doctors, another one called Rescue Africa, but it's harder to establish the link to the not-for-profits because there's no money trail. I'll have them all in the next fifteen, twenty."

Matthews looked at his watch. "Send it to me when you have the list. What more can you tell me about Seattle?"

"There's not much. Hotel security found him in his bathtub with pills all over the place – dead as a doornail. They're treating it as a routine suicide."

"Was there a note?"

"There's no mention of one in the Seattle PD's online files."

Matthews's mind was racing as he tried to limit his questions to the ones he needed answers to most of all. "How long was he in Seattle?"

"He'd been at the Hilton for three nights and was booked for another one. According to his passport info, he came into JFK on September eleventh, via Schiphol. He stayed one night in New York and then flew to Seattle the next day."

"Was he attending a medical conference or something in Seattle?"

"Not that I can tell. I ran his name through pretty much everything I could find in Seattle and nothing came up."

"Can you cross reference his name with Gian Dhillon's and see if anything pops up?" Matthews couldn't help thinking their presence in the same city at the same time was an impossible coincidence, given that there were three different calls to Mwangi's cellphone from Dhillon's in the forty-eight hours leading up to Dhillon's death. There were another half dozen from ten days prior, when Dhillon was back in South Carolina – which explained his wife's confusion about mysterious calls that appeared to preoccupy her husband but were nowhere to be found on their joint phone records.

"I'll check it."

"Okay, and get me that list as soon as you can," he said. "And thanks, Merlin. This is great stuff on such short notice."

"I'll be in touch."

"Wait!" Matthews said, pausing as he thought back to something Dhillon's widow had said. "Dhillon worked for a charity . . . I'm just trying to remember the name. It was Humanity something . . . Scientists for Humanity, that's it. Check if Mwangi was a member as well. And one more thing."

"What?"

"Put a trap on this line."

"You got it."

Tucking the phone back in his pocket and grabbing the tray of coffees, Matthews speed-walked back to the police building to find Luponio still engrossed in his laptop.

"How's it going?"

"I got a couple of calls to a cab company here in Vancouver, there's two from the Seattle Hilton, and I'm still working on the other numbers. Shouldn't be much longer."

Matthews handed him a coffee. "I've got someone else chasing down a list of companies Joseph Mwangi worked for," he said, as his phone dinged, indicating an incoming message. "That's probably it now." He opened the email and started reading through the names of the other non-profit organizations that Mwangi had worked for in Africa. He sat behind the empty laptop and entered the last name, Africa Vision, and started skimming the online information. Clicking on the second set of search results, he learned that Africa Vision was based in Brussels, its stated mission to advance health care in Africa. The main activity seemed to be sending teams of doctors to remote parts of the continent to provide emergency medical care. Matthews clicked on a tab on the left side of the main page, entitled "Prevention" and was directed to another page that described Africa Vision's work in supplying much-needed antibiotics and other basic medicines. He was about to leave the page when something caught his eye on the bottom bar, under the heading "Sponsors". He stared at it for a moment, just to be sure, but there was no doubt that he was looking at WPI's corporate logo.

"You're pretty quiet over there," Luponio said, stirring Matthews from the trance he had fallen into as his mind processed the links between the late Dr. Mwangi, Gian Dhillon, and WPI. Then he remembered his meeting with Tate and looked at the time on the bottom right of the monitor. It was five to ten.

"Shit, I gotta go!" He jumped up and grabbed his jacket off the back of his chair.

"Gimme another five minutes and I'll have the other numbers."

"Text me the details," Matthews said as he rushed out the door of the conference room, down the stairs, and out onto Cambie Street, scanning the street for a cab.

CHAPTER 52

Matthews hopped out of the cab, hurried past the entrance to the Fairmont Pacific Rim hotel and headed toward the water. He muttered a curse as he checked his watch and realized he was almost twenty minutes late and he hadn't even arrived at the monument yet. Unaware that Vancouver had several Fairmont hotels, he had ended up at the one on West Georgia Street and wasted valuable time figuring out his mistake. His anxiety turned to relief as he spotted the lights of the seawall walk through the trees and a few minutes later, he spotted the Komagata Maru Monument – a glass panel in front of a large wooden bench surrounded by rust-coloured steel plates nestled among manicured shrubs. The soft lighting beneath the metal panels cast the area in an eerie light, and he was alone as he approached the large bench and looked around. It was quiet other than the sound of passersby out on the walking path and after closer inspection of the entire area, he returned to the bench and took a seat. Checking his watch again, he saw that it was now almost twenty-five minutes past ten and, as he cursed his carelessness, he wondered how he was going to explain this fuck-up to Croft.

"Shit," he said, the utterance echoing in the cool air of the partially enclosed area. Plucking his phone from his pocket, he noticed that he had three missed calls, presumably sent straight to voice mail while he was on the phone with Merlin earlier. His puzzlement changed to alarm as he saw that they were all from Sawchuk and that the calls had all been made within fifteen minutes of one another, over ninety minutes ago. He was about to dial her number when the sound of voices had him up and off the bench to investigate, but it was just a middle-aged couple who had strayed from the walking path to check out the monument.

He moved away from the central panel and took a seat at the other bench off to the side, his mind turning to his conversation with Merlin about Dr. Joseph Mwangi's work for Africa Vision, which he imagined involved delivering front-line medical services and handing out antibiotics, perhaps giving shots. It was not lost on Matthews that WPI was in the vaccine business, which explained why the company would have funded the not-for-profit medical service provider. It would also explain the connection between Mwangi and Dhillon – it had to. He was convinced now that they had met up in Seattle and had stayed in touch by phone when Dhillon travelled on to Vancouver. Matthews knew both men had ended up dead within forty-eight hours of each other but not what connected either of them to Richard Perry specifically, if there even was a connection.

He thought back to Perry's furtive message, scratched into the bark of the Yukon birch. He had obviously thought it important enough to devote the last few minutes of his life to, but what did it mean? The analysts had dissected the message and come up with nothing, other than the possibility that an impression in the bark next to the last letter might have been the start of an '*o*', an '*e*' or an '*a*'. He glanced at his watch again and saw that another five minutes had elapsed without any sign of Tate. With the same couple still examining the monument's main panel, Matthews's mind returned to the engraving in the bark.

Four days to step v . . .

Four days to step vo . . .

Four days to step ve . . .

Four days to step va . . .

Four days to st—

His mind suddenly stopped churning the jumbled thoughts of Mwangi, Dhillon, Davydov, Tate, and WPI, and then everything became clear.

Four days to stop vaccine . . .

Tomorrow was the fourth day.

He instinctively reached for his phone to call Sawchuk, but realized she was in the air, headed back to Whitehorse. He glanced at the last missed call from her and noticed the time - well after the delayed departure time for her flight. He recalled their last conversation, during which he had mentioned the meeting with Tate. He had even mentioned the location and, as he looked around the dimly lit area, deserted again but for his own presence, he focused on the darkened areas beyond the range of the soft lighting and he felt his stomach churn.

What if . . .

He stood so quickly that his phone fell out of his pocket and when he bent to retrieve it from under the bench his eye was drawn to a silvery glint. He crouched for a closer inspection and his breath caught in his throat as he clutched the silver chain, turning the little pendant over in his fingers and making out the engraving on the back in the faint light: *LS*.

He dialled Sawchuk's number and listened to it ring as he sprinted to the walking path. It was on the fourth ring and he was halfway back to the hotel when the call was answered, though there was no voice at the other end of the line and no sound other than a vague thrum of background noise.

"Lee? It's me, Ben."

There was still no response at the other end of the line, but the thrumming increased and he thought he was listening to the sound of an engine.

"Hello?" he said, suddenly aware of the ragged sound of his own breathing in the expectant silence that preceded a rustling noise . . . It wasn't Sawchuk's chipper voice that eventually came on the line but one with a much deeper timbre, flat and lifeless.

"You will stop your inquiries," the accented male voice ordered.

"Who is this?"

"You talk to no one about your friend, and you do nothing. Otherwise, she dies."

"Listen, don't even think—"

"Do you understand? Please tell me if you don't – I'll be very happy to do it right now."

Matthews stood there in the middle of the pathway, the phone at his ear, as he grasped for options. "Put her on the phone." He waited for a few interminable seconds, then he heard a gasp of breath and Sawchuk's unmistakable voice came on the line.

"Ben? Don't liste—"

"Hang in there, Lee." He paused as the rustling on the other end of the line came to an abrupt end and the accented growl returned. "So, you see her fate is in your hands. Say nothing and do nothing until noon tomorrow. You will be contacted then."

"Wait a minute, you don't—" He trailed off when he realized he was talking to a dial tone, and he started scrolling frantically through his recent calls. He selected Merlin's number and the IT tech picked up on the second ring.

"Did you put the trap on my line?" Matthews was practically shouting the question.

"What? Yeah . . . what's going—"

"What about outgoing calls – can you triangulate on those?" Matthews asked, starting to run again.

"You mean the call you just made?"

"Yeah, her name's Lee Sawchuk."

"Is this official?" Merlin said, his tone jovial.

"I'm not fucking around, Merlin. This is serious."

There was silence except for the faint clicking of keystrokes in the background as Matthews hurried up the steps to the hotel grounds. "Sorry – here it is. The call was picked up north of Vancouver. It looks like . . . in the vicinity of a place called Squamish."

"Where?"

"It's a small town along Highway 99," Merlin said.

"Where does Highway 99 lead?"

"Middle of nowhere basically, though Squamish is about halfway between Vancouver and Whistler."

"The ski resort? Can you narrow down the cell ping at all?" Matthews was already calculating his current distance from Whistler and what his chances of locating Sawchuk were without more information.

"I'm sorry. It's more accurate on the originating end. I can't be any more specific than a cell tower a bit to the east of the town of Squamish."

"All right," Matthews said, his mind spinning. "Can you check the property registries in the Whistler area for the name Walter Tate?"

"I'm on it. Oh, by the way, Mwangi wasn't a member of Scientists for Humanity."

"Shit, okay, I've got to go, Merlin."

"Hang on. He wasn't a member, but he was a speaker at one of their functions."

"When?"

"About a year ago."

"The timing could make sense," Matthews said, reaching the entrance to the Fairmont Pacific Rim and pushing through the door.

"What timing?"

"I'm just thinking . . . Can you cross reference Walter Tate with tomorrow's date? Could be something related to his compensation, but not necessarily." He paused, scanning the lobby and spotting the concierge in the corner. "And one more thing," he said, then hesitated. He wanted to tell Merlin to let Ortiz know that Croft was compromised – there was no other explanation for the evening's course of events – but the threat delivered in that deep, flat voice was all he could think of. He couldn't take the risk. "Forget it. Gotta go."

He ended the call and rushed over to the concierge's desk. "I need to rent a hotel car. Something fast."

CHAPTER 53

Sawchuk stared at the man standing in the doorway and felt a shiver run the length of her spine. His close-cropped hair was dark, but it looked like the result of a bad dye-job and she had no doubt who stood before her. Viktor Davydov looked every bit as dangerous in the flesh as he did on paper, and Sawchuk didn't scare easily. She looked behind him at the open door, the only exit from the dank storage room where she had been sitting in the murk until the door had swung open a few seconds ago. Davydov watched her furtive glance and grinned.

"You must go through me first," he said with a sinister grin, as Sawchuk continued to stare at him – the same man who had killed Dale Oyler – and felt the anger rise inside her, a bubbling rage building to the point that she was ready to pounce. She looked away for a moment and when she focused on him again, there was a shiny blade protruding between the second and third fingers of his left hand.

"You want to try?" His grin twisted into a lopsided grimace.

"Fuck you," she said, resigning herself to the fact that a frontal attack on a knife-wielding man who outweighed her by almost a hundred pounds was not an option. If only she had some kind of weapon of her own.

"Make yourself comfortable," Davydov said, stepping back into the doorway. "At least for a while," he added before slamming the door shut.

As the light from the doorway vanished again and her eyes adjusted to the dimness of the room, Sawchuk resumed her inspection of her surroundings, her mind going through an analysis of options, none of which were very good. She had already determined that the door was too solid to attempt to break and that it was held in place by a sliding bolt on the outside. There being no other doors or windows, escape seemed to be off the table. There was a vent in the far corner of the room, but it was only a few inches square and covered by a metal grille with no accessible screws, even if she had something to unfasten them with.

Returning to the wooden stool in the middle of the room, she sat and fought the urge to panic. She remembered nothing after walking into the little memorial park near the seawall, until she had awoken, trussed and hooded, in the back of an SUV. She had no idea how long they had been driving while she was out, so her current location was a mystery. As for why she was here, that wasn't obvious either. What *was* obvious was that the meeting at the memorial had been a set-up. For whatever reason, Matthews hadn't showed, which she took as a good sign, though it was of little comfort to her now. The other puzzling question was why she was still breathing. She wasn't kidding herself that Davydov, having already murdered a former US vice president and a former Canadian ambassador, would think twice before killing a Mountie. Was he planning on using her as bait for Matthews? She momentarily gave in to the flood of frightening thoughts and images and the panic returned, threatening to overwhelm her, before she caught herself and took a deep breath.

There were a lot of unknowns about her current predicament, but the one thing she felt certain of was that she would die in this room if she didn't have a plan for when that door opened again.

CHAPTER 54

Matthews was headed north on the Sea to Sky Highway and coming up on the Welcome to Whistler sign when his phone went off. He punched the speaker button and Merlin's voice echoed through the car's interior.

"No luck pin-pointing the recipient of that last outgoing call," he said, causing Matthews's heart to sink. He didn't have time for a house-to-house search through the entire Whistler area.

"Fuck."

"I do have something for you, though: Sharon Gallagher."

Matthews racked his brain, trying to think of whether he had heard the name before. "Who's that?"

"Walter Tate's wife."

"Okay," Matthews said, unsure how the information helped him now.

"Point is, her name pops up on a property registry search for Whistler."

"What's the address?"

"It's all parcel numbers and legal descriptions, but I'm working on the civic address."

"All right, that's good. Keep on it," Matthews said, slowing to navigate a sharp bend in the road. "I've gotta go."

"Wait," Merlin said. "There's something else. I cross-referenced tomorrow's date with Walter Tate and there is a connection."

"What is it?"

"It's a bit of a tangled web of corporate and tax paperwork . . . none of this stuff's publicly available. Anyway, tomorrow's the main delivery date for some vaccine that WPI is supplying to the US government."

Matthews remembered the details of the much-touted super-vaccine WPI had developed. "I assume it's a big payday for WPI."

"I'd say the champagne corks'll be popping," Merlin said. "But Tate himself is the big winner. He's in line for a personal lump sum payment of almost a hundred million under the terms of the contract."

In the silence of the car's interior, Matthews's mind began to sift through the pieces of the investigation, from how Gian Dhillon and Dr. Joseph Mwangi fit into the picture, to Richard Perry's cryptic message.

"And none of this is public knowledge?" he finally said.

"Most of it isn't, although he'll have to disclose at least some of the income in his tax . . ." he trailed off. "Hang on, the address in Whistler is coming up."

"What is it?"

"It's . . . 4554 Stonebridge Drive. You'll take a left off Highway 99, then follow Alta Lake Road and then turn onto Stonebridge."

"Got it."

Merlin hesitated before his next words. "You sure you don't want some backup?"

"It's gotta stay between us for now, Merlin. But I'll be fine."

"If you say so. Good luck."

Ten minutes later, Matthews saw the turnoff for Alta Lake Road. Exiting the highway, he found himself first in a residential area and then on what looked like a deserted access road. He took the turn onto Stonebridge and saw that it was dotted with residences, separated by more and more space the farther he continued northwest. He caught a glimpse of the lights of one of the residences as he passed by and saw that these were multimillion-dollar homes, not mere chalets. He was still trying to determine his approach when he saw the number 4554 glowing from atop one of a pair of marble gateposts. He slowed and peered down the laneway but saw nothing other than a winding road and trees.

Continuing on past the entrance, he debated a U-turn, then spotted a little side road up ahead to the right. He parked about fifty feet from the main road and got out. Popping the trunk, he pulled out the camouflage jacket he had picked up on his way out of Vancouver and slipped it on. He checked the clip in his Beretta and set off on foot, crossing the main road then heading into the trees a few hundred feet past the entrance. He made his way up a gentle slope for five minutes, making steady progress as he climbed, then reached the peak of the hill. He stopped and peered through the trees at the lights of the house.

Moving to the edge of a clearing, he sidled up to a big spruce and took a closer look. The large stone and wood house was located on the other side of a little valley separating it from his current position. On the other side, it overlooked another gulley, offering a spectacular view of the mountains rising in the distance. The second floor was lit, as was the large deck. He saw two vehicles parked in front of a three-car garage – one an SUV and the other a sports car. There was no question that somebody was home. Just looking at the house, Matthews was certain that it was equipped with the latest alarms – the Tate–Gallaghers no doubt spending long periods away – which made the prospect of sneaking in undetected highly unlikely. And yet, he had to think of something, and soon. His mind turned to Sawchuk, likely detained somewhere inside, assuming she was still . . .

He broke off the thought and took out his phone, pulling up the landline number Merlin had forwarded and hitting the dial button as he kept his eyes on the house. It rang four times before someone picked up. Matthews scanned the windows on the main floor, hoping to catch some movement as a voice came on the line.

"Hello?"

"Walter Tate?"

"Who's this?"

"It's Ben Matthews."

"How did you get this number?" Tate's voice was quickly losing its confident tone.

"I'll stick to my end of the bargain, but I want some assurances," Matthews said, hoping to keep Tate on the line, possibly even show himself or give something away about Sawchuk's location.

Just keep him talking.

"I don't know what you're talking about."

"Just let me hear her voice," Matthews said, as a dull noise rose above the forest behind him. It didn't register at first, but when it did, he hit the end button on the phone as quickly as he could. A few seconds later, a chopper roared overhead, headed southeast.

"Fuck," he muttered into the dim of the forest around him. He kept an eye on the house below and watched as a man about Tate's size and build appeared by the picture window behind the deck, the phone at his ear as he watched the helicopter fly over. Matthews ducked into the woods and cursed again – his plan had suddenly blown a tire.

"He's here," Tate said, hanging up the phone.

"Who?"

"Matthews. Who do you think?"

"You are sure?" Davydov got up from the chair by the fireplace.

"I just heard that chopper on his phone," Tate said, gesturing into the sky outside. "He's out there somewhere. I knew you shouldn't have brought her here."

"Is not your concern."

Tate held back the retort that was on the tip of his tongue as he took in Davydov's dead-eyed stare. To be ordered to shelter Davydov was bad enough, but now he was a party to kidnapping a woman – a cop, no less. He still didn't understand why she and not Matthews was locked in his basement storeroom, but he knew something had gone wrong. Whatever circumstances had led the man who now sat glowering at him from across the room to his door were irrelevant. There was nothing Tate could do about it now. Maybe that was the point Sasha was trying to make.

"What do we do now?" Tate asked, unable to hold Davydov's gaze as an ugly grin appeared on the other man's chiselled features.

"You do nothing," Davydov said, getting out of his chair and heading to the window. Tate watched him and felt a chill down his spine as he saw the gun in Davydov's left hand as he turned to face him. "Matthews is a dead man."

CHAPTER 55

Davydov knew exactly where he was headed before he hit the last of the stairs leading down from the deck. He moved stealthily into the trees and up the slope toward the high ground where he was sure Matthews was hiding. He stopped about a hundred or so feet from the house, three-quarters of the way up the other side of the valley and scanned the high ground for any trace but saw nothing. Continuing his careful progress, he detoured left to outflank the American. As the ground levelled off, he crouched by the base of a large pine and scanned the area to his right for any sign of life. There was a dim glow from a quarter moon filtering through the forest, creating shadows and pools of light, but his eyes had always been good at night. He scanned a patch of trees just a few feet from a clearing that would afford an excellent view of Tate's house below and, as his eyes surveyed the area inch by inch, he saw it – some camouflage fabric by the trunk of a large tree. He focused on it for any sign of movement as he drew his weapon and crept closer. When he was well within range, he pulled out the phone he had taken from Sawchuk and searched for Matthews's cell number.

Matthews struggled to stay motionless as the tension built within him. He could sense the Russian's approach, but he hadn't seen him yet. Davydov should have been visible by now, he thought, resisting the temptation to scratch an itch on the side of his nose. His every sense was on high alert and though he squeezed the grip of his Beretta, it offered little comfort in the half-light of the forest.

I should have seen him by now . . .

Suddenly, the unnatural sound of his phone's ringer shattered the silence of the forest, jolting his heart as he fought the urge to move. The first ring hadn't ended before he heard the shot, then saw the muzzle flash, followed by another two shots in rapid succession. He aimed the gun down at the spot where he had seen the flash and pulled the trigger just as Davydov seemed to sense something was wrong and looked up into the trees above him, twenty feet from where Matthews had left his underbrush-stuffed camo coat. The decision to leave his cellphone there as well had been a last-minute addition to his plan – one that he now realized had saved his life. Matthews saw those dark eyes even in the dim moonlight and kept firing as the big Russian fell to the ground. He swung down branch to branch and dropped to the forest floor, his gun drawn as he raced to the spot where Davydov had fallen, but the Russian was gone. A semi-automatic lay on the ground and there was a dark slick on the nearby leaves that shimmered in the moonlight. He took a step toward the leaves and saw that the terrain beyond sloped downward.

He has to be in those trees somewhere.

Matthews took another step forward, scouring the dimly lit area ahead of him as he advanced, his gun trained on the treeline. Some sixth sense made him check his blind spot and he was only partly turned when he saw the blurred shape to his right, ducked, and felt a whoosh of air by his cheek. He swung his right hand around and squeezed off a round that went into the trees, before his hand went numb and the gun fell to the ground, disappearing in the undergrowth. Looking up, he noticed that Davydov's right arm was tight to his body and Matthews could see in the moonlight that his sleeve was wet.

"Give it up, Davydov. It's over," he said, noticing the glint of the blade in the other man's left hand for the first time – as though his hand had sprouted a knife – and understood why his own right hand was numb and slick with blood.

"I will kill you slowly," Davydov growled, lunging forward, the knife slicing through the air and missing Matthews's torso by mere inches. He jumped back and glanced around for something to fend off the next assault as Davydov regrouped.

"You're not killing anyone else, asshole," Matthews said, backing up, hoping he might make it back to the Beretta, but Davydov seemed to guess his intent and lunged again. This time, he waited until he was closer to swing the knife and, though Matthews escaped the main thrust, he felt the blade sink into the flesh of his side. He clamped down on the hand holding the knife and kicked at Davydov's left knee, causing a gasp as the other man crumpled and they both fell to the ground, Matthews on top and determined to keep the knife under control. But even wounded, Davydov was powerful, managing to connect a knee to Matthews's ribs that weakened his grip on the knife hand and, as he tried to adjust his body weight to prevent his left hand coming free, Davydov bucked him off. Matthews tried to scramble backward as the Russian collected himself and the knife came up. Matthews put his hand behind him to push himself up and his fingers brushed something cold and hard on the ground.

"Now you fucking die!" Davydov bellowed, his coal-black eyes glowing in the moonlight as he hurtled forward, his left fist with its razor-sharp protrusion thrust out in front of him. Matthews fell onto his back and swung his right hand up, his finger wrapping around the trigger of the recovered Beretta, just as Davydov's hulking frame blocked out the moon overhead. Two shots rang out as Matthews rolled to the left and Davydov crashed to the ground next to him. Scrambling to his feet with his gun safely in hand again, Matthews approached the motionless form and kicked it over. Davydov's forehead was centred by a dark hole and there was a similar wound just beneath his chin. Those eyes still stared up at him, but the dark glower was gone, replaced by a wide-eyed stare of final surprise.

CHAPTER 56

Sawchuk was on her hands and knees by the air vent, listening intently. There was no doubt that those were gunshots she had heard, and they were close by. She stood and kicked the metal screen of the vent, bending it but failing to dislodge it completely. Undeterred, she swung her right leg again, the steel toe of her boot hitting the side of the screen. She knelt down and pulled at a metal shim, cutting her hand as she managed to pull it free. Oblivious to the pain or the blood flowing from her hand as she stared at the jagged piece of metal, she hurried to the door and tried to jam the thin edge of the steel under the hinge bolt at the top of the door. She swore as she tried without success to create a gap between the rusted bolt and the hinge, ignoring the pain her efforts were causing to her already injured hand. She kicked off one of her boots and tried hammering on the steel wedge with the heel, until she felt something move. Changing the angle, she continued to hammer away with the boot, slowing working the bolt upward. She was beginning to think she might actually get it out when she heard two more gunshots. She paused for a moment before resuming her work more frantically than ever. She was running out of time.

CHAPTER 57

"You got him?"

Matthews heard Walter Tate's voice call out as he struggled to cross the crushed stone of the driveway under the weight of Davydov's lifeless body, slung across his shoulders and clad in Matthews's camouflage coat.

"Da," muttered Matthews in his most convincing impression of the Russian's accent.

"Put him in the garage."

Matthews kept his head down as he turned toward the garage, slowing his pace as Tate came up behind him. Matthews straightened up and let the body fall to the ground and was about to pull out the Beretta when he felt cold steel against the back of his neck.

"Drop it."

He hesitated for a moment, but the intensifying pressure of the gun barrel against his skin changed his mind and he let the gun slip from his hand.

"Nice try, but you should have switched boots. I'm very observant," Tate added, as Matthews turned to face him.

"You're in a whole boatload of trouble, is what you are."

"Let's go," Tate said, gesturing to the stairs up to the deck. "Leave that piece of shit there."

"Whatever you say." Matthews walked up the stairs to the deck, Tate following behind with the gun trained on the small of his back. Once inside, Tate directed him away from the picture window and into an ultra-modern kitchen.

"Sit." He waved the gun at one of the stools in front of a granite island.

"You need to think this through, Walter," Matthews said, his voice calm, though he could sense Tate was at a critical point. The next seconds would determine whether he could be talked back from the brink or whether he felt he was past it, in which case Matthews's prospects were not good.

"You can spare me the part about the place being surrounded," Tate said with a derisive snort. "I know you're on your own."

"How would you know, one way or the other?"

"Let's just say information is the most valuable of commodities," Tate said, moving across the kitchen toward a door that led downstairs. "And everyone has their price."

"I know about your source inside the task force," Matthews said. "And I'm not the only one," he added, wishing it were true. The fact was, there was no cavalry on the way to rescue him or Sawchuk. If he didn't do something, they were both dead.

"Why couldn't you just blame it on terrorists, like everyone else?"

"It's time to give this up, Walter," Matthews said evenly. "It's true Croft did his best to sideline me, but people know I'm looking into you and they know I'm here now."

"I don't think so." Tate shook his head and shifted his weight from one foot to another, clearly agitated.

"Where's Sawchuk?"

Tate said nothing, but Matthews noticed the furtive sidelong glance at the basement stairs. "You're not a killer, Walter, whatever else you may have done—"

"They weren't supposed to kill Perry."

"Just Mwangi and Dhillon," Matthews said, eliciting a snort from Tate.

"Those two had it coming," he said. "Just a pair of shit-disturbers."

"But it was you who put Davydov on Perry's trail."

Tate shook his head. "That's not true. I told them Dhillon spoke to Perry at the AGM in Vancouver, that's all."

"And you gave them Perry's travel plans."

Tate was shaking his head again, more vigorously now. "Just that he was headed to the Yukon on a hunt . . . and what outfitter he was using – but it was just so they could keep an eye on him."

"Is that what you're telling yourself?"

"Shut the fuck up!" Tate swung the gun toward Matthews, his hand shaking.

"Take it easy," Matthews slowly raised a hand, palm up. "I know you're different from Davydov and the people he worked for. You probably got in over your head, and there's no reason—"

"You have no idea," Tate interrupted, and Matthews noticed that the gun had lowered slightly.

"So, let's talk it through," he said, eager to continue the progress. "There are mitigating circumstances for you. The first is to stop the launch of that vaccine." He paused to register the glimmer of understanding in Tate's eyes. "Yes, we know the vaccine is what's at the root of all this. Richard Perry managed to carve a warning message into the bark of the tree your friend tied him to before he slit his throat."

"Bullshit," Tate said, but there was concern in his expression. "If it was so fucking obvious, the FBI would have arrested me long ago."

"As you just said, Gian Dhillon met with Richard Perry in Vancouver the day before Dhillon was killed. Before that, Dhillon had been in regular contact with Joseph Mwangi, who'd no doubt come across your secret vaccine trials." He paused again, and Tate's face told him everything he needed to know about his theory. "You didn't think anyone was going to connect the dots? Perry was on the books as a consultant to WPI, no doubt for his ability to schmooze the right people at the FDA for the approvals you needed, but he wouldn't have been too happy to discover a bunch of secret trials that showed serious side effects."

"You don't have any proof of that . . . you're just stalling."

Matthews shook his head. "I'm afraid we do, Walter, but the good news is that it isn't too late for you. You can still stop delivery, maybe you'll even get some credit for—" He stopped talking as Tate raised the gun and pointed it at Matthews's chest. "What are you doing?"

"You don't walk away from a delivery worth billions," Tate said, with a sneer. "And even if I wanted to, I couldn't."

"You're worried about your partners – whoever hired Davydov. But we can—"

"You can't do shit . . . It's too late. I'm sorry but I have no choice."

"Don't do it, Walter. You're not like them. You're not a murderer."

"Just shut up," Tate snapped and Matthews could see him to begin to apply pressure to the trigger and close his eyes. Looking around in desperation, Matthews spotted the cast-iron frying pan on the counter, halfway between him and Tate. He lunged, snatching the pan and throwing it up as a shield just before the shot fired, the roar of the gun followed immediately by a deafening metallic ping. He didn't feel the searing pain in his arm until after he had tackled Tate and knocked the gun from his hand. As they separated, Matthews saw that his sleeve and the front of Tate's shirt were covered in blood.

Appearing to sense Matthews's momentary confusion, Tate reached for the fallen gun. Matthews was on him before he could grasp it and, in their ensuing struggle, the gun was kicked to the side, sliding along the blood-slicked marble floor and ending up near the door to the basement. Matthews was gaining the upper hand and had manoeuvred himself behind the larger man to apply a chokehold when Tate lashed out behind him and dug a fingernail deep in the wound to Matthews's right arm.

Unable to maintain his grasp for a split second, he watched in horror as Tate broke free, dove forward, and grabbed the gun from the floor, swinging it around as he stood and pointed it back at Matthews's chest.

"Don't do it!" Matthews shouted, but he knew from the adrenaline-fuelled glow in Tate's eyes that he was well beyond reason, just as Matthews knew another counterattack from where he lay on the floor, blood freely draining from his arm, was an impossibility.

He felt a wave of exhaustion and despair as Tate advanced a step and took aim, just as the basement doorway swung open and a figure emerged in a blur of motion. Tate had only begun to turn when Sawchuk's closed right fist came down on his arm, just ahead of another deafening bang as the gun went off and its bullet punched a hole in the door of the refrigerator a couple of inches to Matthews's left. Tate was staring at the gun, which had come to rest on the marble tile floor near his foot and was oblivious to Sawchuk, whose left fist landed on the bridge of his nose. He dropped like a stone, cracking his head on the corner of the granite countertop halfway through his fall, and he was out cold by the time he hit the floor.

"That was for Dale Oyler, you sack of shit," Sawchuk said, shaking out her dirt and blood-encrusted left hand as she loomed over Tate's crumpled figure, a muffled groan the first sign that he was starting to come around. When she turned to Matthews and saw the blood her eyes went wide.

"Oh my God," she said, picking up the gun and rushing over to him. "Are you—"

"I'm fine," he said, as his body was racked by an involuntary shiver.

"You don't seem fine," she said, pulling up his sleeve to inspect the wound to his upper arm, then snatching a dishtowel from the counter. "Where's Davydov?" she said, glancing around as she tied the dishtowel tightly above the wound.

"He's gone,"

"Gone where?" she said.

"I mean he's *gone*,"

"You took him out?"

Matthews nodded. "Outside, up on the ridge."

Sawchuk paused, then let out a little breath as a grin bloomed on her face. "Well, I'll be damned," she said. "I'm going to call this in and get you an ambulance. I think the bullet went straight through but I'm not exactly a doctor. Are you sure you're feeling okay?"

He looked up at her with a weary smile. "Honestly, I've never felt better."

CHAPTER 58

Matthews was sitting in the waiting room at Vancouver General Hospital talking to Vanessa Ortiz when Sawchuk came through the doors from the ER, her left hand and forearm wrapped in a white bandage.

"You okay?"

Sawchuk shrugged "A few stitches. How about you?" she said, gesturing to his arm.

"Same here." Matthews said. Sawchuk's initial assessment at Tate's house had been correct – the bullet had gone straight through Matthews's arm and, other than needing a few sutures, it had caused little damage. The ER doctor had also stitched up lacerations to his hand and right side but, overall, Matthews had been very lucky. His arm and side were a bit sore, but he felt pretty good all things considered, and he had managed to lobby for his discharge, despite the doctor's suggestion that he stay overnight for observation.

"What about Tate? Did I at least break his nose?"

Matthews nodded. "Yup, and he's got a concussion, though that was probably more from his kitchen counter than your left hook.

Anyway, his injuries are the least of his worries right now." He gestured to Ortiz. "This is my boss, Vanessa Ortiz."

"Ben was just bringing me up to speed," Ortiz said. "I think we owe you quite a thank you."

She shrugged. "I should probably be thanking him." She laughed and gestured to Matthews. "What's the word on the vaccine?"

Ortiz nodded. "It's been seized. None of it has been used, but we sure cut it close. We're still looking into Joseph Mwangi's involvement, but it looks like he discovered some pretty awful side effects from WPI's trials off the books, some of them fatal. We've also had another look at the post-mortem and it's looking like the actual cause of his death was asphyxiation."

"Just like Dhillon."

Sawchuk nodded. "I assume this means Tate's going to have a long spell behind bars."

"That's a given, but I'm more interested in his silent partner." Ortiz paused as her phone began ringing. "Excuse me."

"Do they know who it is?" Sawchuk asked, after Ortiz had stepped away to take the call.

Matthews smiled. "Ortiz had more faith in me than I gave her credit for. She was keeping tabs on Tate these past few days, and it turns out he flew to New York a couple of days ago and met with a guy named Alexander Kurylenko, who happens to be a big wheel in organized crime on the East Coast."

"You think he's the connection to Davydov?"

Matthews shrugged. "Probably, and if he was, he's got nowhere to hide. The FBI's working it hard, so it's only a matter of time." He watched as Ortiz returned, wearing an uncharacteristically broad smile. "Good news?"

"Sasha Kurylenko's in custody," she said. "And we just picked up your pal Croft at the airport in Seattle, trying to board a flight to Buenos Aires."

"I knew that guy was a weasel," Matthews said, shaking his head. "But I didn't think he was on the take."

Ortiz smiled, as Sawchuk's cell went off. "Listen, Ben," Ortiz said, as Sawchuk turned to focus on her call. "You did great work on this and . . . I've been rethinking the London posting."

"Oh yeah?" Matthews said, averting his eyes.

Ortiz gave him a puzzled look. "You don't want it?"

"I didn't say that."

She stared at him for a moment, then glanced over at Sawchuk and smiled. "Well, why don't you give it some thought."

"Thanks. I appreciate it. And thanks for stopping by," Matthews said. It was a nice gesture, though he knew Ortiz had other reasons for being here in person. There would be no public announcement of Matthews's role in finding Richard Perry's killer or preventing a public health disaster, but that didn't mean Ortiz wouldn't ensure the Agency got full credit behind the scenes. She was probably well on the way to securing herself a promotion, which wasn't bad news for him, either.

After she shook his hand, Ortiz turned to Sawchuk, who had finished her call.

"Sergeant Sawchuk, it's been a real pleasure. If you're ever looking for work south of the border, let me know. Now, do you think you can keep this guy out of trouble for the next little while?"

"Consider it done."

"You going to Cambie Street?" Sawchuk asked, after Ortiz had left and they made their way downstairs and out through the sliding doors of the hospital into the cool night air. He nodded and was about to wave at a cab parked nearby until she stopped him.

"Let's walk out to the street," she said.

"You okay?"

"I'm fine. I just like the fresh air."

They walked along in silence for a while, before Sawchuk spoke again. "When are you going back to Ottawa?"

"I'm not sure," he said, as they strolled down the quiet sidewalk. "Ortiz wants me to hang around here for a while, help with connecting the dots."

Sawchuk took a deep breath of the crisp night air and shook her head. "Who would have thought it all revolved around a vaccine. Perry, Townsend . . . Dale. All gone because of a stupid vaccine."

"A very lucrative, not to mention dangerous, vaccine," Matthews said. "That's why Dhillon met with Perry, to tell him what he and Mwangi had discovered about the drug trials in Africa."

"But why didn't Perry blow the whistle then?"

Matthews shrugged. "I don't know. Maybe he didn't believe it, or maybe he didn't want to damage his old Yale roommate's reputation. Looks like he lobbied Holbrook pretty hard to get the WPI vaccine approved, and those kinds of decisions are hard to reverse. Perry would have needed pretty solid proof before going back to Holbrook to say they'd made a mistake. Either way, Tate and his gangster partner obviously couldn't take the chance."

"And the others – Garcia, Dhillon, Mwangi, and Fenwick? All collateral damage."

"I'm afraid so. At least Alice Wright is gonna make it."

They walked on in silence for a moment, then he reached into his pocket and stopped. "I almost forgot." He took her hand and opened it so that the delicate silver chain and pendant slid into her palm.

"Thanks," she said, as they stood close together on the sidewalk.

"You know, I just realized that tonight's the second time in the past few days that you've had to save my ass."

She laughed. "I'd say I'm the one who owes you this time. I still don't know how you found me, but I'm sure glad you did."

"When do you have to go back to Whitehorse?"

She slid her arms around his waist. "Who wants to know?"

"Just keeping tabs on my favourite Mountie."

"I'm not sure. It might just take a couple of days of R&R for me to recover from this," she said with a grin as she pointed to her bandaged hand.

He smiled, thinking it would take more than a few stitches to slow her down, much less stop her. "The least I can do is offer to share my hotel room with you," he said. "In the interests of furthering US-Canada relations, and saving costs, obviously."

"Well, when you put it that way."

They kissed for a long moment and then she cocked her head and looked at him. "Did I hear Ortiz say something about London?"

He smiled as he pulled her closer. "You remember what you told me when we said goodbye last time?"

She nodded, looking up at him. "About not complicating things? Yeah, I remember."

"Well, I was thinking of ignoring your advice."

Her eyebrows rose. "What are you saying?"

"I can't move to Whitehorse, and I can't expect you to move to London or DC, but what if we met in the middle?"

"The middle?"

"You told me you liked Ottawa," he said, "when we were up on the Plateau."

"I think I said I didn't hate it. That's not exactly the same thing."

"I'm pretty sure there's work there for someone with your skill set."

She let out a little snort. "Just like a southerner – to assume I can't wait to get out of the Yukon, when the truth is—"

"All right, all right," he said, waving a hand in mock surrender. "Can't blame me for trying."

She paused and a smile lit her face as she leaned in to kiss him again. "I suppose not," she said, after their lips parted. "Just don't go thinking I've given up on converting you from a Cheechako to a Sourdough, that's all."

ACKNOWLEDGEMENTS

I have a lot of people to thank for this book. I'll start with Rebecca Rose, who took the project on and put together a wonderful team to see it through editing, design, and all the other important stages in the life of a novel. Special thanks to my editor, Brock Peters, who forced me to address issues that I might otherwise have let slide, greatly improving the book in the process. Thanks also to Samanda Stroud and Sandy Newton for their eagle eyes at the copy-editing and proofreading stages, and to Beth Oberholtzer for the striking cover.

I'm grateful to my sister, Claire, who provided guidance and support early on in the process; it's nice to have an editor in the family! David Jacques and Tate McLeod also provided helpful feedback on various drafts of the book. Many thanks to Superintendent (Ret.) Larry Wilson, for his insight on investigative and procedural matters, and to my long-time go-to on all things medical—and good friend—Dr. Greg Brown.

This book could not have been written without the invaluable input of my friend Cory, whom I first met in the Yukon twenty years ago. I knew immediately that he was someone you'd want around if you were dropped in the middle of nowhere at 40° below! He generously shared his time and extensive knowledge of everything from policing and hunting in the North, to weapons and ammunition, to outdoor survival, to aircraft . . . I could go on, but you get the picture.

Finally, a big thank you to my wife, Tanya—always my first reader and number one supporter in so many ways.

THE AUTHOR

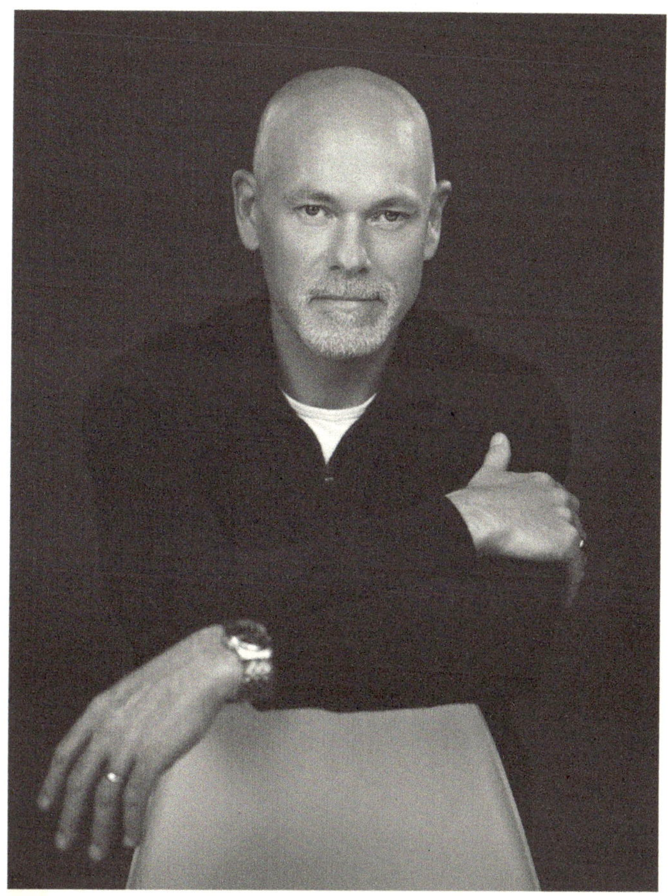

Originally from St. John's, Nick Wilkshire is a lawyer and author who spent five years in the Yukon before settling in Ottawa. *The Hunt* is his seventh novel.

also by NICK WILKSHIRE

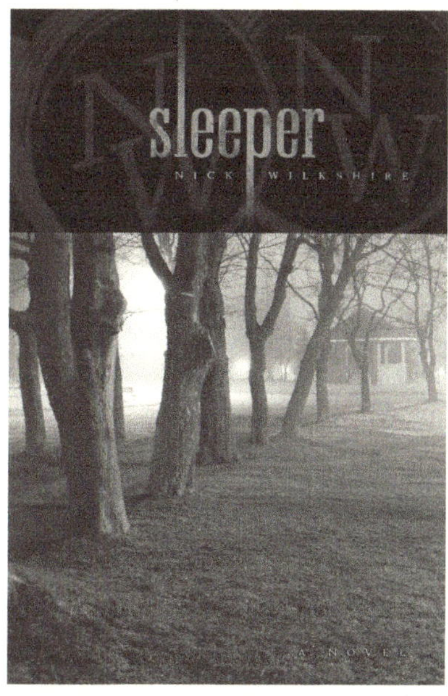

Sleeper (2023)
Breakwater Books

When a prominent Toronto lawyer is murdered on a foggy night in Bannerman Park, the entire city of St. John's is shaken. The crime is quickly pinned on Tom Fitzgerald, a down-and-out drinker with a troubled past. To the envy of the St. John's criminal defence bar a junior associate, David Hall, eventually ends up as the lead counsel on the most important criminal trial of the year. David's determined efforts bring this case to its startling conclusion and reveal that his own life is in danger. Undeterred, David follows the trail of a killer whose true identity will shock the community to its core.